up everything for just one more taste' Melissa Febos, author of *Abandon Me*

'Witty, sharp and painfully insightful' The Pool

'*The Pisces* is a novel that has such depth, and so many layers, that it is hard to put into words … Broder tells a story that is achingly human … She is, often, heart-stoppingly relatable, and a genuine example of the voice who says what we are all thinking … The sex scenes are not perfunctory, or so unrealistic that you cringe, but some of the most honest representations of female sexual experiences I have ever read … If it doesn't make its way onto your list of books to read, then you're probably doing summer wrong' *Erotic Review*

'This novel's journey through the surreal throes of desire is a trip you'll want to take again and again' Alissa Nutting, author of *Made for Love*

'Strangely, almost uncomfortably, addictive … It's rare to identify with a main character in such a way, but with a protagonist like Lucy – passionate, desperate and frustrated with life's shortcomings – it's hard not to. It is precisely the flawed nature of her character that makes this book so impossible to put down … This book appeals to the Bridget Jones in all of us, searching for true love and unhealthily influenced by fairytales. It's a fusion of the fantastical and the real with a sprinkling of the erotic, and is both beautifully written and darkly comic' *Stylist*

'I've never quite read anything like the surreal merman romantic comedy that is *The Pisces*! … Sappho and Tinder, mermaid porn and nervous breakdowns, the banal and the bananas gloriously litter this uncanny marvel that is pretty impossible to put down' Porochista Khakpour, author of *Sick: A Memoir*

'Fearless and perverted, full of desolation and of hope, *The Pisces* is a novel that delves head on into the many dark, absurd facets of human connection and coping in search of meaning and comes back bearing fantastic flashes of a twisted rom-com surreality only Melissa Broder's gemstone-studded brain could conjure up' Blake Butler, author of *There Is No Year*

'An incisive look at modern love. Just brilliant. We absolutely loved it!' Pandora Sykes, The High Low

'The characters in *The Pisces* are so finely drawn and palpably real. These are some of the most real, relatable merman sex scenes I have ever read in any book' Megan Amram, comedian and writer of 'Parks and Recreation'

'A page-turner of a novel ... *The Pisces* is many things: a jaunt in a fabulous voice, a culture critique of Los Angeles, an explicit tour of all kinds of sex (both really good and really bad) ... Broder's voice has a funny, frank Amy Schumer feel to it, injected with moments of a Lydia Davis-type abstraction' *Washington Post*

'The dirtiest, most bizarre, most original work of fiction I've read in recent memory' Vogue.com

'Fearless writing, merrily mixing Sappho and bikini waxes, Greek myths and self-help, and with the most brutally honest sex scenes I've read in a long time' Kerry Andrew, composer and author of *Swansong*

'[*The Pisces* offers] an exploration of how deeply impacted we all are in the corrupted world, and how far we'd have to swim to escape it' *Huffington Post*

About the Author

Melissa Broder is the author of the essay collection *So Sad Today* and four poetry collections, including *Last Sext*. She writes the 'So Sad Today' column at *Vice,* the 'Beauty and Death' column on Elle.com and previously wrote the astrology column for Lena Dunham's *Lenny Letter.* In 2017 she was named as one of *Rolling Stone*'s '50 Funniest People Right Now'. She lives in Los Angeles.

Also by Melissa Broder

So Sad Today
Last Sext
Scarecrone
Meat Heart
When You Say One Thing But Mean Your Mother

The Pisces

Melissa Broder

BLOOMSBURY PUBLISHING

LONDON · OXFORD · NEW YORK · NEW DELHI · SYDNEY

BLOOMSBURY PUBLISHING
Bloomsbury Publishing Plc
50 Bedford Square, London, WC1B 3DP, UK

BLOOMSBURY, BLOOMSBURY PUBLISHING and the Diana logo are
trademarks of Bloomsbury Publishing Plc

First published in Great Britain 2018
This edition published 2019

A catalogue record for this book is available from the British Library

ISBN: HB: 978-1-4088-9098-1; TPB: 978-1-4088-9099-8;
eBook: 978-1-4088-9100-1; PB: 978-1-4088-9095-0

2 4 6 8 10 9 7 5 3

Printed and bound in Great Britain by CPI Group (UK) Ltd, Croydon CR0 4YY

To find out more about our authors and books visit www.bloomsbury.com
and sign up for our newsletters

To Nicholas

These things never happened but always are.

—Sallust

1.

I was no longer lonely but I was. I had Dominic, my sister's diabetic foxhound, who followed me from room to room, lumbering onto my lap, unaware of his bulk. I liked the smell of his meaty breath, which he didn't know was rancid. I liked the warmth of his fat belly, the primal way he crouched when he took a shit. It felt so intimate scooping his gigantic shits, the big hot bags of them. I thought, *This is the proper use of my love, this is the man for me, this is the way.*

The beach house was a contemporary glass fortress, sparse enough to remind me nothing of my life back home. I could disappear in a good way: as if never having existed, unlike the way I felt I was disappearing all fall, winter, and spring in my hot, cluttered apartment in Phoenix, surrounded by reminders of myself and Jamie, suffocating in what was mine. There are good and bad ways of vanishing. I wanted no more belongings.

On the second-story deck of the beach house I escaped the hell of my own smelly bathrobe, wearing one of the silk kimonos my sister had left behind. I fell asleep out there every night, tipsy on white wine, under the Venice stars, with my feet tucked under Dominic's gut, belonging to nothing familiar. I felt no pressure to fall asleep, and so, after nine months of insomnia, I was finally able to drift off easily every night. Then at three a.m. I would wake gently and traipse to the bed with the Egyptian cotton sheets, kicking my legs all over them in celebration, rolling around and touching my own skin as though I were a stranger touching someone foreign, or cradling the big back of the dog to my front to die to the world for another eight hours. I might have even been happy.

And yet, walking on Abbot Kinney Boulevard one night at the end of my first week there, passing the windows of the yuppie shops—each their own white cube gallery—I saw two people, a man and a woman, early twenties maybe, definitely on a first or second date, and I knew I still wasn't okay. They were discussing intently where they should go to eat and drink, as though it really mattered. He had an accent, German, I think, and was handsome and fuckable: hair close-cropped and boyish, strong arms, an Adam's apple that protruded and made me think of sucking on it.

The woman was, as the undergrads at the Arizona university where I worked as a librarian might say, a butterface.

For nine years I had been at Southwest State in the dual lit and classics PhD program. Somehow, miraculously, despite having not yet turned in my thesis, they hadn't withdrawn my funding. In exchange for thirty hours of work per week in the library, I was housed in a below-market-rent apartment off-campus and received a yearly stipend of $25,000. I was supposed to be working on a book-length project entitled "The Accentual Gap: Sappho's Spaces as Essence." This year, as a result of my tardiness, I'd been appointed a new advisory committee, comprised of both the classics and English department chairpersons, and I was no longer flying under the radar.

In March, I had met with them at a Panera Bread, where they delivered the news over paninis—Napa almond chicken salad for the English chair in her coffee-stained Easter sweater and tuna salad for the classics chair, his nose swollen with rosacea—that I was to have a full draft completed by the fall semester or my funding would be pulled and I would be out. So far, this had not made me hustle any faster.

It wasn't that I no longer felt impassioned by Sappho. I did, or sort of did, as much as you can feel impassioned by anyone you have lived with for nine years. But it had dawned on me around year six that the thesis of my thesis, its whole raison d'être, was faulty. In fact, it was not just faulty. It was total bullshit. But I didn't know how to fix it. So I'd just been riding it out.

The book operated under the notion that scholars always assumed a first-person speaker when reading Sappho's poetry. Scholars were kind of assholes and they actually hated mystery—they detested any inability to fill in the blanks. They were victims, like the rest of us, of the way their brains worked: trying to compartmentalize every fragment of information into a pattern. They wanted the world to make sense. Who didn't? So when reading Sappho's work, they took details that they already knew, or thought they knew, of Sappho's life, and used them to fill in the blanks. But they did so erroneously, like a psychologist who, after learning three extraneous things about a person's childhood, believes they know the whole person.

My book presented the argument that one should read the vast number of erasures in Sappho's work as intentional. True, Sappho had not included these herself. They were created by the passage of time and dirt since 600 BCE. Most of her work was actually missing, with only 650 lines of 10,000 surviving. But I argued that to reimagine these blanks as created by Sappho herself was far less of a co-option than filling in the gaps with what little we know of her life, creating our own meanings for them out of a desire to make history our own, and above all, projecting a first-person speaker upon them. I felt that the only way we would cease projecting was if the blanks were read as intentional text themselves. Forget whether she was a lesbian, preferred younger men, was hypersexual, bisexual, or had multiple male lovers. If we were going to ascribe meaning, let's do it with what was there rather than what was not there.

Unfortunately this was a total garbage proposition. I, myself, had a very complicated relationship with emptiness, blankness, nothingness. Sometimes I wanted only to fill it, frightened that

3

if I didn't it would eat me alive or kill me. But sometimes I longed for total annihilation in it—a beautiful, silent erasure. A desire to be vanished. And so I was most guilty of all in projecting an agenda. I knew it, which was why I had not really pressed ahead. I wasn't sure if my advisory committee knew it. But I was about to be cut off and I figured that a shitty book was probably better than no book at all.

So I continued to trudge, not wanting to quit and get a "real" job, not really knowing what I could do anyway. Most of my time in public was spent in the library, amidst the undergrads, and that was where I had heard them use the words *butterface* and *brown bagger*. They used these words to describe women of attractive body and unattractive face, and this woman on Abbot Kinney was, in my opinion, definitely one. I moved quickly behind her to observe her further.

Her visage, when she turned her head to talk to the man, was hard and pronounced, with a jutting nose and chin, but she had good hair and a hot body to save her. She wore a pair of tiny navy silk shorts from which the very bottom of her ass cheeks protruded ever so slightly. You almost felt compelled to touch them. Everything she said was filtered through her own awareness of how good her ass looked, the words she spoke merely an afterthought compared to the glory at the bottom of those shorts. She was almost like a vehicle for shorts and an ass. She sort of danced a little down the sidewalk and flicked her hair.

He was no better. He asked stupid questions—"So how long have you lived here?" and "Do you like it?"—but every question was a chance to put his own hotness into action. Why were they even bothering to speak? Who had time for all of this? Why weren't they just fucking, right there, out in the open? The entire performance was merely a vessel for something else. It was nothingness.

Sure, compared to the greater nothingness—the void, the lack of explicit meaning in life, the fact that none of us knows what is going on here—it was at least something. Their engagement in this dance of elevating a stupid restaurant to high levels of importance, discussing kombucha, making the fleeting matter, the shorts: all of these were a fuck-you to emptiness. Or perhaps these details were symptomatic of their ignorance of nothingness. Was nothingness so imperceptible to them that these things could matter?

Could anyone be totally ignorant of the void? Didn't all of us have an awareness of it, a brush with it—perhaps only once or twice, like at a funeral for someone very close to you, when you walked out of the funeral home and it stopped making sense for just a blip that you existed. Or perhaps a bad mushroom trip where one's fellow trippers looked like plastic. Could there be people on this Earth who never stopped for a moment, not once, to say: What is everything?

Whether these were those people or not, I knew that in this moment neither of them was asking that question. If they had tasted the nausea of not knowing why we are here or who we are, or if they had not, now they were willfully and successfully ignoring it. Or maybe they were just stupid. Oh, the sweet gift of stupidity. I envied them.

But really, I knew that everything came down to her shorts. All of the answers were in that ass line—the reduction of all fear, all unknown, all nothingness, eclipsed by the ass line. It was holding its own in all of this. It was just existing as though living was easy. The ass line didn't really have to do anything, but it was running the whole show. All dialogue began and ended at that ass line. The direction of their evening, their conversation, and in a way, the universe ended there. I hated them.

I hated their ease with everything. I hated their lack of loneliness, their sense of time stretching out languidly like something to be toyed with, as though it were never going to get too late tonight or in their lives. I didn't know who I resented more: the man or the woman.

2.

I have always felt that it would be good to be a man. Not only have I always wanted to have my own dick—just to walk around feeling that weight between my legs, that power—but I have longed to escape the time pressures that my body has put on me. I hated the German man on Abbot Kinney for having that, no time pressure. I hated the woman too, for being so young, for having so much time left to be hot and maybe someday have a baby.

I had never wanted a baby. I never felt the desire so many women describe that suddenly hits them. Having just turned thirty-eight, I had been waiting and waiting for that desire to overtake me, but it didn't. So I always looked on it casually, like something mildly distasteful: a piece of onion I would prefer not to put on my plate.

But I loved having the option of having a baby if I still wanted one. I liked having the future ahead of me. People say that youth is wasted on the young, and I agree in so many respects that it was wasted on me, but in one way I had appreciated it. I always had a sense of my privilege with time. Part of my casualness with the question of having children was that I sensed how lucky I was that I could one day have the choice if I wanted. I liked that that day was very far off. The distance felt luxurious.

I had secretly judged women who regretted never having children and were now no longer of the age at which they could have them. I judged them, perhaps, because I feared becoming one of them. But now at thirty-eight, my time was beginning to run out. I still didn't want a child. I didn't know what I would do with a child if I had one. But I missed having that open space before me in which to decide. And if the ass-cheeks woman had been paying attention to me, I knew she would have judged me as I had judged others my age.

She might have also judged me for being unmarried. When Jamie and I first met, I told him that marriage was an archaic declaration of ownership and it wasn't for me. He said "good," because it wasn't his thing either. But four years into the relationship I wanted desperately for Jamie to ask me to marry him, if only because he wouldn't. I'd never been a jewelry person, but something inside me longed for that ring. Outwardly I shit-talked blood diamonds, while quietly I studied other women's rings, learning the names of the various diamond cuts: cushion, emerald, princess. I swore that married women used their left hands more than their right when they spoke, gestured, or wiped a stray hair out of their eyes, just to rub it in. They seemed to be saying, *Look, someone wants me this much. I have safely made it to the other shore.*

But what would I have even done as a married person? What would I have done with Jamie in my space or me in his? Choosing Jamie to love for so many years was perhaps more of a symbol of my own fear of intimacy than it was of his. He was intoxicating when we first met: a geologist, 6'2", handsome in an L.L.Bean travel vest sort of way, golden brown and unshaven, with sandy-brown hair, ten years my senior. He made me feel like a special little pea. Through his work in the desert with the university, he had received a grant from the American Geological Fund to make documentaries on the national parks. He always directed and edited the docs himself, and the grant gave him the power to travel, be free, and always be producing. Even though the documentaries aired at two a.m. on limited cable channels, he could never be accused of failing. "I'm more with the scientists than the artists," he said. But he had the allure of an artist.

In our earlier years together I traveled to see him on location often. I spent my holiday breaks in an Airstream at Acadia National Park, Glacier, Yosemite. He would go on shoots all day and I would go out exploring, bringing back little souvenirs. He loved hearing what I had seen, correcting my landscape terminology. My favorites were the lakes and oceans, the rivers and waterfalls, like nothing we had in the desert. The rushing water, and traveling in general, made me feel like my life was moving forward, in spite of my flagging thesis. I identified myself with his work. It felt adventurous.

But later on, he began covering more desert locations: Death Valley, Arches. I would stay in the Airstream all day and wait for him to return. Why did I need to explore another desert when I had a desert right at home? And why had I come to see this man who was the same here as he was at home? Same face, same dick. Same ennui of a long relationship but with no desire to commit. I told him I was staying in the Airstream to work on the thesis. But when people asked me what I did for a living, I glossed over my Sappho and the library, and quickly brought up Jamie's work. I pretended it was still exciting. But the only real excitement left was the challenge of roping him into our imaginary future.

On the day of our breakup, I had blown a tire on Camelback Road and called him for help. When he arrived he looked in my trunk and said, "But you don't have a spare." "No," I said. It was late in the evening on a Sunday and the auto-body shops in town would be closed, so we called AAA. While we waited I felt hot and fussy and angry. I wasn't sure exactly why. He looked silly to me, dough-bellied and chinless. Everything had rounded out. He was making little sucking noises with his front teeth, alternating with small whistling noises. It was one of those moments when you look at the person you have loved for a long time and everything is wrong with them. There is absolutely nothing right. You cannot believe you were ever captivated by them in the first place.

"I don't feel happy," I said.

"There are other places I'd rather be too," he said.

"I'm serious," I said. "I think we need to talk. About us."

"Now?"

I watched him so at ease with himself, the fat in the middle, the various layers of padding around the chin, the chin disappearing into a soufflé of neck meat. His chin area looked like it was a second mouth and I imagined it talking. What was it saying?

Feed me, it said. *I don't give a fuck if I'm attractive or not. I don't need to. I have options.*

All of him said that. From his nervous laughter whenever I had brought up marriage—or even moving in together—the years of dismissals, the claims that I wouldn't want that either, to the disappearance of the chiseled, handsome stranger I first met at a party into a honeybear I came to know and love into another kind of stranger: a physical manifestation of time and letting oneself go eclipsing both the stranger and the honeybear until they all but disappeared. I felt irate. How dare he not give a fuck? What a luxury, the luxury of a man. The luxury of someone who looked at the ravages of time and went, "Eh." And that is when I said it.

"Maybe we should just break up."

As soon as I said it, I knew it was an empty threat, something I tossed out. It was how I felt, but it was only a bit of it—a percentage. Maybe 22 percent. That 22 percent was loud right now. It wanted to punctuate the heavy evening ennui, the waiting-to-be-rescued. I wanted drama if only to sever the nothingness of things breaking, the heaviness of having to live in the world, dependent on things, dependent on others, waiting for roadside assistance with a talking chin. I wanted to have him try to stop me, to intervene. Maybe I wanted to hurt him a little bit. Mostly I wanted to hear him say no.

But he didn't say no. He didn't say no at all. He looked at me, sighed, and said calmly, "I think you might be right." And with that the chins disappeared. And all I saw now were his strong shoulders, his deep blue eyes. So many times when we were fucking, his belly bouncing off me, I tried to look only at his eyes—to conjure the attraction I had felt when we first met. Now, suddenly, it was all I could see.

"Or at least," he said, "maybe we can try a separation for a little while."

Now my words had had the opposite effect of my intentions. Or maybe not opposite, exactly. With Jamie taking the bait, but running with it in a completely unexpected direction, he had certainly put a pin in my boredom and annoyance. Fear is a great intoxicant in its own way. Anyone hooked on its adrenaline can tell you that. But in taking this risk, this angry set of words, one sentence, I had lost control of my own narrative. Now he owned the power. I was at his mercy.

I thought the only way to get it back would be to continue testing him. Play it cool, don't panic.

"Okay," I said. "If that's what you want."

He didn't want that, he said. But he wasn't sure what to do. He said he felt that he had not been able to satisfy me in the relationship for a long time.

"Satisfy me or satisfy yourself?"

"Well, maybe a little of both," he said.

The AAA man arrived. Jamie did most of the talking. I could hear what the man was saying but I couldn't really take it in because I was processing what had just happened. I should have kept my mouth shut, I thought. But in another way, I felt that I had been true to myself, I just wasn't sure to which self. The self that wanted to shake things up so as to receive attention and doting? The self that needed to be shaken up, because the ache of living in a body was so fucking dull? Some higher self that said he wasn't right for me? The 22 percent of me that was an asshole?

"Let's sleep on it," said Jamie, after the spare had been put on my wheel. "We don't have to decide anything right away."

"Together or separate?" I asked.

Together or separate was always a big question for us. He wanted no more than two nights a week together. I pushed for four. When I was in my apartment alone, I longed to be in his fold. I hinted and alluded to having free time. I got drunk on white wine, then begged. I wanted the access, the invitation, to feel that I was always welcome. It was a need based on his absence of need. So I pushed for more togetherness. But once I was with him, the closeness was never what I wanted it to be. I suffocated in his presence. When he wasn't pushing me away, the closeness was cloying.

"Maybe separate would be better for tonight. Tomorrow and Tuesday too? Maybe for the week. I have a lot of work and it would be good to maybe just try this on, the space, see how it feels?"

"Sure," I said, though I was scared.

He kissed me on the forehead.

"I love you," he said.

"Yeah, okay," I said.

"Oh, come on, Lucy," he said. He opened my car door, climbed out, and slammed it shut.

"I'm sorry!" I said, my voice trailing after him.

3.

That night I called him.

"So we aren't really taking a break, are we?" I asked.

"I actually think it's a good idea," he said. "I know you were the one who brought it up, but I'd actually like to."

"But what does that mean? For how long? Is it just temporary and then will we get back together at the end?"

"Let's just take it one step at a time," he said.

I could no longer conjure the image of Jamie as I had seen him earlier in the day: overweight, unable to solve my problem, shut down. Now I saw him only as I had seen him when we were first together: strong in the jaw, self-contained in a sexy way, Gore-Tex handsome. I saw him again as a separate person, not an extension of me or something to be coaxed or endured, but his own entity: dry-humored, capable, a real man—whatever that meant. I saw my loss, felt the weight of it, and sat down on my bed. My mouth twitched downward and my stomach heaved. I felt tears rise up. I had not cried in years.

I had felt, for a long time, that if I started crying I would not stop—that if I finally ripped, there would be nothing to stop my guts from falling out. I was scared of what might come out of me: the things I would see, what others would see. I was scared the feelings would eat me. Feelings were a luxury of the young, or someone much stronger than me—someone more at ease with being human. It was too late for tears. I was to keep going, to move forward on the same track in spite of life's unsatisfying lifeness. I was not to ask where I was going or if it was where I really wanted to go. I was not to ask if I was actually going anywhere at all. But now, somehow, I was sobbing.

And so began the melancholy. The days of crying, without notice, in inopportune situations: at work, at the bank, in the Whole Foods checkout line when I saw his favorite protein powder and my spirit gagged at the loss of him. It was as though the powder were him, or transubstantiated him. So strange to know a person's favorite protein powder, their favorite flavor (vanilla almond), and then just have them gone. I didn't call or text. A Pisces and never good at restraint, this time I was dedicated to punitive silence and making him want. He will be back soon, I told myself. He has to be.

Four days went by. I heard nothing. I grew enraged. Eight years and this was all? No inquiry into how I was doing? I could have been dead. On the sixth day he called me. He wanted to see how I was holding up.

"Not great," I said. "You?"

"Terrible," he said. "I haven't been sleeping."

Thank God, I thought.

"I know," I said. "This is so silly. I think we should stop this. Enough is enough."

"I need a little more time," he said.

"Can't you just come over?" I pleaded.

"I don't think that's a great idea right now," he said. "Maybe in a few weeks?"

"A few weeks?!" I said. "How much longer is this going to go on for?"

"I don't know," he said. "I love you."

"Fuck you!" I yelled, and hung up the phone.

Then I texted him.

i'm sorry

i'm just hurt and scared

forgive me?

i love you too

He wrote:

let's just take this time

4.

Then came the obsession. I started reading my weekly horoscopes and his (Sagittarius), parsing every word for a sign that the universe was going to bring us back together. If there was nothing about love I would read a different horoscope. I would read them until I found one that suited me—until it said this was my lucky day or week or month. I consulted a psychic, an old woman in Tempe who worked in the back of a Mediterranean restaurant. She said that I needed to focus on me, do work on myself and my "blocks" and more would be revealed. She suggested a powder made of quartz crystal to put in my bath. She said it would serve as a clearing of negativity. I bought it for $250 and soaked in it. Nothing happened. So I called more psychics.

I realized how much time I had spent with Jamie. Or maybe not how much time I'd spent with him, but how much time I spent alone but knowing, at least, that he was there. It was different now, being totally alone, with no one person in the back of my mind—that little figure, like a cushion. I'd never had many friends in Phoenix to begin with. There was Rochelle, a professor of anthropology, who had introduced me to Jamie.

Rochelle had been married since before I met her. Mid-forties with wiry, pubic-looking hair that she kept cut very short, in a style I secretly called "the Brillo," she wore no makeup and was deeply okay with herself. I thought it was nice that there was a man on Earth who was happy to fuck her—not only to fuck her but to marry her. I wondered if this was where she got her confidence or if it was her confidence that had drawn her husband to her.

When Rochelle first introduced me to Jamie, I was barely thirty, and had the luxury of time, a cool air about my future, zero apparent desperation. She probably thought I was normal. Through the years we would meet every six months or so at the same Colombian restaurant and make the same jokes about how her husband and Jamie both snored, the way they both acted like babies when they got a cold. There was an affected comfort in these casual insults, as if to say, *I know this man is mine. He isn't going anywhere. I could take him or leave him.* I pretended to her that I didn't want to marry Jamie, didn't want to move in together, and had more than enough time with him. I was a woman contented with what she had and did not need more of anyone or anything.

But now I became clingy with Rochelle, besieged her with a barrage of compulsive questioning about Jamie's whereabouts. The questions were coupled with a series of neurotic affirmations on my part that he would be coming back, it was only a matter of when.

Simply being around her in those first weeks made me feel connected to Jamie, though she wouldn't tell me much. She looked at me like I was a woman who had caught a terrible disease that she never thought either of us would catch. She toyed with her dangling beaded earring and said she hadn't seen him in a while, didn't want to get in the middle. Then I saw a picture of them on Facebook, sitting next to each other at a birthday party. They each had glasses of wine and little dishes of flan, so fucking civilized. They were clinking glasses. Rochelle was clearly a traitor.

I felt dissociated from my body, like my head was in a cloud of fog and my limbs were not under my jurisdiction. I started smoking weed around the clock, something I hadn't done regularly since my early twenties, going to work at the library stoned. I made no progress on my book. I only wanted to lie around and

eat sugar and fats: giant chocolaty drinks from Starbucks, bags
of Hershey's minis and gummy candy, tortilla chips with nacho
cheese dip. I had always had a small frame and never gained
weight easily, except in my hips, which were wide. My choice
of clothing made them look deceptively smaller: loose, flowy
cotton skirts and dresses, wide linen pants that kept them concealed. The rest of me would be swimming in my clothes, giving
me a sort of elfin, pixie look, all thanks to my hips. But now my
pants were leaving a tight elastic mark around my waist each
time I took them off.

I also began engaging in weird crafts. I craved creative expression, an artistic order, but did not have the lucidity of mind
for Sappho. I went to the nearby crafts store and bought a hot-
glue gun, beads, tools for needlepoint. I began hot-gluing beads
onto empty wine bottles, making "vases." Eventually I stopped
going to the library entirely. I told them that I needed a week's
hiatus to work on my book. The other librarians agreed to cover
for me. My apartment looked like a frat house mixed with an
arts fair. I stayed up all night beading. Then one week turned
into two. Finally I dragged my ass back, but I still wasn't sleeping. I hid in the university bathrooms on the toilet with my eyes
closed.

And then Jamie did come back, for a night anyway.

"I feel ready to meet now," he said, and so we went to our
favorite Mexican spot.

After a few margaritas he held my hand under the table and
we stared into each other's eyes. I had not remembered being
present for a meal like this, together, both fully engaged, neither
of us on our phones, in years. After dinner we made out in his
car. He tasted different, like a licorice taste had entered his body
in the time we'd been apart. Maybe it was the cilantro. He drove
me home and then followed me upstairs. I went to get him a
glass of water. When I came into the living room he was sitting
on the sofa.

"Come here," he said.

I walked toward him and sat on his leg. I held the water up to his lips. He drank, then put it on the table and kissed me. He undressed me, still sitting in his lap. Then he laid me down on the sofa and undressed hastily as I watched him in the dark. We fucked on the sofa, quickly, our mouths on each other's mouths the whole time. I didn't come. I never did from fucking. Jamie's lack of initiative in going down on me was a source of contention between us, always. He was willing but not ravenous for it. But his mouth on my mouth as he fucked me felt in a way like he had his mouth on my vagina. He didn't stay the night.

Then Rochelle called.

"The girl he is seeing is a scientist," she said. "She's blond."

"He's seeing someone?"

"I thought you knew," she said.

Apparently the woman's name was Megan and she was five years younger than me. Rochelle knew nothing more about her. She had bumped into them at a Chinese restaurant.

"Well, can you find out?"

"I'll try," said Rochelle.

I could tell she was getting sick of me. Or more than sick of me, actually, she was scared of me. She had always thought we were both safe from the crazy-woman disease: that desperation and need. But now I had fallen into it, fallen all the way under, and she saw how a person could just go. One minute you were playfully complaining to friends about a man's farts and the next minute you would kill to have the farts back. Could she catch the disease from me? Was her own contentment in danger? I texted her three times to get the info but she just wrote back:

rly busy

I wanted to tell her I was pissed off, that I felt she had abandoned and betrayed me. I wanted to say that the only reason she had any confidence in her Brillo-self—the only reason she was

18

"okay"—was that there was too much inertia in her relationship for her husband to leave. I wanted to say that this wasn't a reason for confidence, or something to be proud of. As I had seen, that inertia could be disturbed at any moment by an accidental slip of the tongue. But I didn't want her to quarantine me entirely. I might need her.

So I wrote my own narratives. Megan was not only a scientist but an award-winning geologist. They hiked together and discussed the reproduction of cacti. They fucked on a rock. Nothing is more beautiful than the sex your ex-boyfriend is having with his new lover. Nothing more magical and full of gasps. Meanwhile I was in Hersheyland. I could no longer play it cool. One night I parked down the street from his house until I saw him pull in to the driveway and get out of his car. He was alone. I waited until the lights turned on. Then I got out of the car.

Walking down his driveway I realized that I had butterflies for the first time in years. Maybe this was what it took to maintain butterflies in your partner's driveway? A blond scientist named Megan.

I rang the bell. He took a minute, did not ask who it was, then opened the door.

"Lucy," he said.

I felt rage in my chest, in every part of me.

"Fuck you, you fucking asshole!" I yelled. And then I hit him in the face.

I had never hit anyone before. This was not what I had planned. I hadn't planned anything actually. We were both in shock. I didn't know what to say. Two drops of blood ran from his nose, down his lip, and splattered onto the floor. He put his hands up to his face.

"Son of a bitch," he said.

"Jamie," I said. "Jamie, wait, let me see. Let me see."

"Just go," he said. "Go!"

He slammed the door. I pivoted on my heel and walked back down the street to my car. I felt worse.

Later that night I got a visit from a police officer investigating the incident. Apparently, Megan had called the police from the hospital—or she had coerced him into it. I had broken Jamie's nose. The cop said that the couple would not be pressing charges if I agreed to go to therapy. The couple? Now they were making decisions as a unit?

"What did she look like?" I asked him.

"Uh—" he faltered.

"Would you say she's better-looking than me?"

"Ma'am," said the cop, "I'm going to strongly recommend that you seek help for your anger issues. This time we're only going to give you a warning. But if the couple hadn't been so forgiving, you could be facing serious charges of battery right now."

"Battery!" I said. "Do I look like a batterer?"

He was silent.

"Can you just tell me. Aside from the broken nose, did they seem happy?"

5.

I had always thought of depression as having no shape. When it manifested as a feeling of emptiness, you could inject something into it: a 3 Musketeers, a walk, something to kind of give it a new form. You could penetrate it and give it more of a shape you felt better about. Or at least you could make a shape inside it or around it. But this was something new, like a thicker, gooey sludge. It had its own shape. It could not be contained. It was a terror. Of what I was terrified I couldn't exactly say, but it was sitting on me. Every other shape was being absorbed into it. I no longer slept. Was this all because of Jamie? How could someone who got on my nerves so much have this much power over me?

I asked my doctor for Ambien. The Ambien helped me sleep. But in the mornings the goo was right there, waiting for me. I was already in it. It was becoming more dense. One night I took nine Ambien. I was not trying to kill myself so much as vanish. I just wanted to go to sleep and be transported into the ether, another world. I guess that vanishing would have meant death, so perhaps it was an attempt at suicide? But I felt afraid of death, or at least, afraid of dying. Was there something that wasn't death but wasn't here either?

I woke up fourteen hours later, ravenous. Doughnuts! I had to have doughnuts. Stoned from the Ambien, I got in my car and the rest was a blur. I must have blacked out. I only remember waking up on the road, parked, wearing my nightie, with doughnuts strewn around the car seats: powdered, cream-filled, a jelly. I didn't even like jelly. Cars were honking behind me but I couldn't figure out what to do. So I just stayed parked like that in the middle of the road and went back to sleep on the steering wheel.

Then I woke up again. Now a police officer was leaning into my car on the passenger's side. He asked if I could get out of the car. I climbed out hazily. I remember thinking a dumb joke about cops and doughnuts. Then I realized: it was the same cop who had come to my house about Jamie's nose.

"Hi," I said.

He gave me a Breathalyzer to test my blood alcohol levels. Those were normal. Then he searched the car for drugs but couldn't find any.

"I'm really feeling sick," I said. "First the breakup, now some kind of flu. I was going to get the doughnuts for the sugar. I must have fainted. Anyway, if you just let me go home I'll be okay."

"Ma'am, I can't let you drive in this condition. Is there anyone I can call to come get you?"

I thought of Jamie. He was usually my emergency contact. But I didn't want him to know I needed anything from him. I wanted him to think I was just fucking fine. But I did feel sick. Also scared. Would this be my second strike? Would they send me to jail? I just wanted to be left alone. I felt that if the cop left me alone, I could pull my car over to the side and rest a little longer and I'd be okay. I didn't want anyone seeing me like this in my nightgown.

"You can call my sister," I said.

I gave him my sister Annika's number. I didn't tell him that she lived in California. He left her a voicemail saying I had gotten sick on the road and asking if she could come pick me up. She was going to be confused.

"Anyone else we can call?" he asked.

"I'll be okay," I said. "I'm much better now."

"I'm going to have to ask that you pull your car over on that next side street and park it there. You can gather up your doughnuts and I'll give you a ride home."

"Fine," I said. "You know where I live."

6.

"You have to get the fuck out of there," said Annika. "I don't know what that was with the doughnut incident, but something isn't right."

"I'm fine," I said.

"Listen, Steve and I are going out of town for the whole summer. Yoga conference in Provence, then Budapest for two weeks, a month in Rome, and another conference. Oh, and then Burning Man with one of Steve's start-ups. We need a house sitter and someone to watch Dom, love him, give him his medication. You should fly out here. Spend the whole summer. Get the hell out of the desert. It's a nightmare for you ayurvedically."

"I don't know if I can afford to take the summer off," I said. I usually did summer work for the library, even when school wasn't in session.

"Yes, you can," she said. "What happened to the money that Daddy left you?" Annika was actually my half sister, nine years older, but we had the same father. He had left us each about $20,000 when he died in his sleep at eighty-six.

"I spent it on psychics. The rest I'm saving for when I die alone. The cremation," I said.

"I'll pay for your cremation. Also, I will pay you to live here. I want you to treat yourself well while you are out here. Farm to table, spa, all that shit. You need to forget about Jamie. I know he's at the root of this, even though you won't admit it. You were always fucking crazy about men. You don't think I remember when that poet guy dumped you in high school and Dad found you naked in the basement asleep with a steak knife?"

"It was a butter knife," I said. "I was trying to open a jar of peanut butter. I was bingeing."

"Whatever," she said. "I spoke to the cop. You broke Jamie's nose? They want you in therapy and I'm going to arrange it. Group, I think, something for codependents. I'll ask my guy if he knows of anyone good. You need to be around women, no men, and you need to do the work."

"A group? Annika, no—"

"Good, so it's settled. You'll come out here June fourth and stay until September tenth. I'll be back for a week before Burning Man and we can hang out. And I'll pay you double what you would make at the library to watch Dominic. I would be paying someone anyway."

"I'm not doing the group," I said. "And I'm not taking your money. But maybe I can come out there. I have to check with the library."

"Do you want them to press charges?" she said. "If not, you'll go to therapy. Also, I'm paying you, so stop."

I didn't protest any further. I needed the money and Annika had it. Tons of money. In the late '90s she'd gotten into the yoga studio scene in Santa Monica, designed a line of mats made of bamboo. The mats were featured in *Yoga Journal* in a three-page profile about their biodegradable properties and rich texture for asana. Two days later she received a call. It was Hain Celestial. They wanted to buy the patent. Then Native Foods came calling. A bidding war ensued, and the patent was bought by Hain Celestial for $3.1 million, which she used to get into the tech and innovator conferences during the first dot-com bubble. That's where she met Steve, a Jewish hippie investor deep in Silicon Valley 1.0. She got him into kombucha, taught him how to relax (sort of), and they got married in Sonoma. Then she moved him down to Venice Beach, used his money to build a giant glass-and-metal cube of a house right on Ocean Front Walk. Later they got Dominic: a purebred foxhound who became their child. Annika hadn't practiced Ashtanga or Vinyasa yoga in years—only

Hatha and restorative—and was fat now. Steve loved her ass and was always squeezing it. He tried to grow what remained of his hair long like Kenny G and casually ran an investment firm with offices in Century City. He wore linen shorts to work. They joined a hippie synagogue in Malibu and were happy.

Now they complained about the newest wave of gentrification though, what the real-estate agents called "Silicon Beach," taking over Venice. A new kind of yuppie, shiny like the young ass-cheeks couple. The clothes they sold on Abbot Kinney and Main Street still had some boho vibes, but now they cost thousands of dollars. Rich hippies. That didn't bother Annika as much as the chain stores that were moving in, upscale and soulless.

"They're turning this place into a MILF mall," she said. "Soon it will basically be Phoenix."

But Venice would never look like Phoenix, because of all the bums. Phoenix would never allow a homeless community so bustling. Instead they shipped them all to L.A. If you were a homeless person and you weren't living in Venice, then you were doing something wrong. Venice was the place to be. They lined the lawn between the beach and Ocean Front Walk: camps of them sprawled out in the sun. There was a lot of meth and heroin, young people nodding out, barefoot, army surplus–clad and dirt-encrusted. Others had been there longer, hardened, as though the dirt had completely melded with their skin, reeking of piss, fighting with one another, cranky junkies. They pitched tents and got into brawls, held hands and talked to themselves. At night they walked from the beach to Third Street and formed a tent city two blocks long, leaving the street lined with trash, shit, and sleeping bags in the morning. No one disturbed them.

The first time I came to Venice I thought it was weird, all of these millionaires living among the bums. If you moved here in the past decade, you either had a million-dollar home or you slept on the sidewalk in front of one. That visit had been a disaster. Annika and I rarely ever saw each other, although I had promised for many years to take a trip to the beach. I couldn't get Jamie's and my schedules to align, couldn't get him interested, and I was afraid to go alone—to be intimate with her—without him as a buffer. I didn't want to be seen too closely or I might have to look at me too.

"Just come by yourself," she would say. "I don't care about him, it's you I want to see."

This was easy for her to say from the comfort of couplehood. Her independence, even though it had been real once upon a time, was now a performance. How could she judge me for waiting for Jamie when she had Steve following her ass around like a Sherpa? I felt judged, even if she wasn't judging. So I delayed for years. Then, finally, when Jamie was shooting a special on Joshua Tree, we decided I would come out to Venice at the end of his trip and he would take the Airstream out and meet me there.

I was so nervous the afternoon I flew to see her that I got drunk on the plane. I couldn't tell if she or Steve could smell it on me when I landed, although he looked at me funny. I was sitting in the backseat of their Prius and watching him gently rub her neck when the call came in. Jamie's shoot had been extended and he was not going to be able to come. I spoke to him calmly and tried to contain my anger. I didn't want Annika, or especially Steve, to see that I had any rage. If I could fool them then maybe I wouldn't have to feel it myself. But that night I got so drunk on white wine that I puked all over Annika's guest bed. Apparently, in a blackout, I talked to Steve about suicide. I wasn't threatening to do it, just discussing its merits as a practical solution for the problems of life.

I spent the remainder of the trip on good behavior. I used the bums to triangulate, inquiring about them often, giving them money. I thought that in the light of the bums I wouldn't look so bad. I made up a game, "billionaire or bum," in which I would ask Steve to place a bet on which one he thought a straggly-looking bohemian was. Apparently he was offended. She continued to invite me out there, especially once they got Dominic, but I always told her "soon." I didn't invite her to see my world.

Now it was the bums, especially the kids who ran away out here, who kept Venice from becoming a total Google campus—at least so far. They graffitied the palm trees, made sure the drugs were still flowing. I felt drawn to them, particularly the younger ones, how they just let everything go. How they were able to do that. Palm trees in pristine locations depressed me. But with a little grit they were sexy against the setting sun.

"Fuck me," I said to the palm trees.

When I was on Abbot Kinney, the long yuppie strip of contemporary blondewood-and-metal shops that cut across Venice diagonally, I felt out of place, more aligned with the homeless. Here were so many beautiful women: ombre-headed twenty-somethings in boho-chic dresses, minimalist French women clad in black leather with angular jewelry, models even, who made me look at my toe hair and fuzzy legs in disgust. I had stopped shaving since the breakup. My hair, which had always been frizzy, was now even more coarse thanks to an infestation of gray. I was no longer even using henna. The cottage cheese on my hips stood out against my skinny legs. I had stopped giving a fuck.

Looking at these women now, I thought, What if I could get really hot while I was here? What if I became the old me, or the very old me, or someone entirely new? When I get back home, maybe Jamie would want me again.

What would I do? Maybe dye my hair auburn, start wearing lipstick again, wax my vagina into some sort of formation. I had always been more of a natural woman, and I assumed that Megan the scientist was low maintenance in the pubic realm, but how natural was too natural? I had gotten so natural that I was naturally dead.

7.

After a few days in Venice I went to my first group therapy session: a specialty group for women with depression, and sex and love issues. There were four women in the group, plus the therapist and me. But they all blurred together into a multi-headed hydra of desperation.

Judith, our therapist and leader, was definitely unmarried. With her unringed hands she held a ceramic mug of steaming green tea and said very little, periodically murmuring sounds of "mmmmm" and "ahhhh." Occasionally, she asked how some event made a person feel. Everyone called her "Dr. Jude."

Dr. Jude was a collector of things—her office stuffed with tchotchkes: Buddha statuettes, a small Freud action figure, licorice pastilles, air plants, an old gumball machine, angel cards, little signs with sayings like "What would you attempt to do if you knew you could not fail?" and "Trust yourself! You know more than you think you do!" Clearly none of us could trust ourselves or we wouldn't be there.

Alas, our fearless leader was deeply single and trying to be at peace with it. I wondered if she even had a boyfriend. How could she lead a group on sex and love issues? Who would want to take love advice from a single woman who convinced herself she was happy using store-bought sayings she posted on her wall? And what kind of doctor was she anyway? I didn't see a PhD next to her name. Was she a doctor of love?

Dr. Jude had yellowish teeth and a Dorothy Hamill haircut. I guess the yellow teeth meant that she accepted herself and would not be changing for anyone. I was oddly intrigued by

her positivity in the face of the abyss, as though I were an an-
thropologist encountering a new culture for the first time. But
when she quoted E. E. Cummings in an attempt to say that we
could only be ourselves, I decided she was stupid. Also, she used
the words *radical acceptance* a lot. I didn't want to radically accept anything. When I returned to Phoenix I wanted everything
to be radically different. I didn't like her. But compared to the
disaster that was the rest of the group, Dr. Jude seemed like a
winner.

Our youngest member was Amber: mid-twenties, built like
a female wrestler, sweatpants covered in dog hair. Amber had
been in the group longest and was furthest along in terms of
"doing the work" in the personal growth and love department.
She made sure we all knew that. Immediately, in my mind I
called her Chickenhorse, as her head was long and horse-shaped
but she had a beaky nose and big pink gums that resembled a
chicken's comb and wattles. She seemed to get aroused by telling all of us we were wrong.

Dr. Jude had encouraged Chickenhorse to start dating again,
but she had not yet begun. Instead, she focused on problematic
interactions she had with people in her life.

"My boss is emotionally abusive. He's victimizing me," she
said.

"Can you tell us more?" asked Dr. Jude.

"I can't explain it, it's just a feeling," she said. "And as the victim, I don't think I should have to explain myself."

"Understandable," said Dr. Jude.

"It's my truth. And I'm afraid to bring it up to his supervisors,
because this is what happened with my last boss too. He was
another abuser; there's a pattern of abuse. When I came forward
about it at my last job, everyone started gaslighting me by acting
like I'm the crazy one."

Chickenhorse also found herself in a similar altercation at
home. Apparently she had "tattled" on her neighbors to the landlady for playing their music too loud. She left voicemails for the

landlady every day for two weeks in addition to knocking on their door every night and yelling that nine p.m. was too late to make any noise of any kind. Now her landlady was accusing her of trying to start a rift in the building. She was trying to evict her for harassment, which was unfair, because it was she who had been harassed by their music. This, too, was her truth.

I wasn't sure exactly what had happened to get Chickenhorse in here—only that it involved a married man and a restraining order. I wondered if *she'd* ever broken anyone's nose. She seemed more the type to burn your house down.

Seated next to Chickenhorse was Sara, who, apparently, was not only sensitive to men but also to light, cleaning products, mold, pollen, gluten, dairy, and sugar. She had fibromyalgia, chronic migraines, and, as a result of her hypoglycemia, was given special permission to eat during group. She said that made the room more of a "safe space" for her. Throughout the ninety minutes she consumed two bananas, a nectarine, one dried fig, a large box of raisins, and an entire two-liter jug of water. Her emphasis on hydration annoyed me.

From what I gathered, Sara had been in love with a man named Stan—a researcher at the hospital where she worked—for over twelve years. Unfortunately, while Stan was happy to have sex with her, he couldn't commit to a relationship. Then Sara woke up at fifty-one—childless, husbandless—and decided that enough was enough. She entered group and began a "detox" from Stan.

Was Jamie a Stan? Worse yet, was I a Sara? Unlike Chickenhorse's ex, Stan wasn't married to anyone else, but somehow he was still "unavailable." This was a word I heard repeated by all of the women during the session, echoing throughout in chorus. The plight of the available woman and the unavailable man! But somehow, each of these women convinced themselves that they too were emotionally unavailable. As encouraged by Dr. Jude, they'd come to the realization that their choice of unavailable men actually reflected an unavailability within themselves. Well, they all looked pretty damn available to me.

In her attempts to detox from Stan, Sara was taking a ninety-day break from contact with him. She was now on day forty-three and claimed to be doing pretty well. In fact, she said, she barely pined for him at all.

"I'm doing me," she said. "And tonight, I'm going salsa dancing."

Salsa dancing—now, that was the kiss of death, the evidence that Sara wasn't doing quite as well as she claimed. Who salsa danced? Salsa dancing was the last stop on the suicide express. Whether or not she wanted to admit it to herself, Sara was clearly destined for a crash.

But maybe the worst part about Sara was her feet. She wore a pair of ugly white "athletic sandals" that she removed as soon as she sat down. Her feet were small, yet crusty, with one yellowing toenail. Throughout the session, she gave herself different iterations of foot massage: caressing, stroking, rubbing. She also picked at her calluses and between her toes. What a luxury to think that your feet deserved to be rubbed, in front of other people, so languidly! How amazing to be so utterly unselfconscious that one didn't worry what other people thought. I wondered if her feet were even sore or if she simply enjoyed stroking something. Maybe she was trying to gross us out on purpose? I vowed to never touch her hand or receive anything from her. The whole thing, for some reason, filled me with anger. I felt that it wasn't fair to us. I wondered if I could call out her behavior, let the group know that it made the space feel "unsafe" for me. A shoe rule should be imparted. But was she the freak for massaging or was I the freak for caring?

How had I ended up with these losers? I hated the words they used: *inner child, self-care, intimacy, self-love.* We were Americans, how much gentler could life be on us? All we had received was coddling. What had Annika done to me? Did I want to assuage my suffering? Absolutely. But sorry, I was not about to learn to love myself here. It was as though they were each in competition with the other to see who could be grossest while simultaneously loving themselves the most. Is that what it meant to love yourself? To be repellent?

Seated next to Sara was Brianne: a native Los Angeleno, who I guessed was also in her early fifties but had shot her face up with so much junk that she no longer existed in time. Instead of growing old, Brianne's face just kind of grew out: puffy fish lips, cheek skin stretched and shiny—straining to contain all the filler. Somewhere along the line she'd had a botched nose job that left one nostril flaring widely and the other in a small triangular shape. She also appeared to have a skin condition, some kind of rash creeping across her face, neck, and chest, her skin so thin from whatever she was doing to it that you could see all the capillaries in her cheeks.

From under her wide-brimmed hat, hair in two long black braids like a doll, Brianne said that she hadn't had sex or dated anyone since the birth of her son fifteen years ago. From what I gathered, her son's father still came around sometimes—and was maybe even interested in her—but they had never been married. While they usually got along, there had been a recent incident involving an attempted neck massage that did not go well. Now he was persona non grata.

At the encouragement of Dr. Jude, Brianne had been going online since last year to meet men. The websites she chose were Match.com and Millionaire Match, and she repeated them as though reciting a mantra: "Match and Millionaire Match, Match and Millionaire Match." She seemed to be having a rough go of it on both sites, as the men kept disappearing. She would find someone who seemed promising, message with him for a few weeks, and then he would just vanish. On the rare occasion that one of the men didn't disappear and actually asked her for a date, he would suddenly seem strangely repulsive to her. But mostly, they absconded.

The most recent disappearance was a man who claimed to be a retired fighter pilot. She said she liked that, as she liked military men, and he seemed handsome. For two weeks he had sent her messages every day: never saying anything uncouth or sending a picture of his penis. Then, one day, she asked if he might like to meet in person. He deleted his account.

"But if it's meant for me, it's meant for me. And if it's not, it's not," she said quietly, adjusting the strap on her babydoll dress. She was wearing knee socks and Mary Janes too. "I have a very full life. Very full. I don't even know if I really want anyone else in it."

Then she sighed.

The only person I liked was a woman named Claire. She was British, crass, and irate, with long fiery-red curls. Claire kept saying "Fuck this bullshit" over and over. She had left her husband two years ago when she met a younger man at a juice bar and realized, as she put it, that she hadn't had a proper dick inside of her in twelve years. The younger man was happy to fuck her, but he never encouraged her to leave her husband. It was she who assumed they would have a life together. For six months they were off and on, until finally, she threw a plate of pesto kelp noodles at him at Café Gratitude and broke it off for good. Clean and sober for nine years, she was afraid the drama would make her drink. Most recently, though, she was hurt and enraged again by a man named Brad. He sounded pretty bad— bald, baseball capped, and litigation lawyery—but she really liked him. She said that they had begun to get really intimate around his mother's death, then he just disappeared. She wasn't drinking, but she was taking up a lot of bad behaviors again to cope with her depression.

"I left my children with a friend and rented a hotel room, where I could go self-harm in peace," she said. "But then I got scared I would off myself. I didn't know what else to do. So I've come back to this bloody hellhole."

Unlike Brianne and Chickenhorse, Claire was firmly instructed that she should not be dating until she'd done some work on herself. She called this "a load of shite."

"Lucy, I'd like to suggest the same for you," said Dr. Jude. "No dating, no sex, no contact with Jamie for the next ninety days. You'll likely experience a period of withdrawal, if you haven't begun to already. But it will be worth it in the end."

"Withdrawal?"

"Yes, you're detoxing from him . . . from a whole way of life really. A life defined by the pursuit of others to complete you."

"What does withdrawal entail?"

"People in withdrawal describe symptoms of depression, despair, insomnia, a feeling of emptiness."

"Oh, so just life," I said.

"Other symptoms can include nausea, anxiety, irrational thoughts, and even cognitive distortions."

"Great, more to look forward to."

"One more thing. You mentioned spending money on psychics, astrologers, love potions. I would urge you to abandon these pursuits, as they only prolong your inability to find intimacy with yourself. And that's the real treasure here."

"Ah," I said. "Can't wait for that."

8.

There was one place on Abbot Kinney that gave me solace, and that was the Mystic Journeys bookstore. I looked in the window and saw the rows of rose quartz crystals. I knew from Googling that rose quartz was said to bring love. Actually, it seemed like most crystals brought something that you wanted. If crystals really did what they said they did, there would probably be no problems in the world. Everyone would have everything they desired, and all would be peaceful, or at least, all the people who sold crystals would be rich, famous, and well-loved. They probably wouldn't be selling crystals anymore, because they wouldn't have to. Still, I liked to believe that magic was real. I had to go in.

I wasn't really a hippie, per se. But having grown up with Annika as an older sister, I could get down with the New Age vibes. She followed the Grateful Dead around in college and would send me little items that she bought in the parking lot: Nag Champa incense, a malachite pendulum necklace, a blue glass talisman to keep the evil eye away. Annika had been the only maternal figure in my life since my mother died when I was eleven—totemic maternal and from a distance, but all I had—so I always found New Age culture comforting. This store with its cabinets and shelves of crystals and minerals—amethyst, rose quartz, smoky quartz, pyrite, onyx, apophyllite, rock salt, aqua aura—definitely made magic seem real. The air smelled of sandalwood and amber. You could buy enlightenment from a range of Eastern texts: the Bhagavad Gita, the Yoga Sutras of Patanjali. You could buy healing in a white jasmine pillar candle or protection in a black votive. Capitalist magic.

I'd owned enough New Age tchotchkes in my lifetime to know that within a few days of purchase they just seemed like more crap. But as you were shopping, sifting through the stones and their meanings, there was hope that this was a turning point. It was the velocity of buying something that was the high, the potentiality of it. I could capitalist-believe in magic. In the store was hope, and hope was what separated me from the flat expanse of the rest of my life. It was like a line, a gateway that stopped me from being swallowed.

I looked at the fliers for all of the different healers. Some did numerology, others Tarot, others Reiki and chakra cleansing. I could have sat there all day and had my fortune told until someone predicted what I wanted to hear—that I was getting back together with Jamie, that he was coming back to me—so I quickly pulled away. I looked at the crystals. I would have loved to buy rose quartz, giant hunks of it, hundreds and hundreds of dollars' worth. I wanted to make a circle around me; do some ritual shit with rose petals; burn vanilla, gardenia, and strawberry incense to attract love. Instead I bought a sparkly raw chunk of amethyst in the palest purple, which was said to bring peace and stability.

There was also a table where magic candles were sold: red for love and passion, green for money. I bypassed the love candle and selected an egg-colored one for clearing and needed change. Maybe I could just burn the past year away.

At home I ate pad thai and drank white wine, fed Dominic, and gave him his medicine. I'd known nothing about dogs before him—how or where to pet them—but he was patient with me, and I'd soon discovered his favorite places to be touched. His entire head was brown with the exception of two white patches: one a white stripe down the center of his forehead, which I stroked gently with one finger and called his angel mark, and the other a diamond shape on the back of his neck, an arrow pointing as if to say, *Scratch me here.* This was the area that he could not reach with his paws, and, when scratched, would lull him right to sleep. We would play a game where he gazed at me lovingly, trying to keep his brown eyes open, his lids growing heavy, then popping open, then heavier and heavier until they were sealed shut: just two stitches lined with little lashes.

When he rolled over onto his back and showed me his white underside, it meant that it was time for a belly rub. Sometimes I would get crazy like I was waxing a car, Dominic pawing joyfully at the air, fur flying, tongue out, and panting. Other times I would gently stroke and kiss the softness there, relishing his scent, which was somehow reminiscent of a warm roast chicken.

My favorite place to kiss him was smack in the center of one of his big floppy ears. I could tell that he didn't like to be touched there, but he made the supreme sacrifice and allowed me to drape those delicious suede pancakes over my face. The other area I loved was the crook of his neck, just under the jaw, where his skin was soft and loose. Somehow—perhaps through the wear of the collar, or simply with time—he had gone hairless there, so that what was left was only the creamiest of baby skin. I spent most of my time with him with my head burrowed in that spot. I could have lived there.

After we'd both had dinner, I touched the candle I'd purchased, rubbing my fingers up and down it, saying a little prayer for happiness. I said a prayer to the gods I wasn't sure if I believed in—that I doubted even existed. I actually felt like the prayer was saying me.

I said, "Gods, please help me to be happy. Let me do the will of the universe and be willing to do the will of the universe, whatever that even is. Clearly I know very little. Clearly what I think I know leads me only to a place of suicidal longing. I never asked to be born on the planet. I never asked to exist. But I am here now so could you maybe at least try and help me enjoy my life?"

I felt silly asking to enjoy my life. I wondered if this was more than any human being should ask. Did anyone ever say that life was to be enjoyed and not suffered? What if the suffering was the point? But I didn't want to suffer anymore. I couldn't take it. That was clear. So I was going to try to be happy, even if it brought me more suffering. The candle burning, amethyst in hand, sitting on the deck of the beach house, I felt closer to myself than I had since before Jamie. I began to cry. Dominic made a noise, then got up into my lap and licked the tears off my face. He was licking them because they tasted good. He did the same thing when I was sweaty too. But I pretended that they were licks of love, and that's what it felt like. Maybe this group therapy shit was working. Maybe this was self-love. I didn't know and I didn't really care. Where there had been a vile, depressive ooze was now quiet. The quiet itself was a thing: a sweet-filled quiet, as though the depression had been alchemized into something delicious.

I looked out at the ocean. It was as though I hadn't noticed it before, or hadn't wanted to see it. I was scared of its wild ambivalence, so powerful and amorphous, like the depression itself. It didn't give a fuck about me. It could eat me without even knowing.

But now I saw each of the waves individually, one after the other, and felt them to be in rhythm with my heartbeat. They glimmered and splashed in the moonlight. Maybe the ocean was cheering for me after all? Maybe we were on the same side, comprised of the same things, water mostly, also mystery. The ocean swallowed things up—boats, people—but it didn't look outside itself for fulfillment. It could take whatever skimmed its surface or it could leave it. In its depths already lived a whole world of who-knows-what. It was self-sustaining. I should be like that. It made me wonder what was inside of me.

9.

I'd heard it said that when you're feeling good is sometimes when you're the most suicidal. Maybe it's after you decide that you're going to do it that you suddenly seem happier. I don't think that's why I walked across the beach to the ocean that night. I don't think I was planning to jump into the ocean drunk or that I wanted to get killed by a stranger. I knew it was dangerous to be out there at midnight. I rarely even walked the boardwalk after ten or eleven. I think I just felt invincible, connected to myself, like I could do anything and be totally fine. Maybe I was looking for a new high.

I climbed up on one of the big black rocks that lined the ocean in a cluster. I sat there for a little while looking out at the waves, more gray and white now that I was up close. I wondered if the rocks were somehow sentient, lonely out here in the cold moonlight.

"Hi," I said to the rocks.

The rocks said nothing. They had the ocean and they had one another. I wondered if they ever got annoyed by the waves' constant lapping, the daily irritation of their own gradual erosion. Did they secretly long for a tsunami to come eclipse them into the ocean, just to be done with it all already? Or did they enjoy that slow, rhythmic tickling?

From the corner of my eye I spotted something fleshy on the edge of one of the rocks. It was a pair of hands. Fair hands, pale under the moon, with the nails bitten down to just slivers. *Run!* shrieked a voice inside me. A surge of adrenaline rang through my body like an alarm. But I couldn't move.

Then I saw a beautiful face, the wave of brown hair in an eye, and I gasped out loud. Was this the face of death?

"So sorry," the face said. "I didn't mean to scare you. I was just taking a break for a second from my swim."

"It's okay," I sputtered, still frozen in place.

The swimmer leaned on the rock with his arms. They were thick and meaty—not cut like a bodybuilder's, but you could see the muscles underneath what looked like a layer of baby chub. They reminded me of eating a piece of fish with thick skin and a small layer of fat, strong and also soft, very white. I wanted to bite them. His chest was hairless, and I noticed that the color of his nipples matched perfectly his lips, like pencil erasers. He looked like he was twenty-one, at most. If this was death then death was hot.

"Doesn't it scare you to be night-swimming? Isn't the water freezing?" I asked.

"I've got a wet suit on my lower half," he said. "But no, it doesn't scare me. I like the way the splashes look in the moonlight and I like having the ocean to myself. Well, almost to myself."

"Yeah, it's nice out here," I said.

The wine was wearing off. I suddenly felt exhausted. His teeth were shiny white, but not like an actor's. They didn't look bleached or fake. They were practically iridescent, like the inside of a shell. There was something almost feminine about him, pretty, but his jaw was well defined. These surfer boys. I always forgot that they were real. I mean, I knew that they existed. I knew they were alive. But it really seemed to me that the surfing was a costume, like they were only pretending to be so enamored of it. How could anyone be that devoted to something so lacking a destination? Just wave after wave, over and over. I wished someone were that enamored of me. But their love for surfing was real. It was a fact. They really loved surfing as much as they appeared to love it. This one didn't have a board, though. This wasn't a surfer. This was a swimmer.

"What's your name?" he asked.

"Lucy."

I felt old.

"Nice to meet you, Lucy," he said. "I'm Theo."

When he said his name, his hotness increased. He was real, there in the water, real in a way that I wasn't. He was swimming and wet and I was—what was I doing? I thought of all my books, the ones waiting for me in piles back in my parching Phoenix apartment, collecting dust. I thought of the university library. I imagined the library growing and growing, the books piling up on the edge of this ocean. One wave could destroy them all. They were so dry, like they were actually made of dust. My skin, too, felt like an old book: powdery parchment etched with lines that supposedly contained knowledge, but when you looked closer they were only empty scribbles. Not the right kind of knowledge. If you put me in the water, I too would dissolve. I was sure of it.

"Do you always swim at night?"

"Yes," he said. "The waves are more intense but it makes you stronger."

"Aren't you afraid of drowning?"

"No," he said.

I looked at the moon. Then I looked back down at him, and I got scared. Who was he? I didn't want to die. Or at least, I didn't want to feel myself dying or drowning. Here I was, sitting on the rocks at midnight talking to a stranger, my legs hanging off the rock. He could just grab my ankle, pull me off the rocks and hold me under, and that would be that. But why would he do that?

I don't know that we are ever really okay in life, but there are times when we feel closer to it—when we don't remember what it feels like to suffer. During these times we are moving forward in the void, forgetting we are going nowhere, so the void feels less daunting. We feel like we are handling shit. We are handling shit and doing work on ourselves. And then another person comes in, and meets us there, and we think we can handle it. We think we can handle it, because in that moment we feel that we can handle anything.

I always thought I could handle things, until I couldn't. I talked like dying was no big deal, but in that moment I definitely didn't want to die. It was crazy to be out there. I didn't know what I was doing.

"I should go," I said. "It's freezing, and I have to walk my dog."

"Oh, you have a dog?" he said, sounding a little disappointed.

This too was strange. Surfer bros always seemed to love dogs. They themselves were like the beautiful carefree mutts of the sea.

"Yes. Why?"

"No reason," he said.

"Do you have any dogs or cats?"

"No," he said. Then he laughed. "I have fish."

"Fish?" I blurted, and started laughing in spite of myself.

"Where do you live?" he asked.

"Just across the beach," I said. "In one of those houses."

I pointed in the general direction of Annika's house.

"Ahhh," he said. "Venice girl."

"Yeah," I said. "I live with my sister."

I didn't tell him that I was from the desert.

"Well, if you decide to traipse out to the rocks again late at night, maybe I'll see you again," he said. "I'm always out here swimming."

"Yeah, maybe," I said. "Okay, well, bye. Be safe."

"Bye—you too," he said.

He was still holding on to the rocks when I left. He looked like he didn't want to let go, but not because he was scared of the waves, just because—I'm not sure why. I walked onto the beach and took my sandals off. When I turned around he was still holding on to the rocks, with his cheek resting on one of them. He waved.

When I got back to the house I swore I could still feel his eyes on me. I looked back one more time, but he was gone. I didn't see him anywhere in the waves. I felt a creepy feeling go up my spine and was glad the dog was waiting for me.

"Hi, Domi," I said, sliding open the glass door.

But Dominic didn't come bounding toward me as usual. Instead he sniffed the air repeatedly and kept his distance. His ears went flat and he growled. I had never seen him like that before and it made me wonder if I was haunted now. He continued to growl, but the sound was cute to me. He was trying to be like a dog in the wild or a wolf. Did dogs still live in the wild? Did anything? Was there any wildness anywhere, or was all of it inhabited by tech dudes now, juice places and blow-dry bars? Had anything been left undiscovered, or did the Internet snatch it all up the moment it existed? Nothing remained untouched. Or maybe some things weren't completely mapped out yet and there was still a little room for the mystery. Maybe some strange and beautiful boy could still pop out of the sea and surprise you.

"Dominic, no," I said. "Absolutely not. We don't growl. We never growl at Mama."

Suddenly, I felt giddy and silly. No longer scared, not even at all. I wondered if the gods or maybe the universe had actually heard my amethyst prayer. Everything was so strange. Life was okay, though. Life was maybe even kind of cute. You simply had to expect nothing from it. That's what the Stoics believed—Zeno and Seneca, those ancient fuckers. The trick, I now agreed, was you had to remain unattached to any future wishes or vision. You had to never get attached to any other person or expect anything good to come to you, and that was how you fell in love with life and how maybe certain fun and good things could happen to you. They only happened as long as you didn't need anything from anyone. As long as you didn't take anything from anyone or give any part of yourself away to another person, but you just sort of met the other person in space, good things could happen. You had to fall in love with quiet first.

10.

But in the morning the beach was filled with tourists and the amethyst was just a rock. The quiet was gone again and replaced with nothingness. The candle had melted all over the deck and I spent a good half hour scraping wax, which was congealing—thinly—in the sun. I decided I would take Dominic for a walk over to the Santa Monica farmers' market, try to be like other humans on a Sunday. Maybe buy some fruit and be swept away in some bullshit of the day. Maybe I could just be a woman and her dog buying fruit.

The farmers' market was full of families. I don't like families. There was a band doing covers of Crosby, Stills & Nash and children getting pony rides. It made me want to never eat anything organic again. By the locally farmed corn I ran into Claire, the redhead from group. She smiled and waved. I guess she was a little better. At least, she was no longer crying.

"I'm never going back to that group again," she said. "Fuck them and their shite, they know fuck-all about me. I don't believe in love addiction. I don't believe in withdrawal or taking time off from dating or anything that puritanical or black and white can fix my problem."

"Yeah, they're pretty depressing."

"The worst," she said. "And I just had a date with a hot younger man. His name is David, a total crumpet. I'm already enamored, probably on the road to obsession. But I think that if I can just keep them coming—you know, have more than one boy I'm fucking, maybe two or three—then I won't get so fixated on one of them."

"That seems smart," I said.

"I'm already interviewing a harem. I've been going to poly-amory events. I met this one guy, Trent, at an event in Topanga. He is a little older, did porn. He has a ponytail and I can't tell if it's scraggly or scrummy, but I think scrummy. He has a wife. She has boyfriends. I'm going to fuck him tomorrow night. I also met this other guy named Orion; he's, like, barely eighteen, very twee. He was wearing a kilt. He's pansexual. We made out all night. But he lives in Vermont and already went back, so I'm still looking for a third. I might shag this guy who works at Best Buy. We've fucked in the past. He's a Jamaican guy, super cut, really nice to me."

"Are they all poly? Is David poly too?"

"No, he's, like, I don't know what. A computer programmer. Might be on the spectrum. Does yoga, though. Huge cock."

"So fun," I said. "I'm jealous."

"You should really be doing Tinder," she said. "Or come with me to these poly things."

"Oh, I don't know," I said. "I'm worried about getting obsessed with someone else. And Dr. Jude said—"

"Rubbish," she said. "How else do you think you are going to get over him? You think you are going to just heal? Nobody heals. You need to replace! That'll be the thing that makes him come back in the end, but by then you won't want him. Men can smell it when we've moved on. Especially to a bigger cock. Bald Brad texted me."

"Don't text him back!"

"Oh, I won't," she said. "I have no need."

"Well, that's interesting," I said. "I'm glad you found a way to balance it all and not get attached."

"For women like us? I'm convinced this is the only way. The only way you're going to get over him is by having a lot of sex and seeing what else is out there. You might even surprise your-self. You might see that you can do it, you can just fuck and not get attached. I guarantee I will not be getting attached to Trent."

"Ponytail man?"

"Yes." She laughed. "Also, you need to see how hot you are. To feel it."

"I am so not hot," I laughed. "I'm gross."

"Oh, bugger off. You have the disheveled waif ingénue thing going. Like that bitch from *Les Misérables*."

She looked at her watch.

"Fuck, I have to go pick up my kids. Never have children. They'll ruin your life."

"Not planning on it," I said.

"You should just try Tinder," she said. "Just try it."

11.

That night I thought about going to the rocks to see if Theo the swimmer was there again. It made me feel stupid. What was I doing chasing down some boy? Instead I made a fake Facebook profile (I'd shut mine down since I saw Jamie and Rochelle toasting over flan) and created a Tinder account, using old photos: some from five or ten years ago. I was not consciously thinking *I will kill the old me and in her place will grow an electronic me,* but that is what I was doing. I wanted to negate myself somehow, as if you could just sign up to vanish. As if you could sign up to really be alive, but as someone else. Well, I was going to be somebody who didn't care. I was going to be free about sex, my body. I wanted to be the one to no longer give a fuck. Could you sculpt yourself into one who does not give a fuck? Could I remove the giving a fuck from the time in my life before I met Jamie, where I had sex with a lot of people, but always seemed to care whether they loved me after? I had to go into it with a professed mission of not giving a fuck. So I wrote my bio:

Let's make out in a dark alley.

There were a lot of disgusting dudes, particularly actor-type bros. I hated actors. With my levels of social anxiety, I couldn't be with anyone who was faking being relaxed. We all already wore enough masks. I didn't need someone whose profession was putting on extra ones. My propensity was to strip off masks as quickly as possible, lay everything out, so as to relieve the discomfort of having to wear one in the first place. I was almost compulsively confessional. But with actors there seemed to be an unlimited supply of masks, just layers upon layers.

The first person I messaged with was a designer named Garrett. Garrett's bio said he owned his own graphic design firm, with clients like JetBlue, Apple, and MTV, yet somehow he was only twenty-nine. These fucking kids. He was hot though, and I couldn't believe he would be interested in me. I lied and said I had a boyfriend, but we were in an open relationship. I don't know why I said that: maybe so he knew I was wanted elsewhere, maybe to appear less desperate and more preoccupied. Or maybe to point out that if he tried to kill me, there would be someone who noticed I was missing. He said that was funny, because he had a girlfriend and they were also in an open relationship. He was originally from Toronto, now lived in Silver Lake. He said he was in Venice tonight for drinks with a client.

making out in the street, eh? he wrote.

yes, I typed.

what about doing anything else? anywhere else? want to fuck?

I got nervous.

Then I began messaging with Adam, twenty-seven, who kind of looked like a monkey, but in a sexy way. He had one of those man buns. Adam told me straight up that I was hot. I liked this. He said he would love to make out with me in the street, any street. He said he lived right near Venice, in Marina del Rey, and was a waiter at Whiskey Red's, but he was trying to become a writer. This was my man.

I told Garrett no thanks and he seemed disappointed. He asked if I was sure I didn't want to fuck. Could he ask why I was declining? I told him I had met someone who I thought would be a better fit. He said he understood but if I changed my mind to let him know.

Adam and I decided we would meet two nights later and try

our street make-out. It was now 1:57 a.m. I realized I had been swiping on profiles and checking messages all night. I forgot to take Dominic out and it had been eight hours. I rubbed his belly and apologized, then walked him all the way to the Venice canals. Adam, Adam, I thought, and imagined wanting him. More so, I imagined him wanting me. Him lusting for me. I fell asleep masturbating to the thought of this person, as of yet still basically imaginary.

I woke up with my hand inside my underwear. My pubic hair felt bristly and bushy, like a steel-wool sponge. Sometimes I used to put conditioner on it but I hadn't in a while. I wondered what Adam was used to, if any of the girls his age had pubic hair at all. Then I felt my real hair on my head. It was like a bad cloud. I could feel all the gray seeping out, making me nauseated, probably Adam too.

I wanted to be perfect for Adam. I walked Dominic and gave him his breakfast, then went over to Abbot Kinney. There was a salon there called Trim and it looked pretty empty. I spoke with a cute brunette woman with caramel highlights named Allison.

"I have a date," I blurted.

"Nice," she said. "So what are you looking to do?"

"I need to color it. Nothing too crazy. Like an auburn is what I usually do."

I showed her some pictures of myself on my phone, what I looked like prior to falling apart.

"So where are you going on this date?" she said. "Anywhere cool?"

I didn't want to say I would be slobbering on someone like dogs in the street. Or that it was with someone I had never met and that he was over ten years younger than me. I mean, the age difference in itself was kind of cool, but I still felt weird. So I lied and said that it was an older tech executive who I had been seeing. I said we were going away for a few days to a bed-and-breakfast in Santa Barbara.

"Oh, that should be great," said Allison enthusiastically.

It felt fun to be having girl talk like this. I never had girl talk—not since Rochelle turned from ally to rat. This felt hopeful, like there was something to be excited about—both for Allison and me. She was probably just pretending to care. But even if it was all a lie, I preferred the lie to real life.

After getting my color I went into some clothing stores, all of them insanely expensive. It was rich hippie shit: silk kimonos for $700, cuff bracelets and bib necklaces that looked like they came from a tent at Woodstock but were upwards of $3,000, fringe vests for $1,900. But then I found one boutique that advertised everything for $20 or less. I tried on a black long-sleeved dress that showed off my slender legs and waist, but was A-line at the hip.

The saleswomen all said I looked amazing, and I liked their enthusiasm. I liked the attention and it made me high. Now I didn't even care how the date with Adam went. Just getting ready for it felt like something to live for, some net in my life that caught me and strained me out of the ooze. It was as though some wonderful future event were being extended backward in time. The future event needed only to exist so that I could have this excitement and anticipation now.

Next I went to a fancy makeup shop and bought some lipstick to match my hair color, a matte crimson. The women there treated me like an interloper and gave me strange stares. I think I talked about my date too much. I kept mentioning the tech exec and Santa Barbara so they would think that I was rich enough to be there. But they never smiled. Was I not supposed to talk to them? Could you only talk to some women about imaginary dates, while others could smell your reality the moment they looked at you?

The final touch was a bikini wax. I went to a dive—some shithole where they said they could take me right away. I was just going to do the sides, but when the waxer—a bosomy woman named Kristina—saw my vagina, she started yelling.

"Too much hair! Too much hair!"

"I know! What do you think I should do with it?"

"Me? I say take it all off."

"Ha, no way," I said.

"Okay, fine. I take some off. I show you. Just lie back."

I lay back on the small pillow covered in paper. The room was cold and the ceiling was covered in what looked like big pee stains and mold.

"You have boyfriend?" she asked. "What he think of hair?"

"No," I said. "No boyfriend."

"Ah, see!" she said. "I will fix that. Relax."

I felt her spread on the wax. It felt too hot, but I didn't know how warm it was supposed to be. It felt like my right labia was burning. She blew on the wax a few times with frenetic movements.

"One, two, three," she said.

Then she ripped. I felt like my vagina was a tree, its roots being torn out of the ground. It was an ache, a tearing, and a burning all at once. I wanted to kill her.

"Oh my God!" I yelled.

I looked down. There was my full bush with one giant chunk missing. The area was pink and had a few tiny dots of blood. My crotch looked like a furry mouth with one pulled tooth.

"Darling, lie back. That was nothing."

"No!" I said. "Don't do it, please. I'm done. I'm done."

"I can't leave you like this. You're going to go to mans like this?" she asked, pointing to my torn-up vagina.

"I don't care!"

"I go gentler," she said.

I didn't know what to do. We were sort of fighting. I was pushing her hands away and she was applying the wax. With the second strip I started to cry.

"This is fucking insane," I said.

But I let her do my lips, which felt like she was searing off my vulva. I couldn't believe that other women did this. Who were these people? Then she did my asshole, which she said she had to do, because it was "carrying around stink." I'd been carrying around stink for thirty-eight years.

When I got home I lay down with Dominic and held a package of frozen edamame to my vagina. I hated everything. Now the dress, the lipstick, even my hair color seemed stupid. I realized I didn't care about any of this stuff, even the dress, which I had loved. It wasn't about the dress. It was in the acquisition of the dress that there had been beauty.

I thought about different kinds of happiness. There was the happiness I felt in all of the adrenaline of running around, a crazed happiness. This was a different happiness from the quiet peace of just being with Dominic. I kissed his ear.

"Sorry I get so distracted," I said.

He sniffed at me. Suddenly I didn't want to go out with Adam anymore. I fell asleep with the edamame defrosting on my vagina.

But the next morning, my excitement—that sense of purpose—was oddly restored. I woke up to a text from Adam that said,

see you tonight gorgeous.

There was something about the morning of a date that tricked me. It tricked me out of the haze of being alive. Or perhaps it tricked me out of the sadness of knowing that one day I would die. It punctured the nothingness. Now I felt passion and love for everything.

12.

Back at group, the word of the day seemed to have shifted from *unavailable* to *triggered*. In the safe space of Dr. Jude's crap-filled office, everyone, it seemed, had recently been triggered by something.

For Chickenhorse it was an escalation of the issues with her landlady. Apparently, the harassment had increased and was now becoming a question of abuse. Chickenhorse's landlady had entered her apartment without her permission, while she was showering, no less, and had brought her little son with her. When Chickenhorse exited the shower, she was shocked to find a three-year-old boy and his teddy bear. She screamed and accidentally dropped her towel. Now the landlady was accusing her of unseemly behavior toward her son. She was given a thirty-day eviction notice.

"My inner child is triggered, because I no longer feel safe," she said, looking particularly chicken-gummed. "But I'm having trouble getting in touch with my anger. I'm scared I won't have a place to live, so instead of fighting back I'm trying to be 'good' and begging the landlady to let me stay. But I'm the one who has been victimized!"

The group cooed and soothed, letting her know it was not her fault. Was anything ever our fault?

I wanted to tell Chickenhorse that she probably just needed to get laid. Why wasn't she dating again? Maybe it's because Dr. Jude's version of dating, "conscious dating," sounded boring as shit. You were supposed to call and check in with a friend before and after every date, no texting more than once a day, no sex outside of a monogamous relationship. Maybe Chickenhorse didn't think she could follow the rules. She seemed very *Fatal Attraction* to me.

Sara, over a large bag of Calimyrna figs, recounted the tale of how salsa dancing had suddenly turned dangerous for her.

"It brought up all of my body-image shame," she said. "When no one chose to partner with me, it triggered my insecurities over the way I look. Then a man finally did choose to partner with me and I found myself getting high off of it, wanting more from him, the way I always felt with Stan. It was unsafe."

Now Sara was filling her Stanless days and nights by attending an "Opening the Heart" workshop down the street in Santa Monica.

But Sara's heart already seemed pretty open to me. How much more open did she want it to get?

"We'll see how it goes," she said. "Already I feel a little triggered by it, because some of the women at these workshops end up pairing off with the men. It's as though they become a couple for the week. But this has never happened for me. Where is my workshop boyfriend?"

Dr. Jude reminded Sara that she wasn't cleared to be dating yet anyway.

"I know," said Sara, glumly biting into a fig. "But it would be nice to know for once that I could have a workshop boyfriend if I really wanted."

Brianne's son had found a girlfriend, and this was hard for her.

"It's triggering for me, because it means I've been isolating a lot more," she said from under her wide-brimmed hat, face covered in a chalky substance that I guessed was zinc. She looked like she was wearing a clown mask.

"He never had many friends, but now he is out most of the time and I don't have any companionship."

I wondered, too, if Brianne's son was also in therapy. If not, he would be soon.

"I've been staying the course with Match and Millionaire Match," she said, gently patting her lips to make sure they were still huge. "And we will just have to wait and see. If it's meant to be, it's meant to be. If not, it's okay. I don't need anyone. I have a very full life."

I wasn't buying it today.

"So you'd really be okay to never fall in love again for the rest of your life?" I asked her.

Brianne looked at me through her clown paint.

"I'm feeling judged," said Brianne.

"Sorry," I said.

"What about you, Lucy? You don't believe that a person can be alone and be content with that?" asked Dr. Jude.

"I don't know. Probably not," I said.

"Mmmm."

"Do you?"

"Oh, definitely," said Dr. Jude, yellow teeth flashing. "I don't believe we need another person to complete us."

"Not even to fuck?"

"Let's be sure to be conscious of any triggering language," she said.

"Yes, I'm feeling triggered," said Sara.

"Right, sorry," I said.

The room got quiet.

"Are you in a relationship, Dr. Jude?" I asked.

She paused and toyed with an angel card on the table next to her. It said *Awakening*.

"No," she said. "Not at the moment."

"When was the last time you were in one?"

"Well, if you want to know, I'm pretty recently divorced," she said.

"Oh," I said. "Would you say you're content?"

"Hmmmm," she said, sipping her green tea. "Actually, yes. Most of the time I would say yes, I am content."

Nobody said a word. Sara was slowly peeling a clementine

with the hand she used to massage her foot. The amount of time it was taking could not be worth the bite-sized little fruit. I watched her peel and peel the white-and-orange rind, and began to shake. It was the clementine of Sisyphus. Everything was hopeless. Then Sara offered Brianne a slice of her foot-fruit and Brianne accepted gleefully, as though she were giving her a jewel. I felt sorry for them. None of them had anything left to look forward to in the romance department. Maybe they would go on some tepid controlled dates, but no dark alleys. What did any of them have to live for, really? A son who would just grow up and forget all about you? Some man in hemp pants at a workshop saying you had a nice aura? An office filled with shit? At least I still had sparkle in my life. I was going on an adventure.

Of course, I didn't say a word about Adam. I didn't want them reprimanding me or giving me any healthy advice. I knew what they would say: I wasn't supposed to be dating yet. And meeting up with strangers in alleys doesn't constitute conscious dating. But maybe I didn't want to be conscious.

13.

Later, as I waited for Adam on Ocean Front Walk, near Marina del Rey, where the homeless cleared and the vibration of the boardwalk became more desolate, I was so excited that I was nauseated. The Santa Monica Mountains were covered in fog, so the pink and palm-tree silhouettes of Venice looked like their own island—an old beach scene frozen in time. It was windy out and I was cold, but I felt important—momentous—like I was on a timeless mission. I could be anyone standing by any beach in history, waiting for a lover. I could be Sappho, unafraid of Eros, calling Aphrodite to her shrine.

But as soon as I saw him coming, I thought, Oh God no. He sort of looked like his picture, but more the monkey aesthetic than the hot one. Also, he had an additional werewolf essence that the photo had not captured. It wasn't just his jagged teeth, the scruffy goatee, but something else that was distinctly were-wolf. He waved to me, and I waved back, cursing through my teeth, already disappointed. When he crossed the street I tried not to let it show, to be warm, though I wasn't sure why I cared what he thought. I guess I felt bad about rejecting someone with-out even knowing him. I felt sort of ashamed that I was judg-ing him for his looks, but with an alley make-out what other attributes could there be? It figured. Of course this werewolf-monkey creature was the best that I could do.

He might have been disappointed in what I looked like too, but he didn't show it.

"You're really cute," he said, as though assuring both me and himself. "You look a lot younger than forty. A lot younger."

"I'm thirty-eight," I said.

"Not that I don't like older women. I love older women. You've got seasoning. But you look like a young older woman. Or an old younger woman—"

"Okay," I said, relieving him of having to speak. "I got it."

"So what do you want to do?" he asked. "Do you want to stay here and have a drink or do you want to go for a walk?"

"Let's have a drink first," I said.

"God, you're really cute," he said.

We turned in to a little dive. I ordered myself a vodka tonic. Rarely did I drink liquor anymore but I felt that the situation called for it. I needed to be less lucid than I was. He didn't offer to pay for my drink. But he got two tequila shots, offering me one, and a Jack and Coke. I declined, laughing.

"So what have you been reading lately?" he asked, after toasting me with one of his two shots. I had told him over the Internet that I was a librarian, and he loved that. He had asked me to wear my glasses, but I didn't wear glasses.

"I'm almost always reading the Greeks," I said. "I'm doing a project on the poet Sappho that I've been working on for a number of years. Trying to finish it this summer."

"Oh yeah, I read him in high school," he said. "I'm really into the Beats right now. Do you like the Beats?"

I liked the Beats for a second when I was fourteen. By sixteen I realized they were mostly just good for picking out a douchebag. There was something about douche bros and the Beats. They just gravitated there.

"Yeah, I love them," I said. "Who is your favorite?"

"Kerouac," he said. "I'm really into Kerouac, Burroughs, and Bukowski. Kerouac just keeps it so real, like the way he writes his characters it's just so—legit. I would love to write like him someday."

"Right," I said.

"So how about that walk?" he said.

Outside it was almost dark. He lit up a cigarette and offered me one. I declined and watched him squint and inhale, then exhale. Clearly he had studied that move: a James Dean kind of smoking pose. But he was no James Dean, and his hands were even more monkey-werewolf than the rest of him: monkey in the way they curled around the cigarette like they were clutching a banana and werewolf in the way his arm hair crawled well over his wrist and onto the hands themselves. He was hairy to the knuckle. We started to walk and I felt like I was going to vomit. I kept wanting to say, "You know what? Thanks, but I'm not feeling so great and I'm just going to walk home." But we kept walking.

Suddenly he grabbed my hand and said, "Can I kiss you?"

But he didn't wait for me to respond. His palm was sweaty, but his lips were full and I closed my eyes and it felt shocking to be kissing someone new. The new mouth shape was exciting, also strange. After eight years I forgot that lips could come in different shapes and feels. Also, the taste of cigarettes and whiskey was exciting. I was half nauseated and half turned on. I felt rebellious and young.

"What?" he said.

"Nothing," I said, giggling. "You're just cute."

Looking at him, I really didn't think he was cute. But I didn't know what else to say so I shut my eyes and took the back of his head in my palm and pulled him toward me. Then he introduced his tongue, much deeper into my mouth, circling it in a clockwise motion. What the fuck was he doing? He was ruining it. I started to put my tongue out as a guard, to try to stop his rotating tongue, but I guess he just took this as a sign that I was turned on—that I was into it—because he continued with the circling, only deeper in my mouth, almost to my throat, gagging me. I put my finger up between our mouths, pretending to trace his lips, but really trying to create some distance. Then I closed my lips a lot, guiding him into softer and gentler kisses. I kept my eyes sealed shut. I could have just cut it off there. I'd gotten what I said I wanted. I'm not sure why I didn't.

He rubbed my tits over my black cotton dress. I could feel his bulge against me. Then he started kissing my ear and neck, which I think is a turn-on for some women, because men do it a lot—especially when they are younger. I remembered these moves now from when I was in my early twenties: the weird breathing in my ear, the sticky trail on my neck, moves he probably read on Esquire.com. All I could think about was how my neck and ear now smelled like his breath, which had taken on a sour quality: the whiskey, tequila, and smoke forming a noxious stew.

"Let's go back to my house," he whispered into my ear.

"Uhhh, I don't think so," I said. "What if you're a murderer?"

"I'm not a murderer." He laughed.

"If you were a murderer you obviously wouldn't tell me."

"I'm so not a murderer," he said.

"Well, I will just walk a little further and then I'll decide. Maybe I can pick up some more clues in the meantime."

"Yeah, let's just walk in the direction of my house. Or we could go to your house instead?"

I imagined bringing this kid to Annika's house. I didn't want him knowing where I lived. Or in there to begin with.

"No, that's okay. What's your address?" I asked.

Then I texted Claire:

I'm going here with a strange boy from the internet

it's your fault

if i don't text you after then this is where to find the body

His house was one tiny room that reeked of cigarettes. The mini refrigerator, stove, and oven were right at the foot of his bed, and the bathroom just off the head of it. There was beige wall-to-wall carpeting, even in the "kitchen" part, with stains that looked like spaghetti sauce, tar, and generally a lot of lint. He had very few books for someone who claimed to be a writer and loved to read. I counted seven: three of them Bukowski.

"I love Bukowski maybe the best, actually," he said when he caught me looking at the books. "Find what you love and let it kill you. So raw."

I didn't say anything. He put his arms around my waist and began kissing me, then pulled me onto the dirty plaid bedspread and took off my dress.

"You have such a hot body for forty," he said.

"Thirty-eight," I said.

"Mmmm," he said, sliding his fingers into my underpants and tracing my war-torn labia. "I love your pussy. So hot that you have hair down there."

I took off his pants. His cock was hard as a stone, yet simultaneously pink and slimy. I didn't want to touch it. So I didn't. He began fingering me, very dryly, adding further battering to my poor wax-mangled vagina.

He kept whispering, "Can I fuck you? I want to fuck you. Will you suck my dick?"

I kept saying, "No, not yet. I'm not ready."

I guess in an effort to turn me on he inserted two more fingers into my wilting vagina, banging them in and out. My labia burned but I was surprised to find that up inside me I was wet, as though I didn't know I was turned on. Now the wetness began to come down onto my labia and clit. But he ignored my clit and just kept banging away.

"Such a hot, tight, pink pussy," he said.

I didn't know how he knew it was pink. He hadn't even looked at it or licked it.

"Let me fuck it. Please?" he said.

"No," I said.

"Okay, then will you suck me? Just suck me a little," he asked. "I want to see those hot old lips on my cock."

That was it.

"You know what I think would be hot?" I asked. "What would do it for me? I want to watch you jerk off for a little."

He stopped finger fucking me and looked me in the eye.

"Really?"

"Oh, yeah. It's the biggest turn-on. I wanna watch as you lie there and give yourself pleasure. Jerk that hot dick."

I don't know where I was getting this from. When I was in my twenties I used to like to watch my boyfriend jerk off. But not this dude. I think I was just trying to get him to come, and get out of there without having to touch his weird pink dick and mismatched brown balls.

Lying on his back, he complied and began to stroke it. I was just, like, "Oh yeah, baby, that's it." I thought about all this subterfuge, just to get out of a situation that I had put myself in. Technically I didn't even need to do anything to get out of the situation except leave. He kept looking at me and I just wanted him to come quickly. Right before he spurted he asked if I could lick it. I told him no, then I wouldn't be able to watch.

When he was finished I said it was a hot experience, but I had to go home and feed Dominic and give him his medication. He said that he wanted to do something to me—that it shouldn't just be him who got off. I told him that this was wonderful, really, and had been more than enough.

Out on the street I felt free, strangely elated. It wasn't just the joy of escaping him but the fact that I had come out pursued and wanted—something new after my pursuit of Jamie all winter. I hadn't gotten three blocks when he texted me:

u r amazing i'd love to do it again

I didn't respond, but kind of squealed. No longer did Adam have to be real Adam. Now he was fantasy Adam again, and I had him and the fantasy in my pocket. Sure, the experience itself had been disappointing and gross, but at least it was different from the disappointment I'd grown used to in my years with Jamie. When he and I were together and the sex was less than riveting, I felt filled with doom after: ennui in my head and suffocating in my chest. It was the same doom that I felt in the car just before we broke up. There was an *is that all there is*–ness. I would go sit on the toilet immediately after he came. This was partially to avoid getting a urinary tract infection, but also so he wouldn't see me frowning. When he found me sitting there sadly, I told him it was because the sex made me feel such powerful things. But really what I felt was despair: that this was all there would be, forever and ever and ever, until of course it wasn't.

But if Adam wanted me, there were others who would want me, maybe many others, even some who didn't read Bukowski. I imagined a bouquet of dicks, a stack of abdominal muscles like a deck of cards, painted across the sky. The hunger in me suddenly felt bottomless. It scared me a little.

14.

I found myself out on the rocks again later that night. I was throwing shells into the water when Theo the swimmer came paddling up, shoulders white in the moonlight. I hoped he would be there. He seemed happy to see me too.

"You came back," he said.

"I did."

"Hi," he said.

"Hi. You're really not freezing?"

"No, it feels natural."

"Crazy. So I have a question. Do you like Bukowski?" I asked.

"Who?" he said.

"Charles Bukowski; he's a poet."

"I don't know who that is," he said, treading water. "Why?"

"It's not important," I said.

"No, tell me why. Do you like him?"

"Definitely not," I said. "But I just went on a date with someone who is a big fan."

"You did?" said Theo. "How was that for you?"

I couldn't tell if he seemed genuinely interested or if he was just being polite.

"Heinous," I said.

"That can happen, I suppose," he said.

Suddenly I felt too . . . something. I wanted him to know I had gone on a date, because I wanted to see what his response would be. But I didn't want him to think that I was a complainer or needy, or that things didn't work out for me. I didn't want to seem bitter. I wanted to seem youthful and full of joie de vivre.

"It's okay," I said. "There's another possible date on the horizon with someone else. This designer guy. Might make out with him."

What was I saying?

"Ah," he said.

Did he look dejected? His expression was so serious that I couldn't tell.

"What about you?" I broke in. "Do you have a girlfriend?"

"Not at the moment," he said.

"Boyfriend?" I asked.

"Nope," he said.

"Really, I'm surprised. I would think people would be all over you."

I don't know what I was trying to get him to say. Mostly, I wanted to get us talking about sex and love. But he changed the subject.

"So which poets do you like?" he asked.

"Me, no one at the moment. I actually want to kill all of poetry. If there was no more poetry left in the world I would be fine with it."

"I hate art too," he said.

"Really?" I asked.

"No." He grinned.

"It's not that I hate poetry. But I've been working on a project about a particular poet for a very long time. And I'm having trouble with it. So right now I'm feeling pretty over poetry."

"Which poet?" he asked.

"Oh, her name is Sappho," I said.

"I know Sappho," he said.

"No you don't," I said.

I assumed he was being one of those people whom, when asked about a movie they've never seen, responds with an affirmation about how much they loved it.

"Yes, Sappho, she's not exactly esoteric. Greek love poet. Well actually, she was a musician. Of course, most people don't know that."

"Yeah, I know. How do you know that?"

"I know a few things," he said.

"Amazing."

"So what is this project about?"

"It's bullshit, pretty much."

"Is it? I can't imagine bullshitting about Sappho. Her words are so beautiful, what's left of them anyway."

"I don't know if it's bullshit. It's an attempt to sort of read Sappho through the—nothingness around her. Through the destruction of her text."

"That sounds interesting, actually. Nothingness is good. Almost as good as filling up every space," he smiled. "And destruction. Destruction can be sexy."

I shivered a little bit.

"I guess the gaps are sort of a reminder that, in love, things get disconnected," I said. "People just disappear."

"Maybe they leave room for something more infinite," he said.

"Maybe," I said. "All I know is it's not going very well. I'm not enjoying it."

"But you're still doing it?" he said.

"Yes," I said. "I guess I like torturing myself."

"That can also be sexy if done right, I suppose."

Was he fucking with me? I stood up. I didn't know whether to move closer to him or away from him on the rock, so I looked up at the moon, which was a crescent. I thought about licking it or putting it inside me.

"Well, Lucy, I wish you only the best with the self-torture," he said. "And with your next date."

"Thanks," I said. "Maybe I'll see you out here again?"

"Maybe," he said.

"Okay."

"Have a good night," he said.

And with that he pushed off the rock and began to breast-stroke away.

15.

When I got home I was turned on. That little fucker. Who was he, even, lurking around in the ocean? I decided to take immediate action. Brushing past Dominic, who sniffed at me suspiciously and growled a little, I took to my phone. It was time to send Tinder Garrett a message.

Hey I changed my mind. Want to meet up after all? I wrote.

He wrote back within seconds:

guess it didn't work out with the other dude?

haha, I said.

want to come to downtown? i work in a loft down here. meet me on the roof of the Ace Hotel tmrw @ 7

sounds good I wrote, so casually.

Immediately after that message came a text. It was from Jamie.

How are you? I miss you.

My stomach dropped. Claire was right! It was like he could smell that I was out with other men. Now it was raining attention. There was Adam, Garrett, Theo, and Jamie. I wanted to wait to text him back but wrote immediately, of course.

I'm fine. deep in therapy, as instructed

And how is megan?

There was a pause.

She is good

Well, that was that . . .

She's no you, of course

Now this was getting crazy. Was I a sorcerer? Had I conjured all of this? What was he trying to do? It was like I was the other woman and Megan was the one he was stuck with. I suddenly no longer felt hurt that he was with her. I liked being the desirable one. Also, I liked playing with him. I was going to ignore him. Already high on Garrett and our impending date, I would be able to do it. This was what I needed—multiple men at all times. Then I wouldn't need any of them. Put me naked in a clamshell. Let them all fawn around me.

16.

"You're absolutely glowing! You're not dating anyone, are you?" asked Annika.

She was standing on the balcony of her hotel wearing a long embroidered caftan. Through video chat I could see the Provence sunset behind her.

"No, I'm keeping to myself."

"Good," she said. "Get that kundalini shakti recharged. Don't go scattering that chi anywhere and you'll be a warrior by the time I get back. How is the group?"

"A nightmare," I said.

"But you're going?"

"I'm going."

"Let me see my baby."

I held the computer screen up to Dominic. She made cooing noises and he pawed it, whined a little.

"He looks a touch sad," she said. "You're spending ample time with him?"

"We're thick as thieves."

"Good," she said. "Maybe add a bit of coconut oil to his dry food. It keeps his coat nice and shiny."

"Already doing it."

"Thanks, and you should cook for him. That turkey, zucchini, and peas dish I left the recipe for out on the counter. He loves it. Vegetables are good for his blood sugar."

"Will do."

"I hate being separated from him for so long. You don't think I'm a bad mother, do you?"

"No, it's the twenty-first century, don't be a helicopter parent."

"But—"

"That's just patriarchal guilt. Enjoy your trip, Aunt Lucy is taking great care of him."

When we hung up I felt like an asshole. Annika had always tried to be a good sister to me. By the time my mother died she was already in college, out of the house, but she tried her best. She called often to check in on me and never made me feel like I had been forgotten. She sent me mix tapes, weed, and makeup, so that I could feel cool in high school. Before she was even rich she paid for the abortion I had at nineteen so I wouldn't have to ask my father for the money. How was I repaying her? By neglecting the most beloved thing in her life for strangers on the Internet.

I looked around the living room. There were pictures of Dominic everywhere: Dominic on the beach in Malibu with his ears blowing back, Dominic dressed as a bumblebee on Halloween, Annika cradling Dominic as a little puppy, her face serene and dreamlike. Dominic himself now had his head in my lap and was looking up at me from under his dog brow.

"I'm going to do better," I said to him, scratching his white diamond. "I promise. From now on it's only going to be you and me. As soon as I get back from this date."

17.

I got to the Ace at five and had time to kill. I decided I would go up to the roof and maybe try to think about my book a little bit. Once again, I'd somehow shoved Sappho under a man: multiple men this time. I'd come to Venice to purge the influence of dick on my life and had wound up becoming Helen of Troy. What would Sappho think? The advisory committe said the thesis draft was due by fall semester. Did that mean the beginning of the semester? Day one? I knew that it did. But I pretended I had some wiggle room: that I could just pop in there on Halloween, draft in hand, like, *Sorry for the delay!* and my funding would go on.

I'd always been scared not to finish the thesis but maybe even more scared to finish it. What would happen then? Would I apply for teaching jobs in other cities? I had thought that maybe I would, in the hopes that it would make Jamie ask me to stay—that the catalyst of my moving somewhere else would make him finally step up. But somewhere in my mind, I always knew he wouldn't. I hadn't wanted to face that.

On the Ace roof there was flamenco music playing, or bossa nova or something. It all seemed so contemporary and pleasant. The sun was setting and I ordered a white wine. Was this how everything was now? Just nice? I wondered if other people felt comfortable within niceness, or whether they didn't even notice that things were nice. Maybe they expected everything to be nice. Maybe nice was like air to them.

I can't say that I was enjoying it, exactly, or even relaxing, but I felt that I was absorbing the stupidity and slowness of the niceness. Like I was siphoning off its worst qualities. Actually, it did feel good. I just wanted to drool and be dumb. Two glasses of wine later and I was almost there. I ordered another one. Then I got nervous. What was I doing? I should be home actually working on my book. Where was my life going? I couldn't think about it. I ate some olives and stared down the sun. I was wearing the same black dress that I had worn with Adam. I had liked it so much when I got it, but now that it was no longer new it didn't feel good enough. Now that I had owned it for more than a minute it had gotten some of me on it. My mouth tasted acidic. I felt rumpled, like I was wearing dirty laundry.

I kind of forgot that Garrett was coming until he tapped me on the shoulder. He was undeniably gorgeous in real life: six feet tall with a close-cut beard that looked like an evil shadow. Under the beard you could still see the outline of his jaw, which was strong and handsome. His jaw was in attendance. Also, he had the hair—the Tinder hair I called it, because a lot of the boys on there had that same look. It was like a not-so-secret code amongst the young and hip, this haircut where the sides were shaved all butch but the top was long, in what resembled a pompadour. His shirt was gingham and he smelled like the woods. He ordered a whiskey and ginger ale and asked what I wanted. I was afraid that if I drank any more I would fall off my chair, so I told him that I had just met a friend for cocktails prior and was okay for right now. Instead I ordered a sparkling water and avocado toast.

Garrett told me that he would be flying to New York the following day to teach classes in design at different universities. I kept staring at his jawline. I had forgotten they made them like that. He was boring, never asking me about myself, but I was so engaged by his jaw that it made what he said more interesting. It was his jaw that was speaking, not his mouth. The jaw also made me a little sad. It made me forget he had a girlfriend and then remember again. Like, in spite of his boringness, I kind of wanted the jaw to be mine. He did a good job not talking about the girlfriend. It would be easy for someone else to forget he had one.

After his drink and my toast we decided to take a walk. I wondered if this would be the make-out walk, since he had pretty much ignored that line of my Tinder bio and gone straight to the idea of fucking. Downtown L.A. wasn't pretty, but it was sexy in the dark—all empty space, cooling air, and warehouses. Sexy dirt. He pointed across the street at a neon blue lit sign and said, "That's my office." The sign said GO ALL NIGHT.

I thought the sign was stupid, but somehow, in the context of his jaw, it seemed hot. The jaw knew what it was doing, and so the sign did too. The jaw, and now the sign over this cool and modern office, made him seem like he had something creative and successful going on in his life. I wished he would just kiss me and wondered why he wasn't doing anything. I felt ashamed. Maybe he didn't think I was cute. Then the shame turned to anger, and I poked him in the chest. Then I pushed him into a wall. I don't know whether I was trying to get him to kiss me or to wrestle him. But he didn't seem to notice. He was too wrapped up in telling me about his new "health goth"–style fitness client. He was designing their online catalog, only the catalog wouldn't be like a regular catalog. It would be a space that had 3-D printing elements and holographic models.

Finally I said to him, "Can I kiss you?"

"Yeah," he said.

He pulled me to him gently and we kissed in a really sweet way, very soft. That was kind of confusing. He kissed me like someone who definitely didn't have a girlfriend. Like it was more of a loving kiss than a lusty kiss. Or maybe it wasn't loving, but just dispassionate. Then he stopped, looked at me, and started talking about the project again.

"Shhhhhh," I said.

I kissed him again. I felt strangely high. I was still a little drunk, but there was definitely something narcotic about kissing him—just being around him—that made me feel like I wanted to keep doing it over and over. I traced his jaw with my hand and let out a little sigh. He stopped kissing me and said, "So where did you park?"

I told him that I took an Uber, and I would take one back.

"I'm going to get a car now. Maybe we can kiss until it gets here?"

I got higher and higher off the kisses. I just needed more and more of them. I felt that if I stopped getting them I would not be okay, but while I was close to his face everything was humming. I might have been looking at him funny. Maybe too lovingly? Could he smell my strange attachment already? What the fuck was wrong with me?

On the way home in the car, I kept checking my phone but he didn't message me right away like Adam did. I kept turning my ringer off and on. Did I want to be notified? Did I not want to be notified or just be surprised? What if he never texted me again? When I got home, a pile of what looked like brown soft-serve ice cream was waiting for me on the kitchen tile. Dominic had shit on the floor.

18.

The following night, tired of waiting, I texted Garrett.

I had fun last night

I waited to hear back, carrying the phone with me from room to room. There was no response. I felt like Dominic's pile of shit. Was he really going to ignore me? I had gotten a weird feeling after our kisses, that I had suffocated him or seemed too interested. I texted him again.

Would you want to hang out again?

And again:

Hey, sorry if I seemed too eager or something.

And again:

Ok I'll leave you alone now

I went outside to the beach. I saw a girl bike by on the boardwalk. She had long hair to her ass and was wearing a tiny black skirt and a hot-pink crop top with her stomach showing. I thought to myself, *You little slut*. I didn't think it in a mean way but as a celebratory thing. I wanted to be her in that moment. She seemed like such an independent slut. I bet she never waited for texts, just fucked guys like Garrett all the time, casually. Surfer boys who looked like Theo the swimmer too, probably. I bet she never got attached. I wanted to be like this girl, not dependent on anyone else to be okay. Slutty, but an island. She wasn't pretending to be content without anyone while secretly wallowing in misery. She genuinely didn't give a fuck.

I walked over to the rocks to see if Theo was there, but he wasn't: only the waves. It was still probably too early. I waited a few minutes and wondered if he was mad at me for talking about my dating life. Was he jealous? That couldn't be possible. I wasn't even sure if he liked me. Still, now I was being ignored by two men. This felt worse than only being ignored by one, like the hole in me had gotten bigger. Maybe the more men you put in it the more stretched it became. Maybe Claire had been wrong.

But suddenly a text came through. It was Garrett.

fuck you this Sunday?

My heart jumped. It was brazen, not exactly romantic, but it was clear that he wanted me. I felt as though someone had suddenly injected me with good drugs. In an instant the world had gone from black and white to Technicolor again. I began walking back to the house, smiling.

ok yeah

good he wrote. *have you heard of the Shalimar?*

YES, I wrote back.

I had no idea what it was.

Good. i've always wanted to fuck there. wear lingerie and I'll fuck you in your sweet little pussy and asshole

I'd never thought of my pussy as little. Maybe it was big. What if I had a huge pussy? Also, my asshole? I had never had anal and it seemed terrifying to me. I knew, through all of the butt songs the kids listened to on campus, that the ass was a big thing now. Apparently everyone was eating each other's assholes and putting things in them. But then why did he want me to wear lingerie? It seemed kind of retro, not contemporary at all like anal. Now that I thought of it, though, anal sex was a timeless act. The Romans all fucked each other in the ass. I felt like I didn't know anything. But also I was excited.

what color I asked.

It was like I had become a puppet. I just wanted to please him.

Black bra black panties. and garters. meet me in the lobby at 1 pm

All of my underwear was white and kind of threadbare. I had never been a sexy-lingerie kind of girl. It never went with my aesthetic. Also, I had a propensity for yeast infections. Whenever I wore anything other than cotton there were issues. So I called Claire.

"I'm going to be having sex . . . at a hotel . . . he's getting a room for the night . . . the graphic designer, not the chimpanzee one. He wants me to wear lingerie. Do you know where I should go to get something cute? Victoria's Secret?"

"Victoria's Secret? You're joking," she laughed. "That's faff. Let me take you somewhere good."

I skipped group and met her in Brentwood at a place called La Boom Boom. Immediately I could tell it was way out of my price range: a hybrid of Mercedes-keyed tight-bodied moms in yoga pants and potential porn stars. You couldn't tell who were the moms and who were the porn stars, but they all definitely had money. Who were these women buying lingerie in the middle of the day? I guess this was what everyone did in L.A. The place reminded me of being inside a black-and-pink birthday present. The walls were pink with black velvet stripes and there were little pink chocolates on a table. I ate some.

"Come on," said Claire. "Don't be scared."

"How much do you think this stuff is?"

"Just go in there," said Claire, pointing to one of the little pink changing rooms. "I'll bring you stuff. What size are you?"

"I'm a 32 B on the top last time I checked," I said. "But barely. I have no idea what I am on the bottom."

I tried on bra after bra, various panties with little slips of paper in each of them to keep them fresh for whoever bought them. I imagined other women's vaginal juices on the paper. It nauseated me a little but also made me feel like I was part of some kind of ritual, a lineage, like Sappho's all-female cult of Aphrodite. Claire and the saleswoman were the priestesses. They made it a party. The saleswoman was named Bridget and was a GMILF, a hot grandma type. They cooed over me, telling me I had a nice ass, cute little breasts, that I looked great in everything. Claire even slapped me on the ass. I liked the way they encouraged me, babied me even. With my mother dead, and Annika away at college, I'd never had that type of tactile feminine love as a teen. I'd pretended I didn't need or want it. I told myself that I was lucky. As a single parent, my father wasn't home much and I was free. I had zero curfew, no rules. But my longing leaked out in other places. It was in my love for Sappho, the divine feminine. I craved that nurturing, to be swallowed up in the arms of Aphrodite herself, rocked and held. But I was afraid to ask women for it, afraid they would die on me or reject me in some other way. So I looked for it in men who could not give it.

But Claire and Bridget were heaping it on me voluntarily, without me even having to ask. They brought me more and more items: black lace bra with pink satin underneath, black lace thong, bra with leopard straps and black cups, black mesh panties with brown satin insert, demi bra, push-up bra, sheer lace bra with no underwear, black crotchless panties.

I continued to soak in all the attention, the ushering of my transition from woman to whore. But after forty-five minutes of the fashion show, I began to get overwhelmed and hungry. What were we doing? There was a nothingness we all thought we were staving off, using the bras and panties as little lace shields. But now the nothingness was creeping in again and only I could feel it. Bridget's compliments became annoying. What a fake. She didn't really want to mother me and she didn't think I was sexy. She just wanted to sell lingerie.

I asked her straight up what some of the items cost, then began to sweat. $120 for a pair of underpants? $250 for a bra? Now it was too late. I was in too deep. We had become family of a sort. I would feel ashamed not buying anything.

"Don't worry about it," said Claire. "I'll buy them for you. As a gift. A welcome-to-fucking gift?"

I wondered where she got all of her money. She didn't seem to work. I guess the ex-husband had given her a cut in the divorce. Maybe alimony.

"No, I can handle it," I said. "But thank you. I think I only need two items anyway: one bra, one pair of underpants. Oh, and garters!"

Claire laughed.

"What are you going to, a bachelorette party?"

"I don't know, he asked for garters specifically," I said.

"What a wanker. Does he think you're some kind of doll?"

I actually liked being a doll. I wished Garrett would just pick out the bra and underwear too. It made it easier than having to decide on my own. My decisions had never led anywhere good. But Bridget, hopped up on a potential commission, was thrilled to sell me garters. She *tsk*ed Claire and told her that garters were chic for a modern woman. They were a nod to the classic, but you could do them in a modern way.

I settled on the black lace thong, the black lace bra with the pink underneath, a plain pair of black velvet and satin garters, and some sheer black thigh-high stockings. The total was $395. I didn't know what I was doing or who I was being, but I knew that I liked it better than me.

19.

The following morning I packed an overnight bag with everything in it. Then I took it all out, thinking I should probably just wear it all to the hotel. I didn't know if I'd be staying over or if it would just be an afternoon thing. Staying over scared me. The thought of it made me feel trapped, like the way I felt once I begged myself into Jamie's house and then was like "Now what?" I was already having "now what" and I wasn't even in the bed with this guy. What if I sweat in my sleep or farted? I hadn't slept with a new person in years. Farting in my sleep with Jamie was an entirely different situation than farting on a handsome stranger. Also, I didn't know what to do about Dominic and his food and medication. If I left him at home could he wait to use the bathroom all night? I didn't think so. Annika sometimes used a dog sitter named Moira who would sleep over. She had left me Moira's number in case of emergencies. But I didn't want Moira to tell Annika I'd been out all night.

I decided I would just walk Dominic and feed him right before I left, maybe leave him some extra food. If I slept over I would make sure to come home first thing at dawn. And if he peed and pooped on the floor, so what? It could be cleaned up.

Next I took to grooming my body. I couldn't stop thinking about the possible anal. My asshole was definitely not a vacant space. What was I going to do? How was his dick going to get in if there was a shit blocking the way? Would there be a shit blocking his dick? Would he get shit on his dick? In the bathtub I tried to give myself a fake enema, swishing some of the water from the bath directly into my ass. It didn't feel like anything was giving. I wondered how far in the canal it was. So I reached my finger in my butt and felt around. There was the tip of it, not far from the entrance.

Dripping wet, I went over to the toilet and sat down. Dominic looked up at me from underneath his doggy eyebrows. I squeezed and squeezed, sliding around on the toilet, but nothing came out. How did others do this all the time? Who could be expected to have a pristine butthole? I slid my finger in and dug around. I tried to pull some out, and it worked. Now there was shit on my finger, some in the toilet, but still some in the hole. I'd only broken the shit in half inside me, not gotten it all out. So I went back in. Then I squeezed again. I felt like my eyeballs were going to pop out. Eventually the rest of the piece of shit came out. I could tell that it was the end.

I got back in the bathtub and ran the water again. I washed off my finger and my butt four times each with rose soap. It was a fancy tub with jets. I turned them on and put my ass up to the jets, like a bidet. My hole felt tired already and no one had even fucked it yet. But then the jet started to turn me on. I felt a feeling I had never felt before, almost like my butthole was blossoming. I wondered if my whole ass canal was full of water. I imagined it was Garrett's dick. I didn't come but I felt really warm inside. This was exciting. I felt a bit like a Hollywood starlet, someone with something going on. A life was happening.

20.

I arrived at the Shalimar wearing the lingerie under a trench coat that I found in Steve's closet. I'd done a lot of snooping in Annika's house, looking for I wasn't sure what. Something to help me know my sister better? Something to show me that the life she and Steve had together wasn't as beautiful as it seemed to be? But there were no private journals with any confessionals, no secret passageways or locked boxes. Their relationship was like her ample ass: out in the open, giving no fucks, proudly just there. It was what it was.

The trench made me feel petite and Hepburn-esque. Garrett texted to say that he was running late. I got nervous. It felt like my vagina and butthole were sweating. I went into one of the bathrooms in the lobby. It was big, like its own little room, with a marble floor and sink. It smelled like geraniums and I noticed an expensive candle burning. For some reason I thought about stealing it.

I decided to hide in the bathroom until Garrett arrived. I stripped down out of the coat and wiped down my vagina and ass with soap. Each had now been scrubbed multiple times. Then I looked in the mirror. I really did look cute. The light in there was dim and I took a few pictures of myself: hand on hip, ass out, from the back and side. Garrett texted to say that he was waiting in the lobby. I decided I would make him wait a few minutes, not text back, but just appear.

When I came out to the lobby he was checking his phone.

"Hey," I said.

"Oh hey," he said.

He rose and looked me in the eyes. My body felt all needle-y.

"Do you want to get a drink first?" he asked.

"Sure," I said. I wondered why we couldn't just get drinks in the room. I had a vision involving Champagne. Also, my ass was starting to sweat again.

We went to the bar and sat around drinking cocktails. It was dark and tropical in there, with black palm-tree wallpaper like the Beverly Hills Hotel on opium. This time we really didn't have anything to say to each other. I guess he didn't feel like talking about graphic design anymore and I wasn't going to bring up fonts. He still didn't ask me anything about me. It wasn't awkward, though. The silence was thick with knowing that I would be kissing him soon, and other things. I imagined his tongue in my pussy. If only he would look me in the eye again.

"All right," he said as I took the last sip of my vodka and pineapple juice. "This is how I think we should do it. I'm going to go in first. You should wait here. Then in about five minutes or so you come back and knock on all four of them. I will let you into the one I am in."

"All four of what?" I asked.

"The bathroom doors," he said.

"Wait," I said. "I don't understand. Why are we going to the bathroom?"

"To fuck." He laughed but he looked a little concerned. "I've always wanted to fuck in the bathrooms here."

"Oh," I said. "I thought we were, like, getting a room or something."

"Oh shit, sorry. No. The fantasy was that we would fuck in the bathroom. Sorry. Did I not make that clear?"

"Not exactly."

"Are you cool with that?" he asked.

I tried not to look disappointed. But I was. What the hell? Was I not good enough for him to get a room? Did I look like I wanted to fuck in a bathroom? Maybe this was sexier. Maybe this was like an honor, that he thought I would be wild enough. Anybody could fuck in a hotel room. Not everyone could fuck in the lobby bathroom.

"Okay," I said. "I'm game."

"You'll see," he said. "You'll love it. The bathrooms here are super lush. They're like their own little worlds. It will be fucking hot."

I didn't tell him that I was already well acquainted with the bathrooms, that I had already hidden out in one doing a photo shoot.

"I can't wait to make that ass go up and down," he said, kissing me on the cheek.

I ordered another vodka and pineapple juice. Was this weird or was it okay? I didn't even remember what day it was, and I wondered what most people my age were doing right now. Probably something boring involving children and applesauce. I should consider myself blessed. They would probably kill to be fucking in a bathroom at the Shalimar. I wondered what Jamie would think if he knew. Would he see me as hot and exciting? Would he be jealous? Or would I just seem desperate and pathetic? I drank and tried to blot those words from my mind.

There were men and women at the bar engaged in conversations. I didn't know how people could stand it, the regular interactions, conscious dating, trying to pass as normal or interesting. Nobody was that interesting and certainly no one was normal. So why was everyone wearing a mask? Why wasn't everyone fucking in a bathroom?

It turned out that there were three bathroom doors, not four. Now that I was paying attention to them as the place of our fucking, I saw that they were big, varnished oak doors with knockers on them, as though you were entering someone's house. I knocked on the first one.

"Can I help you?" came a man's voice.

"Sorry!" I said.

I knocked on the next door. Garrett opened it and pulled me in. He had me by the hips and kissed me hard, his tongue in my mouth. It made me feel good, like he wanted me.

"Look me in the eyes," I said.

He looked into my eyes and unbuttoned Steve's coat, lifting it off my shoulders and dropping it on the ground. Still looking me in the eyes, he hoisted me up by the waist and sat me on the big black marble sink. I was turned on by the action of what he was doing, but not turned on in my vagina yet. Or maybe my vagina was turned on, but I wasn't there yet. Like, I was and I wasn't. Part of me was acting and part of me was enjoying it.

"Slower," I said, to give myself time to get into it.

He teased me over my underpants for a second. Then he put his fingers inside and started fingering me. My lips kept getting caught and rubbing against his fingers in an irritated way. I felt like they were puffing up like balloons. I kept trying to ask him questions. I wanted to hear that he wanted me.

"What do you think of the lingerie?"

"Hot, baby."

"The garters?"

"So sexy."

I guess he could feel that I wasn't super wet, because he got down on his knees in front of the sink where I was spread-eagle, pushed the undies to the side, and started to lick my clit. I moaned some more, not altogether fake, because I enjoyed hearing myself. But fake in the sense that I knew I was suddenly too self-conscious to be aroused.

I slid down off the sink and got down on my knees. Then I unzipped his pants and started to suck his dick. His dick was long and skinny. I felt like it could stab me. Usually I very much enjoy dick sucking and I'm pretty intuitive at it. I like to lick it first and tease it—really prepare the dick before I suck. But he was impatient. He grabbed the back of my hair and pushed my head closer to his body, as I've seen people do in porn. I gagged a little on his dick, pulled back, then continued, my mouth super wet. He moaned and it was hot. Just hearing the moan come up from the depth of his belly, looking up and seeing that jaw I liked, made me feel wetter. My juices stung my irritated labia. He grabbed the back of my hair and pushed his dick into the back of my throat again, then palmed my forehead away.

"Get up here," he said.

My bra and underwear were still on when he hoisted me by the waist back up onto the sink. Then he ripped open a condom wrapper with his teeth and fumbled to put it on. He pulled off my underwear and spread my legs. I gasped when he put his cock in and began to thrust. It felt good, but also too much, like he was hitting a wall in the back of my vagina. Like a muscle ache. My thighs were chafing on the counter. My back banged against the faucet and I kept getting caught on the sink bowl.

Next, with his dick still inside me, pants around his ankles, he lifted me up and turned around, carrying me back down onto the floor. My back was on Steve's coat. He thrust a few times in a missionary-type position, then commanded me to turn over. I flipped over onto my hands and knees and he began fucking me doggy-style. I could feel his dick up by my belly button. It hurt every time he thrust and now I just wanted for him to come, for it to be over. As hip as the hotel was, the music was terrible. Someone had chosen a range of sad '80s and '90s classic rock ballads: Peter Gabriel's "Solsbury Hill," Eric Clapton's "Tears in Heaven." I was fucking on a bathroom floor to "Tears in Heaven." Sorry, but no. What did it even mean to be alive? I started laughing.

"Rub your clit," he commanded.

I obeyed. I could feel him spread my cheeks wider and begin to rub my asshole. He spit on his finger, then put it in. I could feel it. It felt like I had to shit, like there was something in there that needed to come out. I fucked him harder, trying to make him come already. Every moan I gave was out of pain. I wanted to fuck his finger out of me. But he put a second one in, then a third. I could tell he was trying to stretch my asshole.

He pulled his dick out of my vagina. I felt it bang against my cheeks, then my asshole. He pushed a few times. I felt a searing pain: like a giant hemorrhoid was trying to make its way inside me.

I turned around and looked at him. I was sweating.

"Is it in?" I asked.

"Wait a minute," he said.

He pushed some more. I felt his dick get softer and collapse a little. I imagined it forming a U-shape and going right back into him. I imagined him fucking his own belly button.

"No," he said. "It's too tight. I'm just going to fuck your pussy."

That was fine with me.

He fucked me for maybe a minute or two, then came. I wondered how he could come so quickly when he wasn't even totally hard.

"Sorry, baby. Want me to eat you some more?" he asked.

I looked at Steve's jacket on the floor. It was covered in dirt, and also a blob of semen. The strap of my new bra had ripped by the cup and frayed.

"No, that's okay," I said. "That was really great. Really hot."

He tapped me on the ass.

"You're hot," he said. "But we should get going so we don't get caught."

"Yeah, as much as I would like to sit on the bathroom floor with you all night . . ."

I was playing it cool. Look how chill I was. But I felt angry and sad. This wasn't what I was in this for. I mean, it was something, at least, not just ordinary, hollow life. It was a stab at the nothingness. But I had wanted him to really fall for me, obsess about me. Had I been used? Could you be used if you were also using the other person? Did the one who came automatically become the user? Or was the one who was less attached automatically the user? I tried not to cry as I put on the trench. I felt embarrassed that it was so fucked up, and I didn't want him to see it, even though it was him who had fucked it up. I wanted to seem untouchable.

"Go out first," he said. "So we don't make it obvious. I'll maybe wait a minute or two?"

"Okay," I said.

I saw that he had a tote bag with him and a package inside had fallen on the floor. The package said "R. Garrett Campbell." I wondered what the "R." stood for. How creative could he be with his dumb dick flopping around and a first initial?

I went over to the bar and ordered a club soda, then applied lipstick. I wanted to look hot for him, collected. I sipped the cold soda through a little straw and pretended to be engaged in my phone so that when he approached the bar I would seem disinterested. Five minutes passed and he didn't appear. He was really playing it safe. Then ten minutes passed.

you ok in there? I texted

huh? he wrote

Are you going to come out of the bathroom or do you need me to help?

Oh sorry. I left. headed home. That was fun ;)

When I stepped out into the late-afternoon heat I didn't allow myself to feel sad or angry. In a way I was relieved. If I had come all over his face, then I might have gotten more attached. I would have been disappointed that he didn't even want to say goodbye outside the bathroom. But his stupid pencil dick, his lack of regard for whether I actually came, the clumsiness, made me want him less. In my fantasies they always are dying to taste it, dying to make me come. They will literally die if they don't.

Or maybe I did feel sad. Was I angry about the bathroom itself? I wanted him to like me in the same way that I wanted him not to have a girlfriend. Or I wanted him to like me more than the girlfriend, to care a little more. I knew this was not the nature of the one-night stand. I knew that what I wanted was something that couldn't exist. But that didn't mean it wasn't something I wanted.

21.

At home I found a sleeping Dominic.

"Hi," I said, spooning up against him, my hands wrapped around his warm belly. He snuggled in closer to me as though I had been there all along, sighed a few times, then rolled over onto his back so I could rub him down. Somehow, this small moment felt more intimate than anything I had done with Garrett. I kissed his doggy cheek and he yawned in my face, a long, pronounced yawn showing all of his teeth and the speckled roof of his mouth. He was so completely himself, could not be anything other than himself, and would never understand why I might want to be anything other than me. It would be silly to him, crazy even. We were as we were and that was it.

At sundown I went out to the rocks. The sunset was pink and orange, with the silhouettes of the palms etched into it. Stars were beginning to appear too, between me and the Santa Monica Mountains. I don't know why but I started singing. I thought of the Sirens in *The Odyssey*, their island, how they called the men to them. The men were intoxicated by desire and drowned. What exactly were the Sirens? Were they mermaids? Sea deities connected to death, to be sure, but how did they get the men to do what they wished? Was it only their voices that called men forth or did they have some other kind of power? It seemed manipulative. Maybe they needed group therapy for romantic obsession.

I also thought about Sappho, how her poems were actually songs. How she sang her poems and played the lyre. Most likely it was a sparse accompaniment, though we can only guess what the music sounded like. Theo had been right, it wasn't really doable to bullshit about Sappho. Just because some historians projected their own garbage onto her, it didn't mean I had to project mine. What had drawn me to her in the first place was a feeling, the visceral experience of the words, emotion carried by syllables. How the hell had this led me to theory, the opposite of feeling? I suppose I was scared of feeling. Also, you couldn't get university money for feeling.

Now I had to pretend the spaces left blank in her text were intentional. I could theorize this into being, hopefully convincing readers that the poems could be read in this way. It was true, we didn't want to project our narratives onto her work. Academically, my conceit was interesting enough. But there was no way to deny that something beautiful and magical had once accompanied the poems and now was lost forever. The nothingness had once been full of music.

The surfers began to come in, but there was no sign of Theo. I always wondered where the surfers put their keys, their wallets. Out of all the things they did—choosing a wave, standing up on their boards, staying on their boards, somehow not dying—it seemed the most interesting to me where they put their stuff. Did they have secret compartments in their wet suits? Wouldn't their phones get ruined? Maybe they didn't bring their phones. There were definitely a lot of girls waiting to get texted back.

I waited for hours, but Theo never came. He was probably avoiding me. Or maybe he was on land, out with a bunch of other young people. I imagined them drinking beer on a roof somewhere, setting off fireworks. The group laughed in unison, the tinkling of their voices echoing in the brisk Venice air. They didn't give a fuck about anything. He was at the center of the group, lighting the fireworks and grinning. No, he was sitting over to the side of the group, sullen and mysterious. There were girls in the group—surfer girls with long beach hair, who smelled like vanilla and coconut. They wanted him. They wanted him for his distance. In turns they each came over to him, offering a hit off a joint, or a beer. He could have any of them he wanted. He could kiss them right there, up on the roof, and then lead them by the hand inside the house. But as each girl approached him, he held up his hand, silently. What an asshole, really. Why was he so sullen? Was he thinking about someone else? I pretended he was thinking about me. It made me happy for a moment. Then I felt a flush of shame for being so stupid.

I went back inside and fell asleep cradling Dominic. I had given my power away to Garrett and I didn't like the feeling. It reminded me of the past year with Jamie, only Garrett was someone much stupider. It was like I had taken that longing for Jamie and transplanted it onto the next closest body. How had I ended up here again?

When I woke up in the middle of the night I had to pee like a motherfucker. I raced to the toilet and sat down, but nothing would come out. I squeezed out a few drops and they burned. Uh oh. I crawled back into bed hoping it wasn't what I thought it was. But then I had to pee again ten minutes later.

"Jesus fuck, why?" I whimpered, curling up in a fetal position.

Dominic licked my cheek. He seemed to understand that I was hurting. He whined a little. I whined back at him and we whined together.

I wanted to pretend it was just irritation, maybe the dawning of a mild yeast infection, which could be snuffed out with a bit of Monistat. But this was no yeast infection. It was a goddamn urinary tract infection. I hadn't had one in years, but the feeling was not one you forget. The dull ache in the pelvis, the urgent need to pee, the burning. After my first three UTIs I had learned the secret at my college infirmary: always pee after sex. Pee immediately, within ten minutes, if possible. But I wasn't about to pee in front of Garrett.

I thought about how I was taught to wipe, as a little girl, after I'd gotten my first UTI.

"From now on you're going to wipe from front to back," said the pediatrician. "Do you understand?"

When Garrett tried to stick his dick into my asshole, and then abandoned the mission for my vagina, I did, for a split second, think, This can't be good. Back to front.

I tried to sleep but it was no use. I knew exactly what I needed: Pyridium to take the pain away and Cipro to kill the bug. I started moaning little things out loud in a deeply self-pitying way, like "Noooooo" and "Why meeeeeeee?" Part of me was reacting to the pain. But another part of me liked being melodramatic, babying myself.

I managed to walk Dominic and then summon a car. The closest hospital was in Marina del Rey, not far.

"Be good," I said. "Mommy is very, very sick."

I heard myself talking to the dog, and it reminded me that I existed. Existence always looked like something other than I thought it would.

22.

Somehow, at five in the morning, there were three families ahead of me in the ER. Did children only get injured at dawn? One of them was a boy with a soccer uniform on and one sneaker off, crying. I didn't understand why he was playing soccer at four in the morning. Was he playing in his sleep? His mother and father seemed so concerned about him, comforting him and stroking his hair. I wanted someone to stroke my hair. I thought about texting Annika, who would definitely be awake in Europe, but didn't want to worry her. I didn't want her to ask how I got the UTI.

Instead I texted Jamie.

Hi

just seeing what you are doing and how you are?

He was an early riser. I saw the dot dot dot of him responding. Then the dots stopped. Nothing. I bet Megan the scientist was in bed with him. Immediately I regretted it.

Then I texted Adam the wolf-monkey. I sent him a picture of my hospital bracelet.

Look where I am . . . hospitalized!

I needed to feel seen by someone, even someone I barely knew and did not like. I've always hated doctors' offices or anything having to do with medicine, because I'm always afraid they're going to tell me I'm dying. If I'm going to die, I would rather just die and never know about it in advance. Even at my most suicidal I feared the dying process.

I was exhausted so I lay down in my cloth hospital gown on the little bed. It felt like some kind of surrender, a sweet womb or coma. I curled into a fetal position and rocked myself a bit. Then I felt a little wetness between my thighs and realized I was dribbling pee. My inner thighs felt chafed and irritated, from the sex and from the urine. But everything was going to be fine. I wanted to just lie here forever. I wanted kind nurses to take care of me. Books were nothing in this world. Academia was nothing. Forget about boys swimming up to you in the ocean and graphic designers stabbing at your asshole.

The doctor's name was Dana Ward. She was blond with a severe ponytail and had definitely never made a mess in her life. I imagined that she went to Cornell and had always been self-contained. She had a nice engagement ring—not gigantic— but big enough that she could flash it and make other women feel shitty. She was a left-hand gesturer. I bet she used the word *fiancée*.

"Let's see here," she said. "It looks like you think you might have a urinary tract infection?"

"Yes, I know for sure that I do. I just need Cipro and Pyridium," I said.

"I'm going to have you leave a urine sample and that will take some time for us to get tested. In the meantime I can start you on those medicines. Do you get them often?"

"It's been years."

"Anything different that might have caused this?"

I wanted to say, *Well, I tried to have anal on the floor of a hotel bathroom. It was not a bathroom in a hotel room—just a bathroom connected to the hotel bar. Also, the guy was a stranger. Also, I'm in a group-therapy program for sex and love addiction. But clearly it's not working.*

"My husband and I have been having a lot more sex. We're trying to get pregnant. It could just be too much," I said instead.

I seriously had no idea where that came from.

"Any chance that he could have been exposed to any sexually transmitted diseases?"

Was she implying that my fictitious husband was unfaithful? How dare she!

"Absolutely not."

I wanted to ask if there was a chance her fiancé had been unfaithful with her.

"You can get the prescriptions filled and start taking the medicines. The Cipro could take up to twenty-four hours to really start working, but the Pyridium should provide you with some relief almost immediately. We will call you with your results later this afternoon. If you don't test positive for a urinary tract infection I strongly suggest that you come back in and get tested for everything."

"It's definitely a urinary tract infection," I said.

The CVS pharmacist gave me the Pyridium right away but needed time to fill the Cipro, so I lingered in the magazine aisle. I took the Pyridium with apple juice, which I knew I wasn't going to pay for. It made me feel powerful to steal the juice, drink it casually right there, then stick the bottle behind the magazines. I began to feel some relief from the Pyridium. But I also felt like I had to pee really badly. I figured it was probably just the infection, the illusion of having to pee. While I waited I shifted from foot to foot, reading a magazine about celebrity baby bumps. The whole magazine was dedicated to these bumps, not the babies themselves, just the bumps. If I had a bump, would I be in a better place? Maybe I was wrong for not having one.

Suddenly, I felt a warm trickle between my legs. I looked down and in the crotch of my pants was a spreading stain of orange liquid. Fuck. I forgot that Pyridium turned your pee orange. I had pissed myself the color of a traffic cone.

I ran to the counter, paid for my Cipro, then bailed out of there. I couldn't get in a car like this, I would stink it up and stain the seats. Quickly I waddled down Main Street, past a group of brunchers, disoriented and reeking of piss. I felt like I could see in them what the homeless saw when they walked past these people. I felt hatred for them and shame about myself. But the brunchers didn't notice me at all, or the orange pee stain. It made me want to disrupt their eating, their stupid conversations, and sit in the middle of their tables. I wanted them to be forced to deal with me.

At noon I turned on my phone. There was no word from Garrett, but twelve messages from Adam.

I'm worried about you!!!!! I would come visit u at the hospital but I'm in tijuana

I'm fine, I wrote, *really*

Send pics of the blood, he wrote. *Send nudes with the blood!!!*

There was also a message from Jamie asking how I was. I typed in three different answers:

lovin the California lifestyle!

do you still miss me?

dying.

None of them seemed right. Dying was the closest. Now the urinary tract infection had subsided but I felt sick over Garrett. I kept replaying the night before in my mind. Somehow in my memory it was way hotter than it had actually been: my vagina wetter, his dick thicker, his moans heartier and more passionate. I thought about his tongue and jaw, and tears came to my eyes. What the fuck was happening? And why didn't he want me? That night I slept with my phone next to my head on vibrate, but I didn't really sleep. I woke up every hour and looked to make sure I hadn't missed anything. I decided it might be time to return to therapy and check in.

23.

When I walked in the door at group, everyone gave me looks that were a cross between disdain and *We knew you would be back*. They were actually excited to see me. I couldn't help but think that they just wanted more people to be as fucked up as they were. The more fuck-ups like them, the less alone they were—maybe even the less fucked up they were. If everyone was fucked up in the same way as you then maybe you weren't so fucked up. Compared to them I'd thought I was normal. I may have been obsessing, but I hadn't stalked Garrett outside his office or anything. But oddly, everyone in the group seemed to be doing well.

Chickenhorse felt proud of herself and was tooting her horn. That morning she had spotted her neighbor's two dogs locked in their parked car in the heat and swept in to save them.

"I called animal services on their asses," she said.

Of course, when animal services arrived, the neighbors, who were merely putting groceries away, were livid. They banged on her door and screamed at her.

"You would think I'd be triggered or at least retraumatized!" she said. "But since I'm already being evicted, it felt empowering—as the victim—to stand up for other creatures who were being abused."

Brianne, who looked to have just gotten some fresh Botox in her forehead, had met a man on OkCupid—a new foray for her. They'd even progressed from the messaging stage of the app to actual email.

"Of course, he's on a business trip in Europe," she said softly, her eyebrows arched like a child's rendering of geese in flight. "But he said that when he returns he actually wants to get together with me. Face-to-face. In person. At a real restaurant. And I think I am going to go."

I decided to come clean, sort of, about my two dates. I didn't say that I went home with Adam and watched him jerk off or fucked Garrett on a bathroom floor, but simply that I had gone.

"The first guy was gross," I said. "If they're gross, I'm fine. I can take it or leave it."

"Why did you go out with him if he was gross?" clucked Chickenhorse.

"I didn't know he was gross beforehand," I said. "It was an Internet date."

"And the other one?" asked Dr. Jude.

"Well, that's the one that's the problem. He wasn't gross. But he seems to have rejected me after. So now I'm all spun out. It's not like I felt with Jamie. But it's pretty bad."

"Mmmm," said Dr. Jude, sipping her tea. "What were you hoping to get out of the date exactly?"

I noticed that she had accumulated multiple strands of Tibetan beaded bracelets on her left hand. I wondered how many she would have to acquire until she reached enlightenment.

"I don't know," I said. "I hadn't really thought about it. I guess to have some fun. Casual fun, you know?"

"It doesn't sound like you are having much fun," said Sara, offering me a banana chip.

I declined it. But she was right.

"Well, maybe I don't like fun."

"Of course you like fun," she said. "Everyone does! You just don't know what's actually fun for you yet. I've had to try out a lot of activities until I found my thing. The heart-opening workshop was just okay. But now I've started improv classes and I am really loving it. It's like my inner child is finally coming out to play."

I cringed. Was there anything worse than improv? Maybe open mic nights.

"I also enjoy essential oils," she continued. "It's a form of self-care. Every night I give myself a little rubdown with a home-made blend—rose, bergamot, and a drop of frankincense—on my neck and shoulders."

And probably your feet too, I thought.

"I like to take myself out on artist dates," said Brianne, her face unmoving. "Just me. I will go to a museum or the movies, get inspired and really connect with myself one-on-one in a creative setting. Afterwards I will take myself out for a good dinner and also dessert."

This seemed fucking annoying. I did not want to do any more connecting with myself. In fact I wanted to do less.

"I guess I could do that," I said.

"I dare you," said Sara. "I dare you to take yourself out on a date!"

24.

I left therapy and saw that Claire had called.

"Can you meet me at Pain Quotidien?" she asked. "I'm in hell. I'm dying."

"Of course," I said.

When I got there, she was crying in the corner over an almond Danish.

"I really felt like me and Trent had a connection," she said. "I really felt like with this whole polyamory bit I would have enough going on to keep everything under control. Like I wouldn't get too attached or too crazy about any single one of them. Now that's all gone tits up."

"Which one was Trent?" I asked.

"The old one with the ponytail."

"Fuck him," I said. "What an idiot. You can do better. You know who else was an old guy with a ponytail? This creepy guy who used to come sit in the library for twelve hours a day. He wasn't homeless, he had really nice sneakers, but he would just watch all the undergrad girls all day. At first I felt bad for him, because he was old and would sometimes bring soup and there is nothing sadder than an older man eating soup alone. But then one day he was caught in the women's bathroom. He had been hiding there for hours. His name was Ron. So this guy, Trent or whatever, is basically named Ron. Basically he is a seventy-year-old man with a ponytail named Ron who lurks in women's bathrooms hoping to catch a sniff of them. Whenever you think he is great, just call him Ron in your head."

I thought I had done a pretty good job. But Claire just cried harder.

"That makes it even worse. That someone like him could reject me."

"He's not rejecting you," I said.

"Yes, he is," she said. "His wife said she just isn't comfortable with the arrangement."

"So then it's not even his fault. He isn't choosing to reject you."

I wondered how gross dudes like Trent scored both a wife and a woman like Claire.

"Yes, but he didn't even stand up to her," she said.

I wanted to be like, *Look, this is what you get when you fuck a guy with a wife. This is what the polyamory people are like. You are never going to get to have the whole person.* But I kept my mouth shut. Who was I to say anything? I'd just fucked a guy with a girlfriend on a public floor and wanted him to declare his undying love.

"How did the garters go?" she asked, as though reading my mind.

"Horrific," I said. "I'm giving up men for a while."

"No! But I adore this side of you! You were just getting started!"

"I'm just too crazy."

"It's that bloody group that got in your head, isn't it? Ah well, I guess I'm on my own again to rummage through the cocks. Trent is dead to me, but at least David is more attentive now than ever," she said.

"So pack it all into David. He's younger and hotter anyway."

"No, it's too dodgy with him. He's too hot. I might become too dependent. I need a buffer."

"What about the guy from Best Buy? The really built one."

"It's not enough," she said. "He was number three, remember? I need a new two. Or he can move up to two but I still need a new three. I have to have three."

Seeing Claire's insanity made me realize I was probably doing the right thing by being back in group. She could have a harem of a thousand studs, but the truth was there would never be enough to fill her need for attention—for devotion. That hole was bottomless. It was never-ending. She wanted their devotion, but should one of them—even one of the ones she liked most, like David—want her to commit, it would be over instantly. If he became obsessed with her, really fell in love, asked her to move in, she would grow tired of him in about a month. Maybe even less than a month. When I looked at Claire I saw that there was no human who could do that for us. Fill the hole. That was the sad part of Sappho's spaces. Where there had been something beautiful there before, now they were blank. Time erased all. That was the part nobody could handle. Some people tried to shove things in them: their own narratives, biographical crap. I was pretending that nothing had ever been there in the first place, so that I wouldn't feel the hurt of its absence. I wanted to be immune to time, the pain of it. But pretending didn't make it so. Everything dissolved. No one really wanted satiety. It was the prospect of satiety—the excitement around the notion that we could ever be satisfied—that kept us going. But if you were ever actually satisfied it wouldn't be satisfaction. You would just get hungry for something else. The only way to maybe have satisfaction would be to accept the nothingness and not try to put anyone else in it.

When I left Claire, I blocked Garrett in my phone. I also deleted the Tinder app. Then I went to Whole Foods and bought myself an expensive array of ingredients: a cod fillet, little clams, good olive oil, a bottle of white wine, black truffles, shallots, chanterelles. I finally bought Dominic the ingredients for his turkey, pea, and zucchini dish. Even though I'm not a great cook, we were going to have a little feast.

First I stewed up his mess. I loved watching him eat, how absorbed in it and unselfconscious he was, gobbling quickly and getting right to the point. I loved the sounds he made with his black lips and pink tongue, all sloppy and smacking, totally engrossed in his meal. Occasionally he would stop midbowl, still chewing, and glance at me sideways for a moment as if to say, *What are you looking at? I'm just eating. We all do it, you know.*

Then I cooked the fillet and clams in the wine and oil, browning the mushrooms and shallots to a crisp. It was delicious. I drank the rest of the wine and sat down with my Sappho.

Sappho's gaps are not intentional negative space, and I do not propose we read them as such. The words are gone and they are never coming back, I typed. *We can try to fill the gaps with biographical knowledge, but this will not replicate the music. Guessing at gaps cannot simulate music. Nor can the silence of the gaps simulate the missing music either. But the silence comes closer.*

Had Claire somehow helped me find a new direction, a new legitimacy to my thesis? At least I was admitting that my own idea had been bullshit—that you couldn't read something as intentional if it had never been intentional, even through a perverted academic lens. Yet one crux of my thesis remained: there should be no attempt made to fill in the gaps with biography or bullshit narrative. So what to do with them then—the discomfort of not knowing? How to savor what was there without guessing at what wasn't? I was drunk but the question seemed good. The writing seemed good.

Around midnight, somehow, I found myself back out again on the rocks. It was chilly and I didn't bring a sweater. I looked around, and then, feeling embarrassed, I stopped. It was obvious Theo wasn't there, but I kept imagining that he was—or that he was deeper in the waves, farther out, watching me looking for him, laughing. I pretended to myself that I had come out to the rocks simply because I had wanted to be near the ocean. But I was disappointed.

I turned to go home.

"Lucy," said a voice.

It was Theo. Had he been hiding behind a rock? This kid was confusing. When I felt him watching me from far away, maybe was he watching me from much closer? He sort of bobbed a few feet away.

"You're back," I said cheerfully, but casual. I did not ask where he had been.

"I'm back," he said. "How have the dates been treating you?"

"Disgusting," I said.

"Ah, too bad."

"Each its own little death."

"Funny," he said. "You're like a little death."

"What?" I asked.

"You are. You're . . . gloomy yet charming. I like it."

"Well, no one has said that before."

"You're gently death-ish. You know about death, you're aware of it, and most people aren't anymore. But you're not a killer. You're a soft darkness."

A soft darkness.

"Yeah, I'm aware of death," I said. I was thinking about the doughnut incident. "In high school I wore black lipstick and black nail polish."

"That's not what I mean," he said. "It's not manufactured. You have it in you."

"What about you? What's your story?" I asked.

"Oh God, I hate my story," said Theo.

"I bet you have a great story."

"What do you want to know, exactly?" he asked. He was treading water a little faster now. I caught a glint of his wet suit under the waves.

"Where do you live?" I asked.

"Around here," he said.

"So cryptic," I said. "Are you aware of death?"

Asking that, I felt kind of creepy in a good way. He had a lot of power in not revealing too much of himself. Just that lack of willingness to disclose—that's all it took for me to perceive rejection. So this gave me a little edge. Also, his observation about me and death could have been a bit scary if he wasn't so matter-of-fact. I mean, he was a stranger, male, and likely stronger than me. He could easily pull me off a rock into the water and drown me. But I trusted him completely—at least in terms of my physical safety. And now that he had complimented me about my proximity to death and I had owned it, and thrown it right back at him, I felt cool. We had both decided now that death was my territory. I was the Professor of Death. Much more than a middle-aged woman who was beginning to get serious crushy feelings for a young stranger in the water.

"I know about death," he said.

"Have you ever seen someone die?" I asked. "Like up close and one-on-one?"

"Yes," he said. "I have watched a number of people die."

"Scary, right? The dying process. I don't feel scared about death but dying freaks me the fuck out."

"I'm not scared of dying," he said.

"You're not?"

Now he was the professor and I was the pussy.

"I would say I'm less scared of dying than I am of life."

Actually, I maybe agreed with him.

"I think I'm equally scared of both," I said.

This was the truth. It felt good to say it.

"What is it about dying that scares you the most? Are you afraid of having regrets?"

"No," I said. "I think it's literally the physical process. Like, the suffocation. I'm so scared to be suffocating and panicking. I get panicked even when I go to the dentist. I am not good with discomfort. So I think I'm more scared of the discomfort—my own fear around it—than anything else."

"It might be scary for a moment," he said. "Maybe for a few minutes. But then, from what I've seen, you are very free."

"Maybe," I said. "But it's the fear before the freedom that I'm scared of. If I could just go to sleep—just like that, go to sleep and never wake up—I would do that anytime. I would do it tonight. But I'm scared to be conscious while it's happening."

"I had that feeling about you. That you would be happy to just go to sleep."

"Why? Because I'm so boring?"

"Not at all," he said. "The opposite. But I can feel you've suffered."

He was so dramatic.

"Yeah, well, life is the dumbest," I said, standing up.

"I've suffered too," he said. "I've been sick."

This piqued my interest.

"Yeah?"

"Yes. I have stomach problems, terrible stomach cramps. Problems with my bowel. I don't know why I'm telling you this."

The word *bowel* made me giggle.

"What kind of problems?" I said. "Like you can't go or you go too much?"

"Both," he said. "It depends on the day."

"I'm sorry I'm laughing. I know it's not funny. But it's weird talking about this with a stranger."

"We all do it, you know."

"I know. Have you ever accidentally gone in your wet suit?"

Now I was laughing so hard that tears formed in the corners of my eyes. He was grinning and treading water.

"That's privileged information," he said. "I feel like we're not intimate enough to go that far."

"Ah, okay, I understand. Good that you have your limits," I said.

"I don't, it's just—we would need to be more close for me to disclose something like that," he said, smirking.

"What would be more close?"

"I don't know," he said. "Like if I had touched you before or something."

I felt surprised. I don't know why I am always surprised when a man is attracted to me. Maybe because he was so beautiful and young. But I guess it made sense. Why else was he hanging around these rocks?

"Do you want to touch me?" I asked.

"Yes," he said.

"Where do you want to touch me?" I said coyly.

He swam over to the edge of my rock. I suddenly felt nervous.

"Hmmmmm," he said. "Would you let me touch your ankle?"

"My ankle?" I laughed.

"Yeah, your ankle."

"Okay," I said. "You can touch my ankle."

He ceremoniously lifted one hand, wiggled his fingers like a pianist, and gave my calf a little squeeze. I laughed. Then, he lightly cupped my ankle and massaged it gently, looking up at me. I stopped laughing. Slowly, he ran two fingers up and down the middle of my foot bone. He pressed each of the toes, one by one, and made his way around to the back where he gently massaged my Achilles tendon.

"You have such cute ankles," he said. When he was done massaging he sort of patted the top of my foot like a child's head. Then he hugged my calf with his hand and head. It was weird as hell but it felt so good.

"No," he said. "I've never shit in a wet suit."

25.

"Doesn't Venice make you want to shag everyone?" said Claire the next afternoon. "They're all so scrummy."

She was getting her nails and toenails done at a salon in my neighborhood, preparing to meet David for their first real date—not just sex. I was sitting in the pedicure chair next to her but not getting anything done.

"Beyond scrummy," I said.

"Well, I'm relieved to hear that you haven't totally retired your pussy—at least in thought," she said.

"No," I said. "Actually, I've been hanging out with this swimmer."

"A swimmer," she said. "Like an Olympian?"

"No, like ocean."

"Show me his Facebook."

"I've only met him a few times and I don't have his number or email or anything. I don't even know his last name. He meets me at this rock pile, these breakers, on the ocean. Like, he swims up at night."

"What do you mean 'he swims up at night'?"

"He swims up at night. And we talk. Also, he touched my foot."

"He touched your foot?"

"Yeah."

"Oh so he has a fetish. Like Sara from group."

"Sara touches her own foot," I said.

"More like caresses," said Claire. "She really makes love to that foot. Maybe she's replaced men with her own foot?"

"Ha! No, it was more like he thought my foot was special. Or like through the foot he was touching my soul."

Claire stared at me.

"It's not as weird as it sounds. And I think it's safe for me emotionally, like, I'm not getting romantically obsessed, because I sort of just know now that he will show up. I can rely on him not to ignore me. It's as though he is more of a friend or something. Granted, I don't really want friends. And he's gorgeous and looks like he is twenty-one."

"Twenty-one!" she squealed. "That's brilliant."

"But I think he does like me. I mean, with the foot touching there was an indication that he is attracted to me in some way, though maybe not, because the way he touched it was sort of sensual at first but then it was just sort of friendly. The point is—I don't feel crazy around this one."

"Well, that's what matters," she said. "That you're happy."

"Yeah, I don't even care that I don't have his number or email or even know his last name. I just feel like, I don't know, like the universe put him there to show me—"

"The universe?"

"Yes, that the universe put him there to show me that I can have some of that male energy in my life without going totally insane."

"The universe is a wanker," she said.

26

"There's a light on in your eyes," said Brianne. "Have you been doing inner-child work?"

"Definitely not," I said.

"Trauma work?" clucked Chickenhorse suspiciously.

I shook my head no.

"Must be the self-dating," she said. "You actually look alive for once."

"Thanks, I guess."

I let them know that I was doing well and had blocked Adam and Garrett in my phone. I made no mention of Theo or the rocks, as the group would deem it poor self-care that I had been wandering around there so late at night in the dark. Chickenhorse would probably call it self-harm.

But everyone was suffering too much today to focus on me for long.

Chickenhorse had been forced to move back in with her parents, which was traumatizing for her. Actually, she said it was "retraumatizing" and calling up trauma from earlier in life.

"My mother doesn't accept my pit bulls. Or, she accepts them, but she doesn't like them. Which is exactly the way she was about me as a child. She just tolerated me. But she didn't think I was special. Also, now that I'm living at home I obviously can't start conscious-dating anytime soon."

"Your feelings are certainly understandable. But with regard to the conscious dating, I don't know if that's necessarily true," said Dr. Jude.

"Of course it's true!" neighed Chickenhorse. "You don't know my mother. She has no boundaries. She'll want to know exactly what's going on, who I'm with, what family he is from, and then she'll find some way to involve herself. So, sorry, now that I'm homeless we will have to put off dating again."

Brianne's dating life was going no better.

"Things have gone a little south with the man from OkCupid," she murmured, adjusting one knee sock. "He sent me an email the other day letting me know that he couldn't return to the States yet, because he was waiting for a business deal to close and temporarily was out of funds. Then he asked if I could loan him some funds."

The group gasped in unison.

"I'm not sure what to do. One of the items I put on my vision board is that I want a man who is financially stable. I don't want to compromise my vision board. I'm supposed to be manifesting. My life is simply too abundant to take on someone who is living a life of lack. But at the same time, because of that abundance, I can't help but think that it might be the kind thing to help him out—especially if it will allow us to go on our date."

"Mmmmmm," said Dr. Jude. "I would strongly suggest setting a boundary with him."

"Do not send the money," said Chickenhorse. "He's probably a catfish!"

"A what?" asked Brianne.

"A catfish. Like, a scammer. Someone who pretends to be someone he isn't."

"Oh no, he's not a scammer. I know that he is who he says he is. We're very close."

"How long have you known him again?" I asked.

"About six days," said Brianne.

We all looked at her.

"It's been a rich and rewarding six days."

Sara looked at her quizzically over the pomegranate she was peeling. But she was in no position to judge. Having almost reached her ninety days of no contact with Stan, she had had a slip. A big one. Now not only were they in contact again but they'd been seeing each other.

Stan had reached out with an apologetic one-thousand-word email declaring his love. He also sent her a bouquet of carnations. Of course, Sara was allergic to them and gave them to a neighbor, but that wasn't the point.

"He's been staying with me for the past two days. And I know what you're thinking! Bad idea, he's just going to hurt me again. But this time something truly seems different. He still isn't ready for marriage or an engagement or even to call me his girlfriend or commit to monogamy, but he's showing up for me in a way that he never has before. He's truly present."

"I see," said Dr. Jude. She was wearing what looked like a pair of silk pajamas. "What do you think was the impetus for the change?"

"I think he realized I was serious this time. That I wasn't going to take him back."

"But you did take him back," said Chickenhorse.

"No, I know. I mean before that. I think he realized the gravity of his error," she said. "Also, he lost his job at the hospital and has nowhere else to go. He's been living in his car."

"What?" We all balked.

I struggled to keep from laughing. Compared to the rest of them I was actually doing well.

"I can't forbid you from seeing him," said Dr. Jude. "But I want you to remember the state you were in when you came in here, how much you were suffering. In my experience these sorts of relationships only get worse, never better."

"I know." Sara sniffed. "And I know you're all going to judge me. And Dr. Jude, I know I broke our deal. But he needs me. At the 'Opening the Heart' workshop they said that we can only recover from the past by coming to terms with our core truths. Well, he's been sleeping on a mat in the resting area of the Korean spa. And I'm a compassionate person. And I want him to be with me. So that's my core truth."

I glanced over at Diana, the newest member of the group. She looked horrified. Diana was a Brentwood mommy—a gorgeous, fuckable mother in Lululemon—whose husband was a very new-moneyed TV producer. Apparently he wasn't paying her any attention anymore. It's not that he was bad in bed or turned her off sexually, but after they made love, a progressively less-frequent occasion now, he no longer connected with her. He no longer looked her in the eyes. It was like he could barely see her. Also, sometimes he had a difficult time getting it up. When he took Viagra she could always tell and she blamed it on the idea that he was no longer really attracted to her. So she had started having sex with younger men. At first it hadn't seemed like a problem, but recently she was afraid that she would get caught and it would destroy her marriage. She had been getting sloppier with it: having sex in the back of her Mercedes SUV, compulsively sending text messages from her own phone. She could no longer stay off her phone for more than a few minutes, even during her daughter's piano recital, and that scared her. She felt devastated when she could not get the attention of the young men in her orbit. Or, when she got their interest, they would have sex and she wouldn't hear from them after.

I felt excited by her situation. She was a little older than me and looked like the kind of woman who had never been ignored. With her long blond-streaked hair, large breasts, doe legs, and warm skin, she had probably always gotten all the attention she could need. But now she was seeing what age could do, what those of us who never looked like goddesses had always felt. Now she was mortal like the rest of us.

"I've been going down on the tennis pros," she said, in a way that was sort of proud, but also terrified. "I can't seem to stop. But I keep getting hurt. I've done it with two of them, more than once. The older one is twenty-seven. It started out that we would just go get frozen yogurt and talk. Then one day we took one car and ended up having sex in a parking lot, and it started from there. The younger one is—he's twenty-three. I bet the older one told the younger one that I was . . . a cougar or something. It's embarrassing. I don't need them to be in love with me, I just want them to be there for me when I get in touch. It hurts when I try to contact them and they don't text back. Then I see them at the tennis club and they remember what I look like, and suddenly they want something. So I hear from them again. It's always the same. But I don't know how to stop."

"That's the dopamine talking," said Chickenhorse. "You want your high. Is it that you don't know how to stop or you don't want to stop?"

"It's that I can't," said Diana.

Suddenly I felt a wave of compassion for her. I knew what it was like. I thought about what Claire said, about being careful to stay away from the freaks or else you become a freak. Diana was so hot and polished—the wealth pouring out of her Spandex—with her diamond rings, chypre fragrance, and golden highlights. Did she see everyone at the meeting as sad and pathetic? Did I look as sad and pathetic to Diana as the other women looked to me when I came in?

But after group she came up to me in the parking lot.

"You seem like you're the only one there who isn't totally insane," she said.

"I wouldn't bet on that." I laughed.

"Can I call you? If I have questions about what to do?"

"Sure," I said. "I don't know that I will have the answers. But I can listen."

I saw the sadness in her eyes and the mess of it all. I saw her delusions and the way that things started between her and the older tennis pro as just friends. It was like Theo: you wanted to believe they liked you as a friend. She pretended that's what it was, because if she admitted to herself what it really was at first she would have never gotten in his car. And she had needed to get in his car.

"I'm just afraid of getting worse," she said. "My son has a

friend. He is sixteen and gorgeous. And I see the way he looks at me. I used to think it wasn't that, it couldn't be that."

"You're so beautiful," I said. "How could it not be that?"

"Thank you," she said. "But I'm . . . you should see the young girls at their high school. I thought there could simply be no way. But now that I've been with Ryan, the younger tennis pro, well, I realize what it is with my son's friend. I'm not going to go there. At least, I don't think I would go there. But it scares me that I feel tempted."

"Wow," I said. "That's heavy."

"Yeah," she said. "I didn't want to admit that to the group. I didn't want to say I've thought about, you know, having sex with my son's friend . . . I didn't say it, because . . . it would be very illegal. I don't know what the group's policy is on that. If someone is tempted to do something illegal, are they forced to report it?"

"I don't know," I said. "But your secret is safe with me. Do you feel any better now even just telling me?"

"Not really," she said.

27.

I didn't go back to the rocks that night. I could see myself too clearly in Diana and her suffering. If there was anything in the universe, any kind of guiding force, any kind of greater power, I saw now that it probably hadn't brought me Theo to show that I could be friends with a beautiful member of the opposite sex. Maybe it had brought him to me at the same time as Diana to teach me a lesson. I didn't know if the universe actively taught lessons. But if it did, the lesson was that I could not handle what I thought I could handle. The lesson was that I didn't need to act out with Theo to learn the lesson. I didn't have to suffer again. The suffering of others, Claire and now Diana, could remind me of my own suffering: the suffering of the past and my potential future suffering. Maybe this is why we did things in groups. Maybe this is why people had friends: so we could see ourselves and our own insanity in them.

Instead I went over to Abbot Kinney with Dominic. A few people stopped and commented on him, how beautiful he was, how regal. I felt proud of him, not eclipsed by him, as though being with him somehow made me better. He made me feel purebred. What was money anyway? What was polish? Why was I so susceptible to flights of fancy, my perception of other people's views of me? Look at Diana. I thought she had it together and she was a mess. She actually liked me.

Maybe I didn't need someone else to define me, but oh, I still wanted it. How vacuous was I? How empty was I that I needed a border drawn by someone else to tell me who I was? It didn't even matter whether the person was real, a lover, a new friend, or even a dog. The person could even be imaginary, like the fancy people I saw on the street, who were not themselves imaginary, but became whatever it was I projected onto them. Seeing myself through the eyes of a projection, however uncomfortable the judgment, made me feel safe in a strange way. It was like a box in which to live: a boundary against the greater nothingness, to think one knew something about what others thought of you. It was there I could begin and end. And perhaps it was a prison, to have to begin and end, but it was also a relief.

This is why the Greeks needed myth: for that boundary, to know where they stood amidst the infinite. No one can simply coexist with the ocean, storms, the cypress trees. They had to codify the elements with language and greater meaning, and create gods out of them—gods who looked suspiciously like themselves—so that even if they were powerless over nature, there were better versions of them in control.

Or perhaps it was not for the sake of control over the terror of nature at all that they created their gods. Perhaps it was because the world, with all its beauty, was not enough. Simply being alive was not enough. The Greeks needed a new fantasy to make the world more exciting. With their war, wine, poetry, gods, and food, they needed to get high. Maybe we all did.

Yes, it certainly seemed like the human instinct, to get high on someone else, an external entity who could make life more exciting and relieve you of your own self, your own life, even for just a moment. Maybe once that person became too real, too familiar, they could no longer get you high—no longer be a drug—and that was why you grew tired of them. That was what had happened to me and Jamie. It was only when he was pushing me away—and then after he was gone—that he became a drug. It was so much easier for someone to be the drug before or after the relationship. When they were absent they were exciting. When they were right there it was a different story.

But some human beings did want simple partnership: someone with whom to weather life, like Annika and Steve. How did they stay so into each other living side by side, everything out in the open? How did they simultaneously have each other and still want each other? To want what you had—now, that was an art, a gift maybe. But whenever I felt I finally "had" Jamie, the nights in his bed seemed suffocating. I preferred the acquiring, the almost-getting, the moment before he was mine again. What was left to look forward to after you got a person? To "have" seemed nauseating. Then again, I was the sick one—the one in group therapy—not Annika.

The women in group told themselves they were looking for symbiotic companionship, something like Annika and Steve. They thought they wanted a man to show up for them. But I didn't believe them. They were choosing men who couldn't be present, so it probably wasn't really what they wanted. It certainly wasn't what Claire or Diana wanted. It wasn't what I wanted.

28.

For the next few days I rose at dawn and walked Dominic to Oakwood Park, where he would run around and chase birds. I felt like a wild woman as I ran beside him, a primal lady of the wolves. He thanked me gleefully, jumping up and licking my face, his cold, wet nose brushing up against mine. I couldn't believe that his love for me was still so pure and unwavering, and I didn't even have to work for it. Could a love like that really be trusted? Who was I if I wasn't trying to make someone love me? I knew that Dominic, unlike the men, would never hurt me. But why then did his pure love feel a little scary while the others had strangely felt safe? I suspected that I was afraid it might make me lazy, not through any fault of my own, but because of a lack of friction: a gradual atrophying of the muscles with nothing to push against, nothing to resist. Or maybe it was something else?

Since my mother's death I had been mistrustful of love, or anything, really, that came too easily, as though it were fool's gold and could one day, just like she did, disappear. I had spent so much time creating friction for myself: not only in whom I chose to love but in the work I did. I'd made my thesis impossibly hard—harder than it needed to be, ensuring that I might never complete it. Somehow it always felt safer psychologically to do that. But where had it gotten me?

Well, now I was doing things differently, living in a state of what might be called sisterly purity. Upon returning from the park I would feed Dominic and make myself a breakfast of Greek yogurt, honey, and nuts, like I had done when I'd first started my thesis. I felt that if I could eat like Sappho I could somehow get closer to her. Looking at the ocean, a different ocean from hers but also the same, might have a similar effect.

Unlike my apartment in Phoenix, Annika's house didn't make me feel like I wanted to put my head in an oven. But just in case, I made sure to spend some time away. I would go to a café and drink espresso, writing for hours, feeling a sense of purpose and meaning that I hadn't felt in years. Skater boys, surfer boys, and boys with guitars floated in and out the door: shirtless, shorts low-slung, lean and muscular above the pelvis alluding to what was below. But I felt like a goddess, above them somehow. Something removed them from my field of want, as though I were protected. I wore white. Twice that week I went to group and felt more of a sense of sisterly love toward the other women. Now I was able to help. I was even maternal in a way that didn't feel scary, but strong.

I had figured it out. If you just stayed away from everything dangerous long enough, other people in your life would show you yourself and what you shouldn't be doing. You could get high on their conquests but not have to suffer their losses. Diana, who was suffering, called every day. Most afternoons she went to tennis and was ignored by both of the instructors she had blown. In trying to avoid Caleb, her son's young friend, she found herself on Craigslist now posting about being a MILF. Had she never heard of Tinder? I guess she was afraid her photo would be seen. Now she had begun fucking strangers in cars in dark parking lots. She always felt demoralized after, but before it she was electrified.

Claire had not found anyone to take the place of Ponytail Man as a third member of her harem. It seemed she'd been right: she could not emotionally handle being with David alone—without a buffer of other men. First it started with missed texts. She found herself double-texting him to try to get his attention. Then he canceled plans to go see an outdoor concert in Santa Monica. The night of the canceled plans she called me and said that she just couldn't do it anymore. She was trying not to feel for these men. She was trying to keep her emotions inside, to think and act with her pussy alone, but she couldn't help herself. Now she was in love with David.

"I understand," I said. "I have no desire to feel in a contained way. For me it is all or nothing. I don't know that I can really enjoy the sex unless the person really wants me. And if the person really wants me, I don't want them for very long."

I said this because we were so alike and I knew it would resonate with her. Instead of accusing her I hoped that by telling her my truth she would recognize some of herself in my own admission. It was better than saying, "Why are you doing this to yourself? This isn't going to work. Even a harem of a thousand isn't going to work. You need to stop doing it at all."

But she still couldn't see it. Maybe she could tell that inside me there was some judgment of her actions, that I felt in some way better than her. I didn't want it to show. I didn't even want to feel that way.

"I'm not like you," she said. "I don't live in fantasy. I just can't handle this right now."

"You can get better," I said.

I said this from a place of "I am better."

She told me that she had been hurting herself again.

"Cutting?" I asked.

"No," she said. "I'm not a cutter. I'm more of a beater. I bang my head into the wall. I punch myself until I'm black and blue."

"Oh God, I'm sorry," I said.

I no longer felt better than her, or like this was a game or competition or a question of perfection or who was right or anything. I no longer judged her for being a mother and not having this shit under control, for what she might be putting her children through. I saw that she was me and I was her. It wasn't that she was me when I was in a bad way. Even when I was in a better place, I was completely her.

Yet knowing all this—seeing in these women what I could be like and feel like—did nothing to dull my cravings when they arose. So strange how the book, now in flow, and Dominic, so lovely, could be enough for a few days, and then suddenly they were just furniture: objects in my orbit. They floated in the nothingness but didn't fill it. For the next two nights after speaking with Claire, I fought to keep myself from going to the rocks. In the mornings I would waken glad that I hadn't. I had resisted.

On the third night, it was like I was free again. I didn't need anything. But then, with no warning: no resistance, no fight or second thought or question—no thought of Diana or the group—I found myself bundling up in a long skirt and a thick cream-colored sweater. I took a blanket out with me to the rocks and sat there, waves lapping up and stinging my feet. So strange how Theo had gone from someone who wasn't anything at all to me to someone I suddenly needed. Was it ever real: the way we felt about another person? Or was it always a projection of something we needed or wanted regardless of them?

"It's fine," I said to myself. "It is absolutely all fine."

He wasn't there yet. But the ocean itself was exciting. I could watch it anytime from my balcony, but to be touching it was a different kind of thrill. Why didn't I do things more often that excited me? Why did it take some strange swimmer boy to get me out here? Couldn't the ocean itself be enough, the lure and adventure of its wild, salty licks?

I texted Claire.

i'm sorry if I judged you. or if you felt judged. I only wanted to differentiate things in my mind for myself so that I would no longer have to feel pain

i did it as a self-protective measure

i was trying to make sense of things or have a linear box in the big bad void

Are you high? she texted back.

no, I wrote. *I'm back on the rocks*

I lay down on one of them in the fetal position. When I awoke it was after one a.m. and the tide was rising higher. My body was coated in salt and ocean foam. I felt like I was part of the rock and part of the ocean, and I wondered if this is how Sappho felt, even in her deepest desperation, part of the earth, like that desperation or longing or eternal cosmic want was something to be celebrated—something natural—holy even, or at least, not just something to be endured.

What if everything was natural? What if there was no wrong or right action in terms of who you loved, who you wanted, or who you were drawn to? If the will of the universe was the will of the universe, and if everything was happening as it was, then wasn't everything you could possibly do all right?

I was almost ready to give up, when I saw him in the distance swimming toward me. I started laughing and some tears came to my eyes.

"Hi!" he called.

"Hello!" I giggled.

"It's good to see you. I was afraid you weren't coming back."

I felt emboldened by how excited he seemed to see me.

"Do you want to get out of the water and sit on the rock with me?" I asked.

"No, you come closer to the water," he said. "If I get out it will be too cold for me to get back in again."

"I can't sit on the water," I said.

"No, just come closer to the edge. Put that blanket down on the rock. Lie down on it and just face me. Please? If you don't mind."

I did what he said. I watched myself. Was this natural, what I should be doing? Or was I so sick that I would do anything that this strange boy asked? He couldn't even bother to get out of the water to meet me. Was that a bad sign? But he was so kind in other ways, so attentive and present.

"Now what?

"Do you want to hug me?" he asked.

"Yeah," I said, laughing. "I do want to hug you."

This seemed even weirder than him touching my foot. He was holding on to the rock and I leaned against him. I put my head over his shoulder, the way Dominic liked to support his neck on one of my limbs. He was cold and his skin was very soft. I felt like I was hugging a strange baby, but also like we had always known each other. We hugged and I felt like I dissolved into him, like I was diving into the ocean itself. I looked over his shoulder and saw the cresting waves, the whole ocean suddenly turning white, as though I were on the threshold of heaven. I had been so afraid of dying, but suddenly I knew that death would be okay and beautiful—and even dying would be okay, because there was a heaven, sort of. Maybe it was not the way religious people imagined it, but I saw it as some kind of luminous womb to which we would all return. And because we would return there, in a way we were already there. I started to cry. All the pain and fear of the past nine months poured out of me. Theo stroked the back of my head with his hand. I didn't want to ever move. I was floating above myself and I looked down and saw us there on the rock. I wondered how I had been led to this.

He pulled back. He didn't ask why I was crying.

"It's hard, right?" he asked.

"Yes," I said. "Life is so oppressive and scary and . . . oppressive, and the whole time the ocean is right here. It's like I can't believe it's been there this whole time. I feel like I have a new love for it or something."

"Yes," he said. "I understand."

"Do you want to kiss?" I asked. "I'm not sure if that is how you feel about me? Or maybe you just like me as a friend. I'm not sure."

"Yes," he said. "I want to kiss you very much."

We kissed on the lips, gently at first. His eyelashes were thick and black and he tasted like the ocean. His lips were chapped from the saltwater, I guess, and it felt like I was kissing a flower.

I licked each of them. Then he opened his mouth a little wider and I lightly put my tongue in the front of his mouth. He began to suck on my tongue and I felt that my tongue and the rest of me would go through him, like I was going to be pulled inside him as though he were a big fish. I got dizzy. I took his tongue into my mouth and I felt that I was circling through his body, but also through an entire life cycle of some sort. I felt that I was spinning forward.

He kissed my forehead and I laid my head back on his shoulder.

"So how old are you anyway?" I asked.

"I'm not a teenager," he said. "If that's what you're wondering."

"Will you tell me something about you? About what you were like as a teenager?"

"Tomorrow," he said. "Will you come back tomorrow? I have to go now."

I wanted to ask where. Where could he possibly have to go? We had barely begun kissing. But since I had been the forward one, the one who asked him if we could kiss, I didn't want to be too needy.

"What time tomorrow night?" I asked.

"Ten?"

"Kiss me goodbye?"

We kissed quickly and then I watched him swim off. I wondered if I had been too engaged in the kiss, too desperate and needy, falling down a hole. Maybe he could sense my addictive tendencies coming off of me like bad perfume. Maybe he was just sexually attracted to me? It was hard to say, but I assumed I had done something wrong, because, well, I always did.

When I got home Dominic was in the corner. I had forgotten to give him his medicine and feed him. This was what happened when I followed my desires. I couldn't believe how quickly I had forsaken him. It was as though he simply ceased to exist while I was out frolicking on the beach with a stranger. Was going to the rocks a mistake? For a moment I wished that they weren't so near to Annika's house and that Theo hadn't given me a time for tomorrow—that we couldn't have a day or two apart. But of course, when the time came I knew I'd rush out there to be with him.

I gave Dominic a bowl of dehydrated duck and added a little water. I gave him some extra too, even though I wasn't supposed to.

"I'm so sorry, Domi," I said.

He ate hungrily, then licked my face. Then he started sniffing me, almost compulsively, and growled. Clearly he did not like the smell of Theo. I wondered if it was the scent of the ocean itself that made him angry. Perhaps he liked the ocean and was jealous that he couldn't go there with me. I felt bad, but Venice Beach had a massive fine if you were caught there with a dog.

I washed my face and realized that I hadn't eaten either, but was too tired to make anything. I thought of that song, I didn't know the music, just the words, something like "When you're in love you're never hungry." Was I in love with this swimmer boy? Or was I just completely crazy? It didn't make sense that something could feel so good, holy, and spiritual—like the gods themselves had put it there—and still not be right. It must be right, a gift for all of my suffering. But what if Theo just wanted sex? I thought about whether he was an "unavailable" man, and it seemed unlikely. I mean, I had never spent time with him out of the water. But even if he was available, I was not available— not for long anyway. What would happen when I went back to Phoenix?

I fell asleep spooning Dominic and felt the kind of love I felt the first night I'd arrived in Venice. Only this was deeper, more tinged with dependency, like a heroin vibe, and I knew it wasn't Dominic but Theo I was feeling.

29.

The next morning I awoke to find a long string of texts from Jamie. He must have been drunk and stayed up all night, because the texts were in varying stages of "I want you." He could probably smell Theo from thousands of miles away, how absorbed I was becoming. Men could smell an opening and they could smell a closing.

He said he wanted to see me when I got back to Phoenix. He asked what I thought about giving things another try.

I figured you got a restraining order, **I wrote.**

I miss you Lucy.

I didn't ask him about the scientist. I'm not sure why. Maybe because I didn't want to burst the double bubble of dopamine I now had coursing through me, first from Theo and now from Jamie. I lay around in bed for an hour, high on the potentiality of both of them, texting languidly. Jamie's texts seemed more urgent than they had ever been, asking me questions about my return date, if I needed anything financially, if I wanted him to come pick me up and we could drive back to the desert together.

I enjoyed being coy now, the elusive one for once. The independent one.

That's ok, **I wrote**, *really, but thank you. I will see you when I get back.*

Then I got another text. This one from Claire.

how shall I kill myself?

I grabbed Dominic and got a car to her apartment in West L.A. I saw, for the first time, where she lived. It was not at all what I expected. I knew that her ex-husband had kept their home in Pacific Palisades and she had taken an apartment, but I had imagined a grand courtyard with a fountain: something small yet charming, Old World Spanish with luxe modern interiors. But this reminded me of my place in Phoenix and that I would be going back there. The complex was big, old, and musty, and there was a pool drained of water. A sign hung on the gate read CLOSED.

When I went in she looked completely different, her hair greasy, unwashed, and piled high on her head in a bun, instead of the flowing curls I was used to. Under her eyes were big circles, the faint purple color of the underside of a shell. They were deep and I imagined lying down in them. She was wearing a T-shirt inside out and sweatpants, no bra. Her breasts sort of hung there, facing down.

Depression is real, I thought. It's a real disease.

I don't know why I thought that then. Like, that it just dawned on me. I'd had depression my whole life too but more of a dysthymia—a general malaise. I had never thought of it as an ailment that manifested physically. At least, it had never affected my physicality in the way that it seemed to have affected Claire's. Or maybe it did and I simply couldn't see it. Maybe this was what I had looked like when I broke down after Jamie. Maybe this is what people saw when they saw me.

"Are your kids here?" I asked.

"Arnold has them, thank God."

I was a little scared of her. Even when she said she'd been harming herself there was still a bit of Claire in her, some of the humor and charm, as though the depression was something she could slip out of when she needed to engage with the world. When she needed to protect me from seeing it. But now she was clearly gone. I wondered if it really had to do with David or Trent or any of the men, or if the two just coincided. This seemed so much greater than men.

"You're going to be okay," I said. But I wasn't convinced.

"I'm gutted. I really just don't see the point of going on living," she said. "It just seems so insane. Like, why would you?"

"I don't know," I said, because truthfully I didn't. "I'm probably not the best person to talk you out of suicide."

I was trying to make her laugh but she didn't.

Suicide was one of those things that, having been suicidal, in retrospect, I felt like I could talk about without being judgmental. But at the same time, there was no rational reason I could see giving her to live. Could I say that I was once suicidal but things were better now? Could I say that I was glad I had lived? The thing was, I hadn't really known I was suicidal until I woke up with the doughnuts. Also, even if things were better now, were they ever permanently better? Who was I to put that pressure on her to stay alive?

But what kind of person didn't try to talk their friend out of killing herself? I didn't want to tell her that she had to live for her children. I knew that she felt bad enough about them already. I could have told her what an amazing and fun and funny person she was, but I knew that right now it all felt to her like just a performance. Her charming personality was only more heaviness—another mask that she was going to have to pick up again to prove she hadn't lost it in the depression. The only reason to put it on again was out of fear that she might never get it back. Otherwise, there was no real reason to have to put on a heavy costume every day. It was too tiring.

"Would you sleep over?" she asked.

I felt claustrophobic. I thought about Theo.

"I can't," I said. "The dog."

"The dog can sleep here. We can get him some food."

"I know," I said. "But his medicine is at home."

"I'll give you money for a car to go back and pick it up."

The thing was, I could easily do that. I didn't want to tell her that I was abandoning her for the swimmer. If anyone would understand that I was shirking the duties of friendship over a boy, Claire would understand. But in this situation maybe she wouldn't. Also, I didn't want to hear myself say it.

"I don't think that will work," I said. "I'm sorry."

29.

I went late to see Theo. The fact that he had other plans the night before, and I didn't know what they were, made me feel insecure. Instead I spent extra time cuddling with Dominic, the dog's head draped over my arm so that his neck fit snug like a warm puzzle piece. I pretended that I preferred to be with the dog and could take or leave seeing the swimmer entirely. But I was playing a game: I knew that Theo was not mine alone. I mean, he said he didn't have a girlfriend, but he was so beautiful. Of course there were other women. Everything I saw in him that I liked was available for others to see. But the way he treated me, with such reverence, made me feel like he held me above all others or anything else. If there were a gaggle of younger girls, I was his special older woman. Still, I couldn't help but play a little bit of a game just to make him wonder.

He was waiting for me when I got to the rocks. He was still in the water and was holding on to a rock, his chin resting on it.

I sat down on the rock and leaned forward. With my hand, I lifted up his face to mine, kissed him wetly, our tongues in each other's mouths. He moaned in my mouth and the moaning set off shudders inside me. I realized for the first time that he didn't just like me or think I was pretty, but that he wanted me. In a flash I felt myself get wet inside.

"I just want to take off your fucking wet suit," I said.

He looked me in the eyes.

"Lie down," he said. "With your legs over the rock."

I lay down. He took off my flip-flops and began kissing my feet, sucking my toes.

"Oh my God." I laughed. "Aren't they sandy? Sorry if they taste weird!"

He just moaned more and stroked one of my legs. I was wearing a long flowing skirt and he had one hand up it, his other hand still holding on to the rock. Then his head was up my skirt and I felt him kissing my calves, giving me licks on my knees, and then nibbles on my thighs. He kissed my pussy over my underpants. I was wearing terrible, grandmotherly cotton underpants. He breathed on my pussy through the fabric and it felt warm and wet. Then he licked the skin on the sides of my undies, kissing back into the center and out again, moaning with his warm mouth open on the fabric. He pulled my underpants to one side and gave me a long lick, starting with my hole and slowly tracing over my clit. He did this again, back and forth, bringing the moisture from inside me over my clit. I was shaking. I looked up at the sky. It felt so good, but I was nervous.

"Theo," I said. "It might take me a little while. Is that okay? Will you tell me if you get tired?"

He took his head out from under my skirt.

"I want you to take as long as you need," he said. "Take the whole night. Take forever."

I lay back down. The stars were beautiful but I closed my eyes. I focused on the feeling in my pussy entirely and not what was going on around us or even him. It was a sustained goodness and I felt that in my sexual relationships with others I had missed the point. Had it ever been solely about pleasure for me? Maybe I had missed the point of what having a pussy was for entirely. It was not for having babies or pissing, but simply a locus of pleasure—its own purpose. Now a growing confidence was there, like a crystal inside it or maybe a whole ocean. Perhaps the crystal had always been there without me seeing or knowing. Had I always glowed from there but never realized?

Right above my pussy, my whole pelvis felt full—not of piss or pain—but self-sustaining, pulsing. I felt glad to be alive. Or not even glad, just alive. I was in my is-ness and was not going to fight it. So this was joy. Like my pussy, this part of my pelvis felt like it had existed forever but had disappeared years ago. I remembered feeling something like this as a young child, but somehow that feeling had been eclipsed and forgotten until now. It had been eclipsed by all the matter on Earth. I saw that all of that matter was just emptiness. It accrued and accrued to nothing.

My chest, too, was warm, as though it sought to open, like a light in there was pushing through rusty doors. This I resisted. I was scared, afraid to let the doors swing open fully. But my throat felt like the throat I had known as a child, when all language was new and words hadn't hurt so much. In the past when I made sex sounds, I tried to imitate what I saw in porn. But now what I heard was way deeper, guttural, without the formation of my mouth. It didn't resemble syllables and definitely not words. It was the sound of the planet rotating.

I didn't even think about Theo. For once I was not thinking. Maybe for the first time ever. I felt space in my mind, in my skull, which I had never felt before. Had that too always been there? If it had always been there, then life, it seemed, could have always been beautiful, redeemable, sacred. But if it had always been there, it was strange that I had never found it before. If something so beautiful and pure existed right between your ears, why wouldn't you stay there forever? Why wouldn't you live there?

I started to laugh. I couldn't tell if I was coming, or if I had already come. But then the laughter subsided and I felt a darkness crawl over me—a cool darkness that was dead serious—and I realized that I had not come yet and was going to. His tongue was like a dog's tongue—a little rough—so unlike my fingers or vibrator. It was like a magic carpet or something, in that I came and came and came. It was like the orgasm began, then stopped, then started a couple of times and I felt that I was able to control it, before I rode the carpet all the way up to where it crested and then exploded. I stayed in it longer than I had ever experienced. And just as I came I became aware of him again. I said his name out loud, I heard myself say it. But I also felt a connectedness between me and something bigger—beyond him—as though there were a split screen. He was on one side of the screen and the universe was on the other. I felt love for both of them.

I lay there on the rock and stared up at the sky, silent, for a long time. He kept his face in between my thighs and I hugged his head with my knees.

"Would you like me to come out of the water?" he asked.

"What?"

He took his head out from under my skirt, looked me in the eye, and smiled.

"I said, 'Would you like me to come out of the water?'"

"So much," I said. "More than anything. More than anything I would like you to come out of the water."

"I'm scared," he said.

He looked like a little boy when he said that, scrunching up his nose and squinting.

"Of what?" I laughed. "Are you scared of me? But you just had your face in my pussy."

"I have some imperfections," he said. "I have—something is wrong with my body. I'm afraid for you to see."

"I think you're beautiful," I said. "You are a gorgeous creature. I would never judge you. Anything that could be different or weird about your body I would only see as even more special."

"You can't tell anyone," he said. "About what you see."

Now I wondered what it was that was wrong with him. Did he have a shrunken lower body? Was he missing a leg? Was it just a small dick?

"I don't like people," I said. "I have no friends. I have no one to tell."

This was a lie. I would surely be telling Claire at some point about the pussy-eating in detail and, I figured, probably every inch of his body. As soon as she was better and ready to hear it. It would probably even cheer her up.

"Okay," he said. "But if you don't like it, there is nothing I can do about it. If you feel frightened by it—by me—I can only go back into the water and swim away. I won't be able to see you again."

"Come on," I said. "Would you stop? I won't not like it. There's nothing that can scare me."

That wasn't entirely true, but I believed it. It's an art to believe your own lies. Some people think you have to actively convince yourself in order to believe your own lies, but in that moment, I just didn't know any other reality than everything being okay—no matter what he showed me. I knew only that silence and the wanting him to come up on the rock with me. I didn't think I could be scared of anything. I just wanted him to be with me.

"Okay," he said. "Okay."

He put his beautiful white arms on the rock and hoisted himself up, then flipped himself over so that he was sitting next to me.

Around his pelvic region was a thick beige sash, like an oil-cloth. Below it was the wet suit: scaly and coal black, covered in barnacles. At the bottom were what looked like a pair of fins or flippers, of the same color as the suit, connected to the rest of the black rubbery scales. He looked more like a scuba diver than a swimmer and more like a thick piece of cod than a scuba diver. The suit seemed old—like it had been soaking in the ocean for years—with all of the barnacles attached to it, bits of seaweed. It wasn't sleek or shiny like I had seen on the surfers. It almost looked like the rocks we were seated on. Like he was part of the ocean landscape.

The flippers too really looked like fish fins: thick by where I guessed his ankles would be and then fading to a translucency at the bottom. Sheer black. They reminded me of a black bubble-eye fish I had at thirteen who died while my father and I were traveling to visit Annika at college. When we returned home, the fish was floating on her side at the top of the water, the tank stinking. I remember feeling embarrassed and not wanting to show my father she had died. I wasn't afraid he would blame me for her death, but something about her curvy little body, just floating there, made me feel exposed. It was as though I were lying at the top of the tank, naked and smelling, too intimate an experience to share with my father. I remembered how her tail had already begun disintegrating, and a tiny piece of it had detached and was floating next to her. This is what his flippers looked like.

Then something turned in my eye, or the eye of my mind, like when you look at one of those psychedelic posters that can be seen two ways. For a while you look at something one way, but then, all of a sudden, the image flips. Once you see the second way you can't go back to the first. What I saw was that this was no wet suit at all, but somehow a massive, slimy, heavy tail. It was literally connected to his body. Maybe it was his body? Underneath the cloth were what I assumed might be genitals, then, if he had them? And just below that was an area where the tail, or whatever this was, met his skin. It did not meet in a straight line like the top of a pair of pants, but blended gradually. First there was an area that was mostly skin with a peppering of black scales, like one or multiple birthmarks. From there the scales became more raised, almost like moles or lesions. They began to cluster closer together until they became a solid mass, like rubber or the thick skin of a fish. It looked like time happening, like a wave gradually rolling up on the sand. It was as though whatever this was had happened over time, like some kind of infection—gradually taking over his body.

Except this wasn't an infection. It was like he was part fish.

"Are you grossed out?" he asked.

"No," I said. What the fuck was this? Was Theo a mermaid?

"Freaked out?"

"No. Just shocked and wondering if I'm crazy. How did this happen?"

"I was born this way," he said. "I am what you are thinking I am. Sort of."

"What do you think I think you are?"

"A merman."

"Yeah," I said, rubbing my eyes. "I was thinking that."

"I don't call myself that. None of us think we are that. But to humans we are that."

"Holy shit," I said. "This is fucking crazy. So, like, there actually are mer-people? And Sirens?"

"Sort of. But not the way you conceive of us. Well, we are sort of the way you conceive of us. I mean, obviously I'm very sexy." He laughed.

"You are!" I said.

"Ha, not really. But I mean, we aren't like the Siren myths and stuff. It's not like we are trying to kill humans or keep them imprisoned on an island. We aren't like the way they are in *The Odyssey*. Homer slandered us. But we do live a long, long time. Youthfully. Hundreds of years. We spend most of them looking like we are in our late teens and early twenties. I think it's the saltwater. It preserves us in some way."

"So are you mythic? Are you a mythic creature? Is this a joke you are playing? Am I hallucinating you?"

But from the look on his face I knew it wasn't a joke. There was no way the place his skin met his tail could be fake. The gradations were too rough and eerie. There was no makeup or costume in the world that could do that. He really was part man and part fish. Or something. Had I lost it at some point along the way? Was I worse off than I thought?

"You aren't hallucinating, not really," he said. "I mean, you are kind of hallucinating in the sense that your perspective has shifted. But in a way you were really hallucinating before you met me—in the sense that there was only one part of life you could see. You believed only that which was in front of you. Most people do. Most people believe that which you cannot see or know could not possibly exist. Humans are very arrogant. I don't think you are arrogant, but I think it's just your nature to only believe in what you can see."

"I don't even know what to say," I said. "I have so many questions for you."

"Let's start slow," he said.

"Are you real?" I asked.

He laughed. "I suffer like I'm real. I have wants like I'm real. I fear that I will be unliked or unloved. Men, women, I think that maybe everyone wants the same thing."

"Men want sex," I said.

"Don't you?" he asked.

"I do," I said. "Maybe. But I think I mistake it for love, or something."

"How do you know when you're mistaking it?"

"I think when I get high off it."

"Well, why not? That could be love," he said. "Can't you get high off of love? I don't think I want a love that doesn't make me feel amazing."

"I don't know if that's love or something else," I said. "But I don't think it's love if the person disappears."

"I wouldn't say it's not love," he said. "But it's hard. That is a very painful experience."

I was surprised to hear him say that. I felt that surely he must always be the one doing the disappearing. Merman, fish fillet, whatever the fuck he was, I still thought of him as a surfer who worried about nothing. Someone who was very free to just disappear off into the night at any time.

I wondered what he looked like to the mermaids under there. Were there mermaids? Was he beautiful for the sea or just average? I didn't dare ask. Surely the mermaids must be beautiful—breathing in and out under the ocean. I imagined them long-haired with little waists and shells on their tits. I imagined them all like Aphrodite. I wondered if perhaps they all looked the same and he'd eventually grown bored of them. Maybe that was why he wanted a land woman with calluses on her feet, plain as I was. I was nothing like Aphrodite. But maybe that was the point.

"You're not going to abandon me now that you know what you know," he said. "Are you?"

"Me? No!"

I was delighted. Did it take a mythological deformity to find a gorgeous man who was as needy as I was?

"Good," he said.

He put my chin in his hand and gave me a wet kiss.

I could smell the difference between the top and bottom of him. His head, shoulders, and neck had a clean smell, a fleshy, wet-skin smell. He smelled human, but better. Once in a while, the scent of his bottom half would waft up and it smelled like a fish market—not exactly dead fish, the way my fish-tank emergency had smelled in my youth, but it smelled like blood, the ocean, shit, seaweed . . . a little like pussy, actually.

I felt almost as though his bottom half were some sort of pussy, although it was phallic in shape. Maybe because he was insecure about it, and I had always felt insecure about my pussy. Maybe it was because in seeing it, this part of him, the part he had concealed, I was, in a way, entering him. I thought about dominance and submission—how in some ways he had been the submissive one in eating my pussy. Yet in other ways I was dependent on him emotionally now that I had let him see me like that: splayed, surrendered, thrusting in his face. I was attached to him more than before, because I had opened for him like that. Maybe he felt that of me. Maybe he needed that before he could show me his tail.

I wondered what was underneath that sash around his pelvis. I wondered if he had a cock. Did fish have cocks?

"May I touch you?" I asked.

He nodded.

We began kissing again and I ran my hands through his hair, tickling the back of his neck. I rubbed his chest, smooth as a sculpture, fingering each of the nipples. I wanted to tease him, treat him like a girl a little bit, because I still felt vulnerable and also because I knew, somehow, he would like it. His nipples hardened like pellets under my fingers and he gasped.

I touched his stomach. It was so smooth, not cut or built, but not roly-poly either. A little soft, full, but also firm. It was existing. He existed. His arm muscles felt stronger than his abdominal muscles and I wondered if this had something to do with the way he swam. He had no hair on his stomach or pubic hair sticking out up over the sash. I rubbed my hands in a circular motion over the front of the sash and felt his penis under there, strong, semi-hard, like a thick trunk. His balls felt weighty like peaches.

"Oh," I said. "I wondered what you had."

"Yes," he said. "And an ass too. The tail starts below all that, not like human myths where the tail starts at the stomach."

"Where did you get the sash? Do all of you wear sashes?"

"Shipwreck, obviously," he said.

"Oh, yes, obviously." I laughed.

"And a loincloth does make it easier. Sand, jellyfish, it can all be very abrasive."

"Do you know a lot about Greek myths?" I asked.

"Some," he said.

"Is that how you know about Sappho? Did you, like, date her or something?"

"I'm not that old." He laughed.

What did dating even mean for a merman? Tinder under the fucking sea? Swiping right on a starfish?

"Have you . . . been with any other women who live on land?" I asked.

"Some," he said.

"Recently?" I asked.

"Not in a while. I'm trying to change that," he said, and touched my arm.

I liked that it had been some time, because I wanted to be the only one. I didn't care what the reason was, even if he simply hadn't been near land. Of course, the inability to be with someone else on land did not mean he loved me in a special way. And his having been with other women who had feet did not necessarily equal lack of love. But it still made me feel safe to be the only one in a long time. These thoughts, themselves, were madness. He lived in the ocean and I lived in the desert. This wasn't going to last. Maybe there could be some magic bend in our time together, the way I felt when he was going down on me. That had felt so eternal—as though if it were happening in one moment it was happening forever. But no one could live inside a moment. It was already over. And yet, here he was, still with me. We were sitting beside each other and he had his hand on my thigh, my hand tracing his knuckles. He is still here, I kept repeating to myself.

"I have to go," he said, as if he could read my mind. "It's not a great idea for me to be out of the water like this with the light coming up."

I hadn't realized that it was dawn. The sun was rising over the Santa Monica Mountains, turning the water silver. I could see that a few surfers had made their way to the Venice pier, laughing with one another.

"Are you like a vampire?" I asked. "Are we in one of those teen vampire movies, only you're a mermaid?"

"Ha, no, nothing like that," he said. "It's just not a great idea for anyone to see me out here. I've gotten harassed before. I've gotten hurt. I could be taken to the Venice freak show. I can't exactly run. So it's always dangerous for me to be out of the water."

"Will I see you tomorrow?"

"Not tomorrow, but how about the following night? You should wear a skirt again like that."

"Ha-ha. Okay."

Two nights sounded so far away. It seemed endless.

"Also, you shouldn't tell anyone about me," he said. "As we

discussed. Mostly I say that for you. I don't want you ending up in a psychiatric hospital or in rehab and that's what people will think if you tell them you met a man who lives under the sea."

"But you're just a boy," I said.

"I'm not Sappho-old but I'm older than you think. The salt has preserved me. Also, maybe I'm immature."

He kissed me on the forehead and on the hand. Then he dove back into the water, parting the seaweedy murk.

"Wait!" I called. "What time in two nights from now?"

But he was already swimming out into the sunlit waves. I saw a few flicks of his tail on the surface, like a dolphin fin in the distance. Then he disappeared completely, fully submerged under the water. He was showing me what he was, no longer afraid for me to see that he could go under and not come up for breath. I waited a long time in silence. But he never resurfaced.

30.

I decided to skip group. I was too deeply involved with Theo now. What would I even tell them? I'd met a merman who might disprove all of their theories about love? And why would I choose to recover unless everything was total and complete shit? If there was one sparkle, one possibility of getting as high as I could get off a person, why would I throw that potentiality away? You had to hold out for these moments until you knew for sure they were gone and never coming back. I didn't want group to ruin the way I felt.

I saw this in Diana, with whom I still spoke. She had been in pain but couldn't surrender—not until she knew it was truly over between her and the objects of her affection. It wasn't enough for the tennis boys to ignore her texts. They would have to go further. They would have to tell her she disgusted them and it was never happening again. Even that might not be enough. In truth what she needed was to have no remaining options at all, no one left to fuck. She would have to burn through all of the tennis boys in Los Angeles, maybe in the state of California.

Perhaps again in the future, the pain of not hearing from her conquests—the pain of waiting—would outweigh the potential for sparkle itself. Diana would come back to group and get strong for just a day or for a few weeks. But the moment she got a text, the moment that glitter reached out to her, she would forget what that pain had felt like. She would want only the glitter. Euphoric recall of past glitter would blind her to the suffering it had caused. Then, the group would become just an afterthought: a place for sick people to go, but not for her. She was not so bad off as the sick people.

When she called me I could hear it in her voice. Who could blame her? Somehow she had gotten another taste of sparkle. Now that she had a taste or saw its potential she was going for it again. When she looked back at the group she saw sick, miserable humans, something she would want to block out having ever been a part of. But the women in the group would see her as the sick, miserable one. They thought she would either come back or face devastation. But they'd forgotten the sensation of what it was like out there, to be in the throes of madness. I didn't tell Diana about Theo, either.

I took Dominic for a quick walk. He began pulling me in the direction of Oakwood Park, but I didn't have the energy for it. I held the leash tightly as he yanked and skipped in place, whimpering with his head pointing in that direction. I knew that I should give him what he wanted, a little piece of that effortless happiness, but I couldn't play wolf woman today. My mind was too much elsewhere, already on the rocks, waiting, waiting for Theo to surface and transform my perception. My mind was already in the ocean.

I decided I would call Claire.

"How are you doing, dearest?" I asked.

"I'm better," she said. "David called. I'm seeing him tomorrow. I told him he isn't giving me enough of what I need. I haven't hung myself from any silk scarves. So I guess that's progress?"

"Good," I said.

"And you?"

"I've done it again," I said. "I've fallen hard. Only this time I think it's real."

"The surfer?" asked Claire.

She sounded skeptical, and I wondered what right she had to be skeptical when she had just been in a bottomless pit.

"Swimmer," I said. "All we do is talk. Or all we did was talk until last night when he went down on me for forty-five minutes."

"Nooooo," she said.

"Yes. At least forty-five. What does it mean when a boy goes down on you for forty-five minutes? I feel like it has to be love. Like, I feel like he loves me."

"Either he loves you or he loves pussy. One of the two."

I laughed.

"No, he doesn't seem like that. He isn't a pussy hound. Well, I can't tell. I mean, I think he is gorgeous, but he isn't typically gorgeous. But if I think he is gorgeous then probably a million others do too."

"Usually that's the way it works," she said. "Still, I'm glad you're getting shagged properly. It's important. I think it's very important that you be well fucked."

"We haven't fucked yet," I said. "I haven't even seen his dick."

"Oh really?" she said. "Then it could be love on his part."

"That's what I think," I said.

"But what about you?"

"I'm smitten," I said.

"Of course you are. It's especially intoxicating when there is an expiration date. Aren't you going back to Phoenix in a month?"

"Six weeks," I said.

"Well, there you go. That makes it perfect! A summer romance."

"But what if it's more? He doesn't know I'm leaving," I said.

"But you do," she said.

I thought about this. All I imagined I wanted was the love of someone beautiful like Theo—the kind of love where it stayed young and glittery and never got old. One way to keep it shiny was to have an end date on it. I'd thought it was Jamie who didn't want to commit. But the group was right—it was me who was really the unavailable one. I was picking people with whom

I couldn't have that ultimate intimacy: Jamie, who couldn't make enough room for me in his life, and now these younger men. Their age made it safe to pine for them, to torture myself, because it ensured I would always be pushing against some sort of friction, an inability to really be together. And no matter what any of them felt for me, I would never have to see it grow old, because I would be returning to Phoenix. Even in the case of Theo, where he seemed to actually like me, I would be leaving. I was in control of the way things would end.

31.

Dominic was not doing well. He had started peeing indoors no matter how often I took him outside. I didn't know if it was because he was sick or because he was angry at me for being away so much. I was afraid to tell Annika what was going on, but just to be safe I took him to the vet. The vet ran some blood tests and said that it was further issues related to his pancreas and kidneys, and that his blood sugar was very high. His insulin dose would have to be increased.

I emailed Annika, in part to relay the news, but also because I couldn't afford to pay the $1,300 vet bill. I was scared. Immediately my phone lit up.

"Where is he? Put him on," she said.

"He's right here," I said, aiming the phone at his face.

"Oh no, I can see it in his eyes. Something is not right."

"They gave me a higher dose of insulin to give him."

"I mean besides that. He looks depressed. Hold on, I'm looking up depression symptoms in dogs. Okay. Is he lethargic? Has he been sleeping excessively or showing signs of clinginess?"

"No, that's just me," I said.

"Lucy! I'm serious. Loss of appetite?"

"Definitely not."

"Weight loss?"

"No, it's just been the peeing. That's it. Which I think is directly related to the insulin."

"How long has this been going on? Why didn't you tell me that something was wrong right away?"

"Only a few days. And I didn't want to worry you."

"Lucy, he is my child! You have to tell me when anything like this happens. Are you able to give him the care he needs? What did the vet say specifically? Should I come home?"

"No, no, don't come home. The vet said he is going to be totally okay as long as we adjust this insulin to the new amount. I can do that. It's easy."

"I still think he looks depressed," she said.

"I'll take him to group."

The vet hadn't exactly said it would all be fine, but she didn't seem particularly concerned either. I felt strangely jealous that Annika would come home to see the dog. After my mother died, I longed for my sister to take some time off from college to be with me. I verbalized this one time, a few days after the funeral, that maybe she might delay her return to school. She was sitting on my bed behind me, playing with my hair, which was something my mother used to do every night before I went to sleep. It was very quiet; the only sound I could hear was the gentle brush of her fingers against my scalp.

"Please stay with me," I said. "I need you."

But she told me she had exams, and while she wanted to stay with me, she had to go back or she wouldn't complete the semester. I felt totally rejected, but I did not judge her. I looked up to her, and my world had already been so destroyed by the death of my mother that I couldn't afford to be angry with her. But it hurt, nonetheless. So instead I judged myself. I made myself wrong for needing someone, for revealing that need. I needed more than the universe could give me. Clearly my feelings were too big for the universe to hold, too disgusting. I would not put them out there like that again. I didn't even want to have to feel them myself.

Well, now I was feeling again and I did not want Annika coming home. If she returned there was no way I could just wander out to the ocean alone at night. I guess I could still go to the rocks and not tell her where I was going—I could lie and say I was going across town or to a café to see some acoustic guitar bullshit. But if she saw me out the window, what would I say I was doing? She would start asking questions.

Also, I had a new fantasy. I wanted to ask Theo if he would maybe come with me to the house and stay for a night. I didn't know how I would get him there. Certainly he couldn't drag himself across the beach. I doubted he would want me to carry him. But maybe I could get one of those little sand-wagon things, or a bicycle with a wagon on the back.

I had already planned this visit, fully, in my head. I wanted to have sex with him on a bed. I didn't even care if he slept over or not. I just wanted a place to be with him where we could relax that wasn't freezing and where we weren't looking around for people to catch us. The way I felt when we kissed or when he went down on me—I wanted to create that feeling and live in that for as long as I could. I wanted to build a tent of it in the warmth of my sister's house: a container where I could bottle the feeling, like a little ship, and hold the glow.

Here was a bit of magic that could happen in my life. After all the nothingness, maybe this fantasy was worth living for. I suppose that whenever you're addicted to something, this is what they mean when they say you forget about the consequences and don't care about the other side. All I cared about was my plan.

32.

Theo was waiting by the rocks, hanging on to the side of them. I ran across the beach and climbed up, feeling like Catherine running to Heathcliff across the moors, in my long skirt. I imagined that I looked like a child. I knew that I wasn't, but I felt time to be slowing as I ran—or at least, I wasn't getting any older anymore. I was alive and that was it.

"Hi," I said, and crouched down to kiss him.

"I'm coming up," he said, and twisted himself up onto the rock. For a second I was shocked to see his black tail, the sash still around his pelvis. He kissed me hard and laid me down onto the rock. Then he pulled himself on top of me and I could feel his cock, my skirt and his sash between us. It was all so natural. My legs spread and his pelvis and tail were between them, just where his legs would be if he were a regular man.

As we kissed I imagined eating his tail with garlic butter. I wanted to suck his cock and also to see it. I rolled us over and sat up on top of him, kissing my way down his torso, my skirt fanned out around both of us, covered in ocean water and sea-weed and black slime from his tail. I felt like an octopus or an anemone. I sucked on his neck, his nipples, the insides of his arms. I licked his meaty rib cage, kissed my way down his belly, sucked on his belly button.

My head hovered over his sash. I teased him, kissing the outside of it, licking it. Like a salt lick, the sash had accreted so much salt. I wondered how many sashes he had, if he ever changed them.

I unfastened the knot on the side. His cock rested on a nest of beautiful dark pubic hair. He wasn't totally hard anymore. I felt self-conscious and wondered if I had turned him off somehow. But he had an ample, beautiful cock, uncircumcised, white and pink, with two round pink balls.

I kissed his cock, rubbed it against my face and cheek, so soft. I looked up and he was smiling at me. I began to lick it, to make out with it. My mouth was very dry from the salt and I felt like I had a fur tongue. I put his whole cock in my mouth and aimed it toward the back of my throat, gagging, making some more saliva. He moaned and softly tousled my hair with his hands. He got a little firmer but not totally hard yet and so I had to hold it in my fist. I sucked and jerked gently, but he would not get fully hard. I began to lick his balls. I put them in my mouth. My chin rested on the place where his tail met his skin. The scales were slimy and hard at the same time. But his balls were delicious, like raw oysters.

"Oh my God," he whispered.

He reached down and began to jerk himself as I licked his balls.

"Don't stop licking," he said. "Don't stop."

It wasn't the romantic jerking I would have liked to have seen, his beautiful body in a slow search of pleasure. This was the second time in one summer that a boy jerking off wasn't what I would have wanted it to be. He was more frantic and urgent, like he was trying to get it done, like he wanted to prove to me that he could get it up and stay up. Maybe he just needed a lot of friction in order to feel pleasure. I wondered if his cock being exposed to saltwater had made it numb. Maybe this was just how men jerked themselves when no one was watching. Maybe he was comfortable around me.

"It feels so good," he said, his voice hoarse. "I feel you so much. I'm going to, oh my *God*—"

My pussy surged. I took my mouth off his balls and put it on the head of his cock, grabbing his balls with my hand and rubbing them in a circle. They were tight. His come in my mouth didn't taste bitter, like some men, but it wasn't exactly sweet either. It was a feminine taste. It tasted like the smell of his tail, oceanic, a little fishy. I felt as though I had eaten his pussy, that I was yang or yin, or whichever the male was, and he was female for a moment.

I thought of the god of the sea, Poseidon, the father of Triton. Was Aphrodite his lover? No, Demeter was his lover—the earth goddess—they were siblings but also lovers. What did that make Aphrodite on her clamshell, then? To Sappho, Aphrodite was the ultimate sex deity. In Hesiod, Kronos, the king of Titans, castrated Uranus, the sky god, and Aphrodite rose out of the water from his spilled seed—transformed into a woman out of sparkling seafoam. Perhaps they were all one person. The gods were always switching identities, changing genders, inhabiting new bodies as though they were clothes. So Poseidon, with his long beard and muscular chest, was in a way also a woman. A woman, a man, what was the difference between the two anyway? It seemed in that moment very little.

I felt that we were twins—two strands of the same DNA or one egg split in two—sibling lovers, like Poseidon and Demeter. At the very least we were two eggs sharing one womb. He was both the womb and not the womb. And I was both the womb and not the womb. We were the womb for each other and made of the same material, but also contained together in a larger womb. I felt so good, and for a moment I wondered, Maybe it is not him who makes me feel this way? Maybe I already contain him, as the gods contain one another. Perhaps I do not even need him, to feel like this?

No, I needed him and maybe it was okay to need him. This is how love was spiritual, when it felt like this: unity with each other, the self, and all. And if this wasn't love, then this was how lust could be a thing of value: a peak experience, something worth the pain of coming down. Was this true or was it a lie? So many things were both true and a lie, depending on how you felt in the moment. In this moment it felt like love.

I was bold and ready to ask him.

"I was wondering if you would ever possibly come to my house?" I asked. "I mean, it is my sister's house but I live there alone."

"I would love to be in a house with you," he said. "I would love to make love to you without having to look over our shoulders for anyone coming. To be totally alone."

"You would?" I giggled.

"Yes," he said.

"Have you ever been in a home on land?"

"Yes," he said. "A few times, many years ago."

I didn't press him.

"But this was a home very close to the water," he said. "It wasn't really a home. It was a deserted boathouse right on the ocean. An old fishermen's boathouse. I just don't see how I could possibly come to your sister's home. I think it is too far. First of all, I can't be seen. How would I get across the sand?"

"I've been thinking about this," I said.

He seemed so excited by the idea that I didn't feel weird letting him know that this was something I had spent a lot of time thinking about. It was like I had let go now and decided to trust him. Something in me had suddenly decided that it didn't really matter what would happen. Either I was going to scare him off or I wasn't, but if it was going to happen, it would happen. I didn't have to stifle my fears and desires. Just being around him, inside his supernatural aura, gave me the confidence to speak, like the way wine gives you confidence. I was languid and casual. Later I would likely replay everything and pick apart what I had said. Had I been too forward? And God forbid it ended that night when we said goodbye. If he disappeared and I never saw him again, I would blame myself for pushing him away with my omnivorous need. But for now I didn't feel at risk of losing him, since he was very much here with me.

"What if I took a shopping cart and brought it to the ocean?" I asked. "It's Venice and there are so many people with shopping carts. We could hoist you into it and cover you up with a blanket. I could wheel you across the beach and you would be my secret. To everyone else I would look like any of the other bums who live here."

"But are the street people allowed on the beach at night?" he asked. "The boardwalk people? It's one thing when you come to me alone at night, looking as you do. You're one body, a woman in a dress. Coast Guard, the police, none of them are looking for you. And even if they were to come over, when we are on the rocks I can go right back into the water. I can go under the water and they would never see me again! But if I was in a shopping cart, far from the water, and they found us, how could I get free? They would lock me up or make me into some kind of terrible show. Remember that on land I am helpless."

"What if it wasn't a shopping cart?" I asked. "What about . . . a child's wagon? And what if it wasn't at night but at dawn? It's legal to be on the beach then, but no one is around except maybe a few surfers. What if we loaded you onto the wagon and covered your bottom half in a blanket? People would just think you were my child. Only grown."

"I feel that there would still be a danger if I was seen getting into the wagon."

"They might just think you were wearing a wet suit. Haven't others thought it was a wet suit? I did at first."

"Yes," he said. "Others have."

"See!" I said.

"I want to do it," he said. "But I'm scared."

"Okay, I understand."

"But I really want to."

"Well, then listen to my plan. Just hypothetically, this is how we would do it. I would go to the hardware store, or maybe the toy store. And buy a wagon. Something big enough that we could get most of you in there without too much dangling. I could come tomorrow morning at dawn with the wagon. Or not tomorrow, this dawn, but the next day. You could come up onto the rock as usual. And then just slide right down, right into the wagon. I would bring a blanket, maybe even a couple of them. We would make sure that you would be totally and completely covered. We wouldn't even have to go anywhere. We could just see how you felt. See how it worked. It would be like practice."

"Okay," he said. "I think I could possibly do that. Just practice."

"That's all it would be."

33.

Buying the wagon wasn't sexy like shopping for makeup and clothes. I wondered if real love always devolved into this: moments of non-sexiness. Maybe the moments of non-sexiness gradually moved together to become one solid thing, like the way that Theo's scales started as almost freckles or moles and eventually raised and congealed. I went to three hardware stores before I found a wagon that was big enough. It was tin and red and looked like an antique child's wagon. I pretended for a moment that I had a child, and was buying the wagon as a gift for him or her. Was the child's name Theo? I imagined myself hand-in-hand with a little brunette boy and wondered what it would be like. Would I feel as deeply for him as I did for my Theo? Maybe I was only fooling myself with my romantic adventures, looking to fill a hole that could only truly be satisfied by the love that women said they felt for their kids. If you didn't have children, they liked to remind you that you were missing out—and that there was no greater love. No, fuck all those childbearers and their "fulfilling" lives, never getting to have adventures like mine. I was glad that this wagon wasn't for some snot-nosed kid that I felt I had to pretend to be all excited about but secretly loathed for destroying my body, my freedom. It seemed depressing.

My romantic adventures were something to really be excited about—something that could really keep the nothingness away. As I walked home tugging the wagon, I decided not to think about anything that would happen after. I wasn't going to think about my languishing thesis again. I wouldn't think about Claire or her phone calls. Certainly not Jamie or Phoenix. I would think about Dominic enough to make sure that he stayed alive. But I didn't have it in me anymore to really spend quality time, snuggling and imbibing his warmth. I had begun to feel differently about him now, not as a delight or a gift, but just another responsibility.

I decided also that I wasn't even going to think about what would happen if Theo got frightened and refused to come with me. Instead I busied myself, cleaning the house, playing with the lighting, picking out music. Everything on Annika's iPod seemed primed for a spontaneous bout of triangle pose, but not really for sex. I needed to get the moment just right if it was going to remain eternal, stretch over the face of the time-space continuum, and suck up all of the nothingness everywhere.

34.

Claire called, but I didn't pick up. Then she texted:

What's your favorite suicide method?

Where are you what are you doing?

I hate to be needy so I'm going to pretend I don't need you but seriously where are you?

Lucy, I am so on edge and hate everything namely me

I couldn't get out of bed to drive my kids to school do you think I am an awful person?

Don't have children they destroy everything

Do you want to go shopping?

I didn't mean to be cold, but something about her really scared me now. She'd passed over to the darkness, the edge of nothingness, and she'd done it by trying to access the light, the glitter. Those highs, even if they were fake and we knew that they wouldn't last forever, felt so real when we were in them. That's where I was now. I just couldn't discern the ephemeral nature of what I was experiencing, and didn't want to. Perhaps what I had with Theo was as synthetic as what Claire had with her men, but it felt so good—how could we ever even care when we were in it?

Craving the fake light was a completely real feeling, even if those around you could see that you were just another junkie. I think this is what was most frightening: me and my Theo haze and Claire and her druglike need were the same thing. I didn't want to look at it; I didn't want to look at her. To look at her would be to see the danger that I was facing on the other side of Theo's visit, the darkness that inevitably fell when you spent too much time basking in the sun of a man. To look at her was to know that I was inevitably the cause of my own darkness, my own nothingness. The more you went for the ephemeral light, the more the void opened on the other side. It was waiting for me right there.

I set my alarm for five. I wanted time to try to look beautiful, even though the wind and salt air always washed away anything I did to my hair or face. Dominic, never an early riser, was still asleep—sprawled in the bed where I had been, one ear above the sheets. I picked him up, carried him to the little white loveseat in the bedroom, and covered him with a blanket. He didn't stir. Then I changed the sheets on the bed so they would smell clean and not like wet dog. I got in the deep tub and soaked. It was cold out and the hot water felt good to my bones.

I brushed my teeth, then drenched myself in one of my sister's expensive body oils: something called Exotic Seduction made with jasmine, ylang-ylang, vanilla, and lavender oils. I dabbed two extra drops on my nipples and one in my belly button. I applied spearmint lip gloss and rubbed some honey wax in my hair. Then I put on a knee-length gray cotton sundress and a wool sweater. I brought two large blankets outside and placed them in the wagon, unlocked the gate, and started dragging it across the sand. It was quiet. No one was out. If anyone saw me they would have thought I was using the wagon to carry my beach stuff out for the day. I was simply having a beach day.

I got to the rocks and saw the rosy dawn, the sun rising over the mountains. The rocks were cold and wet, and each wave that came in slapped against them—making its own little crash for a moment, then vanishing. I hadn't slept much and felt giddy. What the hell was going on? I was out here looking for a merman. Was I crazy? Was I becoming just another Venice lost soul, belongings in a wagon, having insane visions by the ocean? I laughed aloud to myself. I imagined moving onto the beach at the end of the summer when Annika returned. I could sleep under the stars, meeting Theo every night. Then I could go eat breakfast and shower in their multimillion-dollar home. The thought of moving to the water's edge seemed romantic in that moment. Sappho had always lived by the ocean, imagining love as a luminous divinity rising from the waves. This would be my living thesis.

Then I saw Theo's head surface, his thick wet hair draped over his left eye.

"Hey!" he said, spitting out water.

"Can you see when you're underwater?"

"Yes," he said. "I live there."

"Well, I'm here to kidnap you," I said.

"No, I'm willfully coming," he said. "I'm coming up. Land ho."

He looked around to see if anyone was coming.

"Wow, you weren't kidding about a wagon. You are really committed to doing this, I see."

"Uh-huh," I said. "I think we should at least try, anyway. I will protect you. I just want to be safe with you, no elements, just a soft place to land together, by ourselves."

"I really want to be with you," he said.

I shuddered.

He climbed up onto the rocks belly first, then flipped himself over, grunting.

"Need help?" I asked.

"I'm okay."

I rolled the wagon over to the edge of the rocks and held it steady. As he dragged himself on board, he looked like a paraplegic pulling himself onto a seat. He rolled over just using his arms to rearrange himself and tucked where his knees would be up to his chest. I draped the blanket around his shoulders and let it collect in front of him, covering the bulk of his tail. We were good, it seemed. But hoisting the wagon off the rocks proved more difficult than I thought. I pulled left and right, and the tin axles ground. He tried to push off the rock with his arms, like a man in a wheelchair, face straining. With him pushing, I gave a final tug and the wagon fell onto the beach, toppling over and dumping Theo in the sand.

"Oh my God, are you okay?" I asked.

"I'm fine, I'm fine," he said. But I noticed he was shaking.

"Would you cover me up with the blanket quickly? Please?"

The wagon and blanket were only a few feet from where he had fallen, but I realized how hard it would be for him to even crawl that far. I wondered if his tail was heavy, what was inside it. Was it human flesh or fish flesh? I covered up his bottom half and he just lay there for a second.

"Maybe this is a bad idea," he said. "Maybe this is a warning."

My stomach dropped. I wondered if he really felt this scared, or if he was embarrassed from the fall, looking for reassurance to show him how much I wanted him to come home with me. No, he probably really felt that way. And anyway, I wasn't going to beg.

"Whatever you want," I said.

Theo closed his eyes. Under the blanket he looked like a child. I stood in the sand, tracing half-moon shapes with my toe. My life now came down to whatever he decided. But I didn't convey any desperation. Just being with him relaxed me. When he was right near me I could feel strangely casual, as though he could disappear and I would be okay. I could just be there, languidly drawing my little sand prints. It was only when he wasn't with me, when I was away from the ocean, that I felt like I was disintegrating.

"Come here," he said. "Come under the blanket with me."

I got in and pulled up the blanket as though we were going to bed. We hugged for a long time. Then we started kissing and I felt his cock get hard against me.

"I want you so much," he whispered in my ear. "You are my earth girl."

"I want you too," I said.

"We shouldn't do it here," he said. "Not on the beach at daylight."

"What do you want to do?"

"Okay," he said. "Let's go."

But he began to finger me, first tickling my clit just a little, then teasing my hole. I was already soaking wet.

"Come on," I said into his mouth.

"Okay," he said, fingering me harder.

"You're finger fucking me on the beach and you're a very young man. This is your first time fingering a girl. What do you have to say about that?"

Of course it was not his first time. But I wanted it to be.

"I'm finger fucking your beautiful vagina and it's my first time. You're the most beautiful girl I've ever seen. I can't believe it. I can't believe I get to finger you."

He intuitively knew exactly what to say to have me writhing. Or perhaps I planted the words in him, as so much of what our lovers do and say is imagined. We turn them into who we want them to be. We fill in their bodies and words for them.

He pulled out his finger and sucked it, then put it in my mouth.

"Taste yourself," he said. "You are delicious."

"I am?" I asked. I nibbled his finger a little.

"You are," he said. "But it's not safe here like this."

"What should we do? Do you want to go back in the ocean?"

"Not particularly."

"So then let's try again."

I rolled over, out from under the blanket, and stood up. Then I brought the wagon over to him.

"Okay, hold it very still," he said, and hoisted himself on backward. I covered him up in the blanket. This time he stayed on.

As I pulled him across the beach, there were just a few stray joggers and assorted weirdos nearby. His blanketed tail jutted off the wagon, but it wasn't the strangest thing to happen in Venice. No one seemed to notice or care. It wasn't like I was smuggling a dead body.

35

I wheeled him up to the side gate of Annika's house.

"Wow," he said, gaping up at the glass structure. "The other place I was in was just a wooden shack."

"Yeah," I said. "My sister's place is really nice."

I could hear Dominic barking from inside. I had never heard him sound so loud and unhinged.

"Oh God," he said. "I forgot you had a dog. I'm very frightened of them."

"Dominic is really sweet," I said. "But I can put him in another room if you want."

"Please," he said.

I went inside. Dominic was baring his fangs.

"Okay, chill," I told him. But he growled and showed his gums to me. I also saw that his penis was out, the red lipstick of it extended from its sheath. I knew this happened to dogs when they were angry or excited. Why was he so agitated?

"Come here," I said, and he began to whimper. "You're going to go in this room."

I opened the door to my sister's pantry and put in his food dish and water. Then I dragged him in there by the collar. He put his head on his paws and his tail between his legs, but when I went back outside he began barking maniacally again. I didn't know what to do. This was not the glowing bubble I had envisioned.

"How scared are you?" I asked Theo. "Maybe if he just comes out and meets you."

"The problem is that if he attacks I can't get away."

"He won't attack," I said. But I had never seen Dominic this irate and I wasn't sure.

When we imagine a situation—when our hearts decide this must happen—we will go to any lengths to make the fantasy happen. In my fantasy there was no barking. There was only me and Theo on the soft sheets and a universe of silence.

"Wait one second," I said. "I'll be right back."

I remembered I had seen some doggy tranquilizers in one of the kitchen cabinets for things like airplane flights. I got two pills and hid them in a treat, then went into the pantry and stuffed it into Dominic's frothing mouth. Two was double the dose. Was I awful? Would I be punished? Next I turned on some music, something ambient of my sister's, a soft electronic yoga chant meant to soothe the most stressed-out human or animal.

"He should be quiet soon," I said, coming out the side door.

Then I realized that Theo was still in the wagon.

"Oh God," I said. "I'm sorry, let me help you out of there."

He smiled nervously as I pulled the wagon into the house. In my visions, Theo would be able to go anywhere on his own. He would be part Paralympic champion and part giant snail, easily gliding from room to room and up the stairs. But there really was no way of getting him up there.

"Maybe we can relax on the sofa," I said, pointing.

My sister's sofa was white and I felt nervous about getting it covered in kelp, sand, the sheen of sea dirt that accrued and attached itself to Theo's tail. I was covered in the beach and ocean salt too.

I took the blanket off of him and laid it on the sofa. He flipped himself onto the floor and began to drag himself over. I felt proud of him that he was unashamed to do this in my presence, to let me see him so vulnerable. It was adorable—him flopping around out of water, trying to be strong for me, arms straining. Who was this magic creature in my sister's home? How had this even happened?

He hoisted himself onto the sofa and lay down on his back.

"What's that?" he asked, pointing to the big flat-screen TV.

"It's a television," I said. "It projects images and sound. But right now it's off. It's sleeping."

"Do you enjoy it?"

"Not really," I said.

"Come over here," he said.

I got on top of him. We kissed each other with open mouths, sucking at each other like we were eating mussels. Then we kissed slow and gentle. I noticed that Dominic had stopped barking. How long could Theo stay with me? Would we be able to bend time in any direction we wanted, or would reality have to come snapping back? As long as we still had one more moment I felt safely enshrouded by a womb of light, protecting me from the nothingness. But as I lost myself in his kissing, I felt a strange darkness creep through that barrier and overwhelm me. I was part of him again, twins again, and I felt the surge of the ocean—the real one or maybe the ocean of consciousness—but this time the ocean was scary and dark, and I couldn't breathe. I felt nervous, responsible for him, like I needed to pretend I was fine. He flipped me over. Now I was trapped under a strange fish.

He stopped kissing me.

"Are you okay?" he asked.

I was the one who was supposed to feel comfortable, in this home, on land. It had been so brave of him to come, to do something so risky, but it was me who was suddenly afraid. I lied and said I was good. My sister's home looked like a strange submarine to me, spinning in a vast ocean. There was nowhere for it to land. We kissed some more, but I was being consumed by terror and scared that I would float away or drown.

Just let yourself go, I said to myself. I wondered if the darkness and sadness were coming from him or from me. I stopped kissing him again.

"You have experienced great sadness," I said.

"Yes," he said. "But I suppose we all have."

"But you're so intuitive. I can really feel you, I can feel the way you feel. You feel other people's pain, don't you?"

"I guess I do," said Theo.

I wondered if he could feel what I was feeling. Did he know that if I stayed there any longer I might choke on this new darkness?

"Let me check on Dominic to make sure he's okay," I said.

Dominic was asleep on the floor of the pantry. Everything was peaceful in there, as though there were a halo of okayness. Suddenly I wished it were just me and Dominic. Now the dog seemed like less responsibility than the merman. Why had I been so urgent to get Theo back here? Perhaps it was only because I thought that I couldn't. Maybe this was my way: now that he was here, that I knew I could get him here, I didn't want it. Maybe the group was right. I was intimacy-averse. I took a deep breath and gathered myself. I couldn't just leave Theo in the other room.

"Do you want something to eat?" I called.

"No, just come back in here."

I wondered what he ate. Plankton? Fish? His breath always tasted fresh, a little salty but not fishy. He tasted like ocean air.

In the living room he was sitting up in the sunlight that shone through the big glass windows, the blanket wrapped around him.

"I'm sorry," he said.

"Why?" I asked.

"I think I brought some darkness in here with me. The sadness, moving from sea to land, sometimes I can't shake it. I thought if anything I would feel scared, but coming here I couldn't help but think, What's the point? I mean, I guess the point is that we have an experience. I guess that is the point. I just, well, I am going to live a long time. And have lived a long time. I have seen a lot of people come and go."

I wondered how many people. How many women, human women? Mermaids? I wanted to say I would be with him forever. But I didn't know if that was what he wanted me to say. I couldn't make that promise. I realized it wasn't my impending departure for Phoenix that stopped me from offering the words. And it wasn't my fear of intimacy. It was still my fear of rejection.

"But you seem so young," I said.

"No, I'm not. I've been alive for a very long time. I'm not eternal. I can die. But we don't usually get sick, not in the body anyway. Something about the saltwater. It brines us and keeps us young. It keeps illness from entering."

"So how old are you exactly?"

"Honestly, I don't really know. It's not a thing down there. Maybe forty?"

"That's how old I am," I said. "Almost. Wow, I'm younger than you."

"I told you you're young," he said. "I might be even older than that actually."

"Who are your parents?"

"They are like me, but also very much not like me. They look like me, or my mother does anyway, but more content with their existence. They never leave the water. They aren't scared, they simply have no interest," he said. "Anyway, hoisting and dragging myself like that, on the sand, it made me feel tired. Sometimes I get so tired, even in the water. It's like physical things don't make me physically tired, but they make me mentally tired. Mental things make me feel that way too."

"Everything is just so much," I said. "All the time."

"It is," he said. "And I was scared I wasn't going to be able to, you know." He laughed.

"Get it up?" I said.

"Yeah," he said. "Not because I don't want you or because I don't have it in me physically, but because of that mental exhaustion. I can doubt myself. I become more susceptible."

"Theo," I soothed him.

Now that I knew he was the one who had brought the darkness I felt that I didn't have to be as afraid anymore. The gloom wasn't coming from me. I was still responsible for him but not for the atmosphere. So many times I had tried to fix things, people's feelings, the shifting moods of men, by adjusting my own behavior. But in this case it was beyond me. He was, after all, supernatural. Did he even exist? I decided that he existed like a mood. In some ways, my moods did and did not exist. People said that you could will a mood into being or will it away. Just think positively. But I never felt that way. My moods were their own entities, even if no one could understand why they were there. That was what made me scared of feelings. I realized now that what I had to do, in spite of what others said, was not try to change a mood but surrender to it. I had to surrender to whatever feelings arrived and in doing so I could maybe ride them, floating on the waves. I decided I was going to surrender.

"We could rest a bit," I said. "I'm tired too."

"Yes, let's rest," he said. "I'd like that. Come here, come lie down with me."

I got on the sofa with him and we lay there face-to-face. He closed his eyes and I kissed his eyelids and cheeks. He gathered me in his arms and his upper body was warm. Everything above his tail was soft. I didn't know what to do with our lower halves. I couldn't intertwine my legs with his tail as if it was a pair of legs, so I wrapped one leg around him and pressed the other leg straight against his tail. Usually when I cuddled with another body, I would have to separate before falling asleep. I would feel too trapped or get too hot pressed so close against them. But Theo's tail was cool, almost like a built-in fan or compress, and I was reminded of what my friend's aunt taught me years ago as a trick for insomnia: keep one leg under the blanket and one leg out. It was as though I had one leg under a towel in the sun and one dipped in the sea. When I thought of it this way I slipped into the waves. His breathing was rhythmic and the slight scent of fish drifted up from him. The sun came in the window and shone on our heads, and we both drifted off with our faces in a glow.

We woke up around noon. Theo stirred and pulled me closer. "Mmmmmm," he breathed in my ear. I kissed him on the lips. His breath tasted less fresh than usual, a bit like wet leather.

"I like how you taste," I said. "I like tasting you in this state, no saltwater to cleanse your mouth. It's so primal. I feel like I'm getting another part of you."

"You really do?" he asked.

We kissed deeper, our tongues in each other's mouths. I could feel his cock hard now against me. I pressed my body against his with pure want. I felt that I had a hole, not just my pussy itself but an existential hole, and that for the first time it was on the verge of being filled: the inertia of our mingled desire caulked it up. It was stuffed with anticipation. My anticipation of his cock was solid, its own entity, as though my desire were a second cock. He too seemed to exude complete want and devotion, which made me feel confident in my own wanting—as though, in his mirror, my lust was good and pure. He made me feel innocent and part of something bigger, like nothing had ever been my fault.

I did not say "I love you," or even whisper it, but somehow I felt that I was praying it into his mouth without speaking. I was saying it with my breath, my chest, the magnetism between our pelvises. It was a swimming into each other. I also felt that he had a hole, or holes, and in some strange way my cock—an existential one, really—was filling him. I felt that we were moving in and out of one another's holes, nursing each other, symbiotic and magnetic. I felt the Earth rotating around us, or that we were the planet—spinning on its axis. In my head came a deep buzz of the Earth again and I didn't know if I was actually humming out loud or if it was all inside me.

This is how you exist in the world, I thought. This is how you are alive.

"I want you so much," he said.

Under the blanket, so we would stay warm, he lifted my dress up over my head. I was naked except for my undies. He put his face between my small breasts, cradling and then sucking on them. He kissed and licked my stomach, then down the front of my underwear over my clit. He teased around my underwear, the crevices of my thighs, the crease where my lips met. Then, caressing my ass, he slid my underwear down and put his face between my thighs. He inhaled deeply like there was oxygen in there.

"God, you smell so good," he said.

He peeled my underpants down my legs.

"And your vagina is so gorgeous. I just want to put my face in it all the time and live there."

"You should," I said nervously, and giggled.

I watched the top of his head as he ate me. Even though he had said before that he wanted to eat me all night I still felt nervous about how long it might take me to come. I made moaning sounds. My clit felt good but my mind stayed disconnected. I wanted him in me, wanted to fuck him, face-to-face. As if he knew how I was feeling, he put a finger inside me. I gasped.

"I want your cock so bad," I whined.

"How much?" he said with his face still buried in my pussy.

"So bad," I said.

I could see that he was stroking himself as he ate me. I could feel his cock, hard against my shin.

"Give me your cock please," I said. "Please can I have it?"

He climbed back on me so his face was over my face and his chest on my chest, his cock nestled between my thighs, resting on my wet clit and lips.

"I'm on the pill," I said. "We don't need to use anything."

Then I started laughing at the absurdity of everything. Was I really talking about birth control with a merman? It was true that I was on the pill, sort of. I wasn't great about taking it. Sometimes I would forget for days at a time. Occasionally I would just go off it for a month. Jamie knew this, but in all our years together I never got knocked up. He would always pull out and come on my belly. He feared me getting pregnant, how that would impinge on his freedom—the emotional fallout from an abortion, or worse yet, a baby. He was afraid, but not enough to wear a condom. I couldn't remember if I had taken my pill the day before, but could a merman really impregnate me? Would the child have legs or a tail? Perhaps it would have legs and a tail, or multiple legs, like an octopus.

I couldn't imagine Theo was riddled with disease either, considering he spent his life in saltwater. He was like a saline boy. I didn't know how many others he had fucked, and now I didn't really care. Let him give me his diseases, I thought. Let him give me some strange sea syphilis or whatever. I want it. I don't care.

Looking into my eyes, he rubbed the crease of my pussy with his cock. Then he slid his cock into me, so slowly. I gasped, he moaned, and I wanted to eat his moan. He was inside me. I couldn't believe he was there. I had never thought of it like that before in the heat of things—about a person really being inside another person. "Entered," like they say in romance novels. With every thrust he kissed me deeply and I gasped in his mouth. He was surprisingly dexterous given his tail.

We looked in each other's eyes as we moved. I felt that we were creating something together. The sounds I was making became primal and real. But then I felt him in me just a little less, then almost not at all. Somehow he had gotten soft.

He pulled out and jerked it a little. He looked ashamed.

"I'm sorry," he said. "Sometimes I just get nervous the first time with a new person. It's the pressure. But you feel so good and are really gorgeous. I want to give you so much pleasure. I want to make you feel so much."

He pulled out of me and wriggled down my body. His desire to get me off made up for him having lost his hard-on. I let myself go completely, like when we were on the rocks. I focused only on the feeling and not on anything else. This time when I came I did not come for the gods or the stars, but only for him. I called out his name as I came into his mouth. I came for so long I felt suspended in time or air or space, as though the divisions between seconds had been obliterated.

Afterward, as my pussy settled, he kept his face down there, his cheek resting on my inner right thigh. I could feel us attaching and knew that any chance of breaking apart from him emotionally was not possible. I was his now.

36

I read somewhere that it takes women one and a half fucks to get attached—that it happens in the middle of the second fuck. Now I knew this was true of pussy eating too. Theo lay with his head in my lap and I gently tickled his face. Then I heard Dominic barking from the other room.

"Do you want to meet the dog?"

"I don't," he said. "Also, I should probably be getting back soon."

"What do you have to get back for? What if you just stay here with me a little longer," I said, tousling his hair.

"How about you come into the ocean and stay with me forever?" he said, smiling.

"I would get too cold," I said. "But I'm coming to see you as much as I can. I want to come see you all the time. When can I see you again?"

Now it wasn't enough just to be with him. I felt that he was already gone even though he was right there. I could see past his body to his absence, feel him slipping away, as though he flashed back and forth between here and gone like a strobe. I was already worried for that moment when he would be gone. What would it take for him to be enough? Even if I were to cook him up and eat him, fry his deliciousness with butter and a bib, swallow him up and digest him inside me, it still wouldn't be enough.

"Soon," he said.

Dominic was barking wildly.

"I should probably walk him first and then I will take you

back to the ocean," I said. "I won't bring him over to you. I'll keep him over on the other side."

But as soon as I opened the door to the pantry, Dominic came darting out and jumped onto the sofa. He lunged at Theo.

"Oh my God, Dominic, no!" I yelled, yanking him sideways.

I was terrified. For a moment, I couldn't see Theo clearly. It was as though he were vanishing, or I couldn't hold my fear and vision at the same time. He flashed in and out of focus, then I saw him again, first his dark head and torso, then his tail, all the way to the translucent fin at the bottom. He looked fragile.

"Damn," said Theo. "This is what happens. It's exactly what I was trying to tell you, why it's unsafe for me to be out here."

"I'm so sorry!"

"Could you please walk him later and just take me back now?"

I still had Dominic by the collar and I shoved him back in the other room again.

"I'm sorry he scared you."

Theo looked ashamed.

"Just please take me back."

We loaded him into the wagon and covered him in the blanket. The beach was cold and the sand was freezing on my feet, moist from the tide. It was just after sunset, the sky darkening, and we were both silent as I led him to the rocks. Had I ruined it? I should have just kept Dominic in the pantry, but I never expected he would attack. I don't know whether Theo was scared or if his pride was just hurt. Perhaps both.

"Will I ever see you again?" I asked.

"Of course," he said. "I just need a little bit of time back in the ocean. Let me refresh myself. How about you come back out on the rocks tomorrow night? At eleven? I will be there."

He didn't kiss me goodbye, just wriggled into the water and swam away. I felt my chest tighten and my face crinkle up as I began to cry. I had faith that he would be there tomorrow—that wasn't it. But how could we ever really be together? We were relegated to a relationship that could only exist on a rock. At some point soon this would come to an end. I felt my body shivering. This was new; I'd never had that symptom of love loss before. Dr. Jude never said anything about the shakes. I was going into a new type of withdrawal.

It doesn't matter whether we know what's good or bad for us, I thought. It doesn't fucking matter one bit.

37

I walked Dominic and then kept him shut up in the pantry the rest of the night. In him I saw a symbol of everything standing in the way of Theo and me being together freely. It wasn't a problem with the sea but a problem with the land.

I went to Abbot Kinney to try to distract myself. If I could be light about this, like the way I felt shopping for those other dates, maybe I could fool myself into thinking there would be life on the other side. But as I stood in the sun, each of the boutiques looked like fake storefronts—empty, like a film set. At one of the cheaper boutiques, I decided I was going to steal something: an adjustable ring with a blue stone in it. I brought it into the dressing room with me and stuck it in my bra, then walked out. It made me feel high for a minute, an adrenaline rush, but then the doom set in again. I felt sick and sad. Under a pair of palm trees on the street corner I threw up on a grate. I couldn't believe how physical or immediate my loneliness was. I needed help, some kind of comfort, to get through until I could see him again, a place to vent. I needed someone warm who might not judge me.

I called Claire and left her a long message on her voicemail.

"Hi, it's me. I'm over my head with the swimmer and fucked up. I think I might be dying. Have you ever felt like you are dying from your experiences with these guys? I mean, I know you have. But what about, really dying? Like, in a totally physical way? I think I'm actually sick, Claire. I puked in front of a bunch of Euro tourists on Abbot Kinney. I hate people and their normal lives. Anyway, can you call me back? Please? I'm sorry if I have been horrible."

I threw up again in front of a boutique called Safe Sox that sold expensive patterned socks: argyle, stripes, superheroes, marijuana leaves. I didn't give a fuck if anyone saw, what anyone thought. Fuck them and their stupid socks. Why were people personalizing their feet with something no one else would ever see? Didn't they know their socks were futile?! Could you get any more Sisyphean than a pair of socks emblazoned with sushi rolls? I wandered in and out of stores, like a ghost. I looked at all the people and they seemed inconsequential: deluded and interchangeable. Anything I used to worry about meant nothing now.

But nothing terrible had happened. In fact something beautiful had occurred—or, at least, it was supposed to be beautiful. Would the pain begin to outweigh the beauty? How much pain would I have to get into before I gave up on pursuing beauty? And what would I do then anyway? No, I wouldn't stop. Even if the experience became only pain, eclipsing the beauty entirely, I would wait at those rocks. I would wait for that little bit of relief that fed the pain in the first place.

And what if I really were to stay in Venice and not return to Phoenix? Would it even be possible? Would Theo even want me here? I knew nothing about his patterns of migration or anything about his life. Maybe he took off for other places at other times of the year. How did I know that he wouldn't be leaving? And what about Annika? Her love had always been across a distance. Even in her act of kindness this summer we were never together in the same space. How would she feel about me taking root where she lived? Would it expose a less geographic, more profound internal distance in our relationship? I was scared to need her, to ask for more than she could give. I didn't want to be rejected by her again.

Venice looked like nothingness to me now—the same nothingness that I had fled Phoenix to escape. The only difference was that I still had Theo. He hadn't gone anywhere. I would see him tomorrow night. In the past the emptiness came when the person rejected me and would not be coming back, like Jamie or Garrett. But I was going to see Theo again, this I pretty much knew. We were connected. So how, in spite of this, had the emptiness made its way in anyway?

I wandered into a fancy convenience store, crying next to the chips. I realized that I hadn't eaten all day. I got a pint of strawberry ice cream and sat on a bench outside the store, watching people walk by. I wasn't sure what time it was. There were a lot of couples, hand-in-hand. I imagined that when these couples broke apart for a time, when they took a day apart, they didn't crumble and get sick like me. I was different from most people. Whatever this thing was, I definitely had it and it was only getting worse.

38.

That night I went out to the rocks even though he said he wouldn't be there. Where was he in the ocean? I pictured him breathing under the waves. I imagined him lying in a sand bed on the seafloor in pure, total darkness. He was sleeping. His eyes were closed and he was faintly smiling. I wanted to be there with him, in quietude, a better abyss than the one up here. I wanted to swim to the bed and curl up beside him, kiss him on the forehead, the water rippling out around us, brining us both.

A passing submarine rang above us. It was my phone. I looked at it. I didn't recognize the number so I didn't answer. But I held it up to my ear and pretended that I could talk to Theo through the waves. What would I say to him? How are you? Who are you? Are you me?

There were so many questions I had for him that I didn't ask. I didn't want to puncture what we had. I feared chasing him away with curiosity and neediness—too much of a desire to pin him down—when he was already giving me so much. I didn't want to know his limits, where his dimensions—both physical and emotional—began and ended. I wondered who else could see him as I saw him. I didn't know the exact constraints of his world or his existence and I didn't want to fracture it. My greatest fear was that I would make him disappear.

Was this how it was with all men? Did they all exist in a totally different reality—one in which you couldn't ask certain questions or the spell would be broken? But it was the same for me. When a man held me at arm's length I wanted him. But if he came closer, stayed too close for too long, the spell was broken for me: the myth dissolved. He wasn't who I thought he was. What was love without the spell?

The spell was broken for me around Jamie. It broke twice: once before the breakup, re-congealing in my need for him, and again now. He'd been frantically texting me every day. This contact, his pursuit, which had gotten me so high just weeks before, only bored me now. I no longer felt excited by being chosen by him. Even the prospect of being the other woman, a hot escape from Megan the scientist, did nothing for me. It only hammered home my feelings around the need for distance in love. He only wanted me because I was far.

I wondered how long Jamie had pined for Megan the scientist. Probably for a long time. Maybe they had even started an affair while we were together and he had fantasized about her, wished he could be with her instead of me. But now that he was with her, I had become her and she had become me. We've all heard of men who leave their wives for a mistress, only to miss the comfort and predictability of their wife. But I felt certain that this wasn't the case. He wasn't missing my predictability. He was wanting me because he could no longer have me. He could tell I was gone and that was a new spell for him.

39.

In the morning my phone rang again from the same number that had rung twice the night before. I hadn't checked the message yet.

"Hello, is this Lucy?" It was a male voice.

"Yes," I said. "Who is this?"

"This is Arnold Schuman. Claire's husband."

"Oh," I said. "I didn't know Claire was still married."

Then I covered my mouth with my hand. Fuck. Who knew what he knew about her dating life?

"Well, the papers haven't been finalized yet, but yes, for all intents and purposes we are no longer together," he said.

"Oh, okay, I'm sorry about that," I said. "Is everything okay with Claire?"

"As a matter of fact no, not right now. Last night she made an attempt on her life. She's in the psych ward."

"Oh my God," I said.

"It was really bad," he said. "She took a handful of pills and then tried to hang herself from her closet doorknob. Luckily the kids weren't there, but some man showed up and broke in. He found her and got her to the hospital. Her boyfriend or something, I'm not sure."

I wondered for a moment which of her men had saved her life. Was it David? Best Buy Dude? Even if it was Ponytail Man, I was genuinely grateful for his existence.

"Oh no, poor Claire. I'm so sorry."

"He didn't take her cell phone so I went to her place and grabbed it to see if I could reach out to some of her friends. I heard your message. Sounds like you aren't in great shape either."

"I'm totally fine. Fuck, what hospital is she at?"

"She's at the UCLA Neuropsychiatric Hospital," he said. "She is allowed visitors from ten to three. I just saw her for the first time this morning and she is doing well, all things considered. But I think she could really use a shred of normalcy right now, and a friend. She really hates it there, but she's not getting out anytime soon. I'm going to try to get her to go to treatment for drugs and depression following her stay. Apparently she'd been taking pills again."

That's not gonna do it, I thought. It's not the pills or the depression. It's the sex and love. But you can't tell a person's husband, one who probably still very much loves her, about her addiction to other men. You can't say, *Oh, the real problem is in her heart and cunt.* Who was I to know what the real problem was anyway? Maybe her real problem was drug addiction, and this love and sex thing was only a poor substitute. But if that was the case then where was my drug problem? And why was she crying for men but never for drugs? Why was it that whenever one of them left or did not give her enough of what she wanted, she dissolved into a disaster? And why was I vomiting on Abbot Kinney last night?

"I'll go see her," I said.

I walked and fed Dominic quickly and then I went to see Claire, just like that, no fear of what I would see, no recalling the memory of having almost been hospitalized by the doughnut incident. There was only this person who needed me. It wasn't a reflection of me that I was seeking, a way to feel good about myself. There was just this human being for whom I could maybe bring some love. For once I could actually do something of service. The thought of getting out of my own mind, and the situation with Theo, made me feel good for a moment.

The psych ward smelled like institutional mashed potatoes and the nurses said that Claire was with a doctor. I wondered if this was where I was going to end up. Or would I end up in a hospital in Phoenix? As the patients moved back and forth, shuffling around the locked ward, I felt very aware of my freedom. One woman about my age sat in a chair, in her gown, digging her nails into her scalp: red sores scabbing all along the hairline. With every few digs she would intently scrutinize the skin she had scraped off and then put it in her mouth. I did not feel like I was a better person than these people, but perhaps stronger, or luckier, or something. Then I felt ashamed of my strength and freedom. I was one of them, only I was out here.

But I wasn't one of them, was I? I had been alive a long time and had not ended up in one of these places. I had come close but never completely lost my freedom. Didn't it say something about my ability to make decisions, or at the last moment save myself and evade disaster?

Maybe I could have two lives. Maybe I could be with Theo and also go to group. I had been avoiding them, thinking that the two could not coexist. But what if they could? Why couldn't I, then, stay in Los Angeles? I could get a job at a library or something. I could live somewhere on the beach in a little bungalow, if cheap bungalows still existed. I could be a woman who didn't kill herself over her problems, but triumphed. I would be balanced, a measured human being. There wouldn't have to be any more sadness. I would have love and sanity.

Or, like Claire, would I just keep getting worse? It was so hard to reconcile fantasy with reality. It was hard to believe that something as beautiful as the way Theo made me feel could put me in the hospital or kill me.

Did chasing the light inevitably lead us here? If we didn't chase the light, did people like us just end up here anyway? If Claire had never left her marriage, where would she be now? She said that she was depressed during her marriage and ended up here once before. And that was before she began her odyssey of love and sex. If you were just going to end up here, regardless of what you did, it seemed worth it to really push things like she did. The nothingness was going to eat you alive anyway. It was going to be mashed potatoes at the end no matter what. So why not just grab for whatever you could get?

"Well, I've really mucked it up this time," said Claire. "I'm back in group therapy now, only here with a pack of sad arses who are completely catatonic—which is maybe actually better."

She laughed. It was good to see her sense of humor back. Her hair was still greasy, piled on top of her head, but the circles under her eyes had diminished and there was a glint in her eyes again.

"You seem better," I said. "Like you're not just staring at the wall."

"Yes, with my last suicide attempt I woke up completely miffed that I was still alive. But this one was oddly refreshing. Maybe I just needed some sort of sorbet—a life palate cleanser."

My God, I loved her.

"I get it," I said. "I mean, not really, because mine wasn't really a consciously active attempt."

"No, yours was more of a gesture."

"Exactly, a gesture. I'm not the suicide pro that you are. But I think I understand."

"Love, if I were a pro I wouldn't be here."

"Right," I said. "But I mean I'm not as, like, experienced with suicide or whatever. Like it's not as much a part of my oeuvre. I'm more—I don't know what I am actually. But I know what you mean by a palate cleanser. Sometimes everything is just so bleh that you need to fucking cut it with a knife."

I was trying to ask her in a roundabout way if it was worth it. We felt the same nothingness, of that I was sure. But I wanted to see if she knew if we were going to be okay or not. Or, at least, if I was. I was asking life advice, couched in the language of suicide, from a friend in a mental hospital. This was the direction my life had taken.

"So are you glad about everything? Like, everything that led you up to this point where you feel okay, maybe even good about being alive? Are you glad for that trajectory of your life?"

"Yeah," she said. "I feel strangely good about everything. Sure, no regrets. I regret nothing."

"I regret everything," I said.

"Lucy."

"I'm still fooling around with that swimmer," I said. "More than fooling around, like, I'm completely, totally in love with him. But the thing is that he's totally in love with me. I mean, it's the most passionate, real, most spiritual experience I've ever had with someone. And yet, I'm not even totally sure if the whole thing even exists."

"What do you mean?"

"Well, we don't function well in the real world."

"The real world is rubbish."

"But we're mostly relegated to a rock. We're tied to a rock."

"Sounds like most marriages. At least ones with children."

"I just—I'm afraid it might kill me. I can't tell if it's a sickness or the best thing that ever happened to me."

"That's brilliant!"

"Tell me, was it definitely men who landed you in here?"

She paused.

"Yes, I suppose it was the men," she said. "But really it was me."

40.

That afternoon I got my period. When I saw the blood, I wept. I wondered if that was why I had been feeling so anxious and afraid. I had cramps that felt like I was being stabbed in the uterus. Usually I enjoyed getting my period, the release of it—I always had. It made me feel connected to some primal goddess energy. But today I just felt heartsick. I had only five more weeks left with Theo and now the next week would be spent bloody, unsexed. What would we do together? I supposed we could just talk. I could put his cock in my mouth.

He was waiting for me when I got to the rocks. He put his arms on the rock and his shiny body came shooting out of the water. He looked like he wanted to stand to greet me, to come running over. I imagined him standing, how or if that could ever happen. I would have to prop something up for him, almost like a frame or a podium. I wondered how much weight his tail could withstand.

"Guess what?"

"What?" he asked, kissing my cheek.

"I have my period," I said, dejected.

"I know," he said.

"What do you mean you know?" I laughed.

"I just know. I know because I just intuited it. I could feel it. I'm in sync with your vagina. We're always in contact," he said.

We were both laughing but his eyes seemed serious.

"Also, don't forget," he said. "I'm an oceanic creature. I'm always with the moon. I can tell these things."

"Well, I guess we won't be able to fool around for a while," I said.

"Oh, I don't care. I'd be happy to be covered in your blood."

"You would?"

"Yeah, I want your blood all over me. I want your blood on my face and in my hair."

"You're crazy," I said.

"No, it's true."

And with that he began to kiss me down my body, lying between my legs with his face up my skirt.

I felt scared. Did I smell? Jamie had never gone down on me with my period, and certainly no one before him. I had a tampon in and no blood was on the outside of me, but even still. I was shocked.

But after a minute or so he sighed.

"I can't eat you the way I want to with this rock under me. And I'm certainly not going to be able to fuck you here. It's cutting me up," he said.

I could see that some of the scales near his sash looked irritated and misshapen, like a fish that had been packed at the bottom of a full grocery bag.

"What should we do?" I asked. "Do you want to get back in the water?"

"No," he said. "I don't know. I guess you'd better get the wagon."

"Oh my God, really?" I squealed.

"Yes," he said. "But keep that creature in there under full lockup. And throw away the key."

"Of course," I said. "I'll be right back!"

I went skipping away. Or maybe I was running. My joy of having him again, being near him, was unabashed. You could not separate me from it. I was the happiness and the happiness was me. The nothingness was nowhere near. It couldn't touch me. I felt no need to be or do anything other than the way I felt. And if I did, it wouldn't have been possible anyway.

I tripped on a dune and skinned my knee running across the

beach. I cut it on a shard of shell. That made me pause for a moment. Was it a sign that being with Theo was deeply misguided? My knee hurt and there was sand in the cut. But all I wanted was for him to take care of my knee. I wanted to show it to him and be babied.

When I got back to the house I didn't wash or bandage the cut. I wanted him to see what happened—to know that I hurt myself and needed to be taken care of. Even though he was entering my world, it wasn't all easy for me. I was making sacrifices and taking risks too. He wasn't the only one for whom this was difficult. I've always felt that injuries are a bit romantic, in the sense that you're forced to be vulnerable and have someone else take care of you. I wanted to stay vulnerable.

I wondered if he would suck the blood out of the wound like a vampire, the same way he wanted to lick my menstrual blood. Of course, he wasn't a vampire, he was some other kind of mythic creature, but it didn't matter. Even if he had legs, no tail, and was a real vampire, I wouldn't care. I would put my knee to his mouth and say, "Drink, please. I hope you enjoy it." I wanted him to help heal and soothe me, even if it meant consuming me away. I realized I was tired. I couldn't be more tired.

Dominic was already whimpering. I guess he could smell Theo on me.

"It's time to take a nap now," I said, and got the tranquilizers from the cupboard. I didn't know how I would explain to my sister where all of the tranquilizers had gone. Maybe she wouldn't notice or maybe she would think that I had taken them. Perhaps I could score some more tranquilizers to give to him, or go to the vet and get more. Maybe a different vet so that no one would know what was happening. I gave him the tranquilizers in a pill pocket and put his head on my lap.

"Nothing is beautiful and everything is nothing," I said to him. "Everything is nothing and everything is beautiful." I had no idea what I was talking about but I felt hypnotized with joy and potentiality.

When his sighs deepened, I closed the pantry door and tip-toed away. Walking back across the beach with the wagon, I was limping.

This is how we get injured for love, I thought. *This is how love can hurt us.*

I felt great and noble, like a woman coming to claim her man in battle, or perhaps a man who was coming to rescue his woman. I had to be the rescuer, because he was more handi-capped than I was. His legs were in worse shape than mine. At least mine could move on earth. Why was I even comparing the two of us? Was this a competition, a competition for pain? Besides, when he was licking me he was entirely my rescuer. He was strong in his softness. We could take turns.

Then I saw him under the moon and it was like the first time I had seen him. He was just meant to be mine. In my mind I heard more words, and they said, *No one knows what they are doing on Earth or even off it.* The gods didn't even know what the gods were doing, assuming there were even gods. Did the void know what it was doing? Did it know itself? Maybe the void didn't even know what to do with itself and didn't even like itself. Maybe the nothingness knew only to fill itself with people, and in that way was a creator of sorts. Maybe the noth-ingness was a god, but not intentionally cruel—not confident in itself. Maybe it was not evil or saying ha-ha to me, just lonely, hating itself, wanting something else to stick inside itself to re-lieve itself of itself. It seemed as though Theo didn't know what he was doing. I obviously didn't either. In that way maybe we were like gods.

"I fell," I said. "I cut myself."

"I know," he said. "I saw. I tried to climb up onto the rock and then drag myself to help you. I wanted to call your name but a jeep came onto the beach and I had to drag myself back into the water."

That he wanted to protect me felt good. I didn't want to be the weak woman, but really it had nothing to do with femininity or masculinity anyway. Simply as a human being, I liked that someone else was worried about me—someone as beautiful as him. There had already been plenty of people worried about me, more than enough, and I didn't like that. But having Theo worry about me felt sexy.

"Let me help you onto the wagon," I said.

"No, I can do it. You're hurt," he said.

He dexterously slid off the rock right onto the wagon that was underneath it.

"Here, just help me adjust the blanket," he said.

His arms were so strong and thick, like marble, only supple. I couldn't help but think, This is mythic . . . what you are seeing is mythic. You injured yourself for him, an injury for love, and he is injured too. But his tail was only a handicap on earth. On land he was half a person, but in the sea he was complete. On earth I felt like half a person too. But I didn't know if there was anywhere I was whole. On earth he was like the god Hephaestus, the clubfooted, cuckolded blacksmith. He needed me. But underwater he was as powerful and graceful as Poseidon, only younger and gorgeous. Maybe he was the son of Poseidon, the wayward son. Maybe he was Aphrodite herself.

"Let's go," he said. "Let's get you back to the house. Then I can kiss all your wounds."

41.

Dominic was sprawled flat on the floor of the pantry like a pancake and didn't stir. I wanted to take Theo upstairs to the bed, but didn't know how. So I moved the wagon over to the sofa and let him haul himself up again.

"I want all of your blood," he said.

I wasn't sure if he meant from my pussy or from the wound, but I sat on top of him on the sofa and kissed his mouth. He flipped me over, kissed me down my body, then gently kissed around my scraped knee.

"I'm so sorry," he said.

"It's okay," I said.

He went up and down my leg until he was licking the crevice between my pussy and my thigh, then peeling my underpants off and licking my pussy. He flicked his tongue on my pussy, in the front, on my clit. Then he put his finger inside of me. It felt like two fingers were there because of my tampon.

"Can I take this out?" he asked.

I nodded and he pulled out my tampon and put it on the glass coffee table. The colors were both red and brown with a clump of purple blood on the side. I felt embarrassed. But he just kissed me and slipped two fingers in my pussy. Then he kissed down my belly back to my clit. Looking into his eyes, I thought, I will never forget this. He licked my blood off his fingers. He loves me, I thought. He completely and totally loves me.

Soon there was blood on his face. I closed my eyes and rode his face. I came very quickly, for me. He had my blood dried and smeared across his cheek. I put my fingers in my pussy and smeared blood under his eyes like No Glare. It was funny to be dressing him up in my blood. Here he was, a man with a tail, and I was making him look even more bizarre. I was used to the tail by now. To me he was just a man or a boy or a boy-man, and I wanted to paint him with so many of my fluids: sweat, spit, blood. I wanted to brand or mark him.

I imagined that in the ocean, blood would never stay in the entrance of a pussy. When I took baths with my period, or went swimming, my blood always stopped. We learned this in junior high school at swim practice: that your blood stops in water. Perhaps it just slowly dissolves, or maybe it stays up in the uterus. Maybe it trickles out so faintly that time slows down and that's why you never see any trail of pink in the bathwater.

Did mermaids menstruate? Perhaps this was part of Theo's attraction to me, my feet in the dirt and the blood in my pussy. My feet on the desert sand, dirty feet, dirty legs, bloody legs, blood dripping down my legs and onto all the earth. Both of us dry on our chests, but me wet in the pussy like a red hearth: the only wetness for days, no other water. Did mermaids even get wet in their cunts? Was it hard fucking them in the water, as beautiful as they were? I remembered trying to fuck in a pool years ago at a motel in Phoenix. It wasn't easy. You got dried up from the water and couldn't slide around right. So what would happen in the ocean? What did they use for lubrication?

I gasped when I saw his cock. It was harder than I'd ever seen it, thick and pink, aiming straight at me like a meaty arrow. I gasped again when I saw the pool of blood on my sister's white sofa. I was not so blinded by passion that I didn't care if I had ruined it. I couldn't destroy Annika's house just because my new boyfriend was a merman with a penchant for period sex.

But Theo saw the stain as a memento and looked proud: as though we should both autograph it. Saltwater stained boats, but in a beautiful way—weathering them, rendering the wood a soft, gray color. So too was our stain to him an act of nature. Perhaps he saw it as a triumph, even, a miracle marking our existence together on land, rather than any cause for alarm. And so I pretended to own my bodily secretions, as though I was proud of what we had made, instead of feeling inwardly ashamed. I pretended to celebrate by kissing him. With his tongue in my mouth and little bits of dried blood flaking off of his cheek, he put his dick in me. I couldn't believe how strong it was.

"Fuck me," I said. "Fuck me with your Triton spear."

We both laughed. We were looking in each other's eyes and he was rubbing my organs from the inside. My flow was very heavy and he was sliding in and out, pumping inside me. I had never come from sex before, but maybe I would this time. Maybe I would.

"Oh my God, I'm either going to come or piss," I laughed. "I'm either going to come or piss, I don't know which one."

"So come and piss," he said. "Come and piss!"

But I couldn't. I just couldn't let go, or maybe I wasn't about to come—only piss. Whatever it was, I couldn't reach it. But it felt so good to fuck him and I felt so connected to him and to all of the lovers throughout time. Missionary was so classical: simple, romantic, and ancient.

I can't believe his dick is inside me, I kept thinking, that it is his dick inside me, that it's your dick inside me. A beautiful look came across his face: flushed cheeks, glazed eyes, lips wet and full. He looked intoxicated, and I felt so proud to be the one intoxicating him. Or was it simply being in a pussy, a wet pussy— not dry-wet from seawater, but wet with secretions—that made him look so drunk? Could it be anyone's pussy? I wanted to believe it was me and that he felt about my pussy like I felt about his cock: amazed, because of who it belonged to. It was me alone: my body and my spirit that made this beautiful creature look so high. In that way I felt that I was beautiful now too.

And then his expression changed again. Now he looked more pained, or perhaps engulfed in a pleasure that overwhelmed him. He was moaning "ungh, ungh" into my mouth, but not like the guys in porn saying stupid, phony lines like "Fuck me, bitch." This was pure sound. It was as though his mouth emitted pure nature. His mouth was like a shell that you could put to your ear. Or maybe we were nature together? Were we shells or were we animals? Or one shell and one animal? No, we were two fish swimming in circles around each other, playful and spared of memory, unaware that we had ever been born and that we would ever die. We were connected now not only with all of human history—all the human lovers of the past—but with animal history as well. I'd been having sex for years. I'd had it hundreds, maybe even thousands, of times, but now it was like I finally understood what sex was. There were only so many things in our lives that connected us to all of our ancestors, to all of humanity and to the animals. Poetry was one thing that bridged generations. But this was the big thing. This encompassed every species. Otherwise what was there? There was birth and death. There was eating food, drinking fluid, pissing and taking shits. There was this.

And what of love? I felt certain that this could be nothing but love, and if this was only lust or infatuation or a simulation of love—well, then give me lust or infatuation. This was how I wanted love to feel. This was the love I wanted. I didn't want the other kind of love, whatever that love was. I didn't want the "conscious" kind. Had anyone ever tried to strip Cupid of his quiver? Had anyone tried to send the Sirens to group therapy or Sappho to the UCLA psych ward? Homer gave the Sirens a bad reputation. Falling in love with a Siren meant certain death, but perhaps this was the greatest love: to die in feeling. This was the greatest annihilation—the highest purpose—and the Sirens themselves were not evil. They were simply giving human beings the greatest gift they could possibly give them, to die intoxicated by love and lust. What better way to die?

"I love you," I said into his mouth and did not regret saying it.

"I love you," he said back into mine.

"I love you I love you I love you I love you," we said.

In between our moans he looked at me with our noses almost

touching, his dick going in and out of my pussy, and he said, "I'm going to let go, I'm going to let go."

It was such a funny way to say it. Maybe this was how they said it underneath the ocean. It was a testament to his different-ness, the sense of an old soul I got from him in spite of the way he looked, and it made me love him more. As he began to come, his voice moved up an octave: a full scale that went through my whole body making me feel as though I was Sappho's lyre. I gyrated against him too, making him come, helping him to let go. I was a vessel. I was gladly a vessel who was helping him so that he could abandon his own vessel: discard the wants of liv-ing in a body, the pain, the hard husk of it. He could discard his scales, which I still didn't fully understand, and also his arms, which I knew well by now. I didn't know what it felt like to be a man or what it felt like to have a tail, but I certainly understood the prison of the body. I knew, too, the desperation of not know-ing exactly why we are here. I was proud to be a conduit for his escape.

When he came he looked like he might cry. I felt him gush inside me and in that moment experienced the most maternal surge I have ever felt toward another human being. I felt both lusty and maternal. Then he lay there after with his bloody cheek pressed against my breasts, shaking. My breasts, which never were ample enough, suddenly seemed all I could need. Now I felt I understood that the heart was not the breast it-self—it was the current underneath. You did not nurse from the breast itself, but from a place beyond it. The breast was only the bridge. Grown men needed nursing too. Perhaps he needed nursing most of all. So I nursed him and tried to sustain that gift I had given, which was to disappear in the nothingness and thus no longer have to be aware of it.

42.

Every other day at dawn it started again: me pulling up to the rock with my wagon, Theo dragging himself up and in, the return to my sister's house, where he assumed I would continue to live long after the summer. He didn't ask when my sister would be coming back and I stopped worrying if I would see him again. We now had just enough permanence for me to have faith—a sense of knowing that he would be there. Yet there was still a feeling of wonder and mystery brought on by the gaps in between visits and my knowledge that in a month I could be gone. It was the perfect balance of love and longing, or lust and longing, or lust and love: what I had always sought.

I felt more at ease, because I knew that it could be me who would create the ending if I wanted. I would be the one returning to the desert if I chose. I would never be left. Only leaving. I already contained the answer. When I thought of the thing itself—the actual end—I felt a sense of impending dread. I didn't want to go. But I made no plans to stay either. I lived in what was there—keeping the date of my supposed departure in a corner of my mind, like a little magic peach pit. It radiated just enough control as to the way our future could unfold that I no longer feared rejection or his retreat.

On the days when I would be seeing Theo in the evening, I worked on my book. Its whole contention had changed. I no longer wrote about the blank spaces in any theoretical way or tried to convince anyone that the only way to understand Sappho was to perceive the spaces as though they were always there. I no longer argued with past scholars about their biographical projections on the texts. I wrote, instead, about Eros in the text it-self and its relationship to the spaces. The verb *eratai* less closely meant "to love" than it did "to desire." Yet despite the best attempts of history, time, weather, and churchmen, the desire in Sappho's poems had survived as though it were love eternal. Perhaps desire was not so ephemeral after all. Was a feeling the only eternal thing, despite the fact that everyone said it would pass? Could you get away with academic discourse about a feeling? I was going to try. I informed the advisory committee by email of my changes. They asked me to send an outline of the project and a sample. I bullshitted an outline and sent it over to them. At the same time, it wasn't bullshit at all, because I was already living it. The book was me.

On the in-between days, after returning Theo to the ocean, I mostly hid from feeling. I stayed deep under the covers and slept. I tried to ignore the rest of the world. I was like a hungover person, biding time until she could have more alcohol. The hair of the dog alone would fix me. I was a drunk waiting only for her next drink.

I felt I loved him, yet I kept my secret from him. To contain the answer as to how this would all end—to withhold that knowledge, as well as the lie that I would continue to live here alone—felt strange. I was so close to him, it was odd that I could keep a secret that might upset him. It was as though we were one person who was able to completely compartmentalize different elements of themselves in different parts of their mind, and the two parts never intersected. They were not allowed to meet. When living in the illusion of our eternality (which was perhaps not an illusion if the feeling rather than the facts were to be believed), I prevented the truth from entering. Actually, it was as though the truth didn't even knock. But when I was alone, I would wake in a panic from my daytime naps and there it would be: my impending departure.

43.

One afternoon I received a call from Rochelle. I could tell right away that she had been sent by Jamie as a spy to suss me out and see where I was in my feelings for him. She played nice-nice with me, as though we were still seated across the table from each other at the Colombian restaurant—as though I had not seen the scared look in her eye, despite her feminist branding, when I went from safely-coupled-off confidante of inane relationship stories to single-and-psycho nosebreaker. While I knew Rochelle was not to be trusted, I enjoyed her sniffing around me again: that I was once again desirable enough to her to be allowed back into her fold of banality. It wasn't that I liked this fold more than I liked being in Claire's inner sanctum of sexual camaraderie or the group's nest of pathos. I found her truly intolerable now, and vowed that when I returned to Phoenix she would never again be rewarded with my presence at another dinner. Let her pontificate to someone else about her husband's farts. But it felt good to know that I was welcomed back into her fold if I wanted, that I was approved, as though I had once been sane, then gotten sick, then gotten well again.

The truth, of course, was that I had done nothing to indicate to her I was in any different place than I was when I left town. It was all on Jamie's end, this mirage of "health"—his renewed desire for me made me safe and appealing to her once again. After she lectured me on the differences between beach culture and a landlocked lifestyle from an anthropological perspective, she lowered her voice.

"Do you want to know what?" she asked conspiratorially.

"What?"

"Jamie has been asking me about you."

"Oh yeah?"

"I keep telling him we haven't spoken, but he keeps asking."

"Well, that's fine, because I talk to him too. He texts me all the time. Sometimes I text back," I said.

"Oh," she said, sounding dejected that she was not the sole liaison. "Well, I just figured I would tell you."

"That's nice," I said.

"You know, I think he really misses you."

"Yes, he tells me that too."

"Oh," she said.

"But if he really missed me he'd break up with the scientist," I said. "Then I'd know he's serious."

But I knew why he hadn't broken up with the scientist. Nobody broke up with anyone unless they had someone else locked down. Even Jamie, who—when we were together—seemingly only wanted to be free, had not initiated the breakup. In fact, that had been my fatal error: breaking up with him before I had anyone to trapeze onto. Of course, all of that had led me here, to Venice and Theo, so perhaps it hadn't been such an error.

"Well, we'll just have to see what happens when you're back in Phoenix," she said knowingly.

"*If* I come back," I said.

"Really? You might stay there?" she asked.

She sounded impressed.

"I don't know, maybe. I just love being so free right now, not beholden to anyone or anything," I said, lying completely.

I was only trying to fool her, as I hadn't really planned out the idea of staying. The truth was, I couldn't fully admit to myself that I wanted to stay. To do this would mean putting an end to the peach pit, blasting it to smithereens. And though it was parked in the far corner of my mind, I needed it. I didn't actively acknowledge that I needed it—this escape or safety valve—but on a primal level I knew. Perhaps this was what living in the moment was about: an active state of denial about the future. I also felt that somehow Theo just "knew" that not only would my sister be returning soon but that I would be leaving. Maybe this was what past men had assumed of me? That I simply knew everything was temporary between us.

I felt as though it would be evident to anyone, even Theo, that Venice was not my natural habitat. As beachy as I looked in my long white dresses, which I wore solely now—never black anymore—there was something about me that didn't belong. I was like a cactus, a storer of water, and not a creature who naturally immersed in the water. I didn't take things lightly. I hoarded. And our differences were evident each morning when his tail would begin to go dry and crack, and we would rush him back to the ocean. I couldn't hoard him. He did not ask to hoard me. And so I assumed that he never asked if my sister would be returning, or when I planned to leave, because on some level he already knew.

But he didn't know. And sometimes when we were fucking, despite the relegation of the peach pit to a far corner of my mind, I would begin to cry. There would be the eternality and then a sudden break in the eternality that brought tears. Before the doughnuts, I didn't even know I wanted to die. Now, I attributed my crying to joy. I hadn't known that I'd wanted joy either. I had not ever known that I could have it. Now I was crying because it felt like a miracle—not only that I would want to live at all but that I actually could.

The time I cried the most was the day at dawn when he fucked me in the ass. The ass fucking did not hurt, or not in a way that made me wince. I did not cry from pain. This ass fucking was the tenderest fuck I could ever have imagined. Earlier on, when we were whispering to each other on the rocks, he had said, "I want to make you feel things you've never imagined and explore places you didn't think could be explored."

"Oh yeah?" I had asked.

"Yes," he had said. "Like deep inside your asshole."

I'd laughed.

But this was romantic. It felt like a loss of virginity in some way, and completely opposite what had happened in the hotel bathroom with Garrett. For one thing I was lying on my back, not doggy-style. Also, Theo licked my asshole a lot first. I was scared, of course, that it wouldn't taste very good: as much as I washed before I saw him. I was afraid but he softly licked and sucked it, making me come with his finger gently rubbing my clit. I kept coming on his fingers, when he also put one in my asshole and kissed me from my belly to my neck to my face. Then he kissed my mouth and forehead. His cock was so hard it pushed all the way out of his foreskin, already glistening, straining for me. I grabbed him and it was warm and pulsing.

"Are you ready?" he asked, and I nodded.

He nudged my cheeks apart and opened my asshole slowly. First he put the tip of his dick inside me while continuing to rub my clit gently with the hand he hadn't used to stroke my cheeks and crack. Maybe he knew about urinary tract infections? Could mermaids get them too? I loved his dick moving slowly in and out of my ass, a new intimacy. I never imagined that anal sex could be loving. I never thought of it as an intimate act, one of trust, only a pornographic and brutal one. So I cried a lot, but not because it hurt.

44

I didn't mention Dominic to Theo again. It was taking more and more pills per day to keep the dog relaxed and asleep, and I went to three different vets to get more prescriptions. In an odd way I had become a drug addict of sorts, like Claire after all— going from doctor to doctor to get the pills. Only I wasn't getting high on the medication itself, but on the time and intimacy with Theo that it afforded me.

"We travel a lot," I heard myself say to the veterinarian. "I'm going to be touring through Europe and I can't bear to leave him home with a sitter. He's my child, basically. So I'll need some for the plane ride and each of the train rides from city to city."

"How many cities?" she asked.

"Ten?" I said.

She raised an eyebrow.

I had heard of addicts going from doctor to doctor to get pills as their tolerance for the drugs deepened. Anything involving addiction always escalated, never the other way around. I felt this to be true within myself, and that when and if I returned to Phoenix I would need a thousand lovers to ever take the place of how good it felt to be with Theo.

One night, when we were lying on the sofa tangled up together, after a day of lovemaking, I asked him how many other women who lived on land he had been with.

"There have been a few," he said.

He told me about a woman named Alexis with long black hair who was a heroin addict. He had licked her menstrual blood too, the first he ever tasted, and watched her shoot dope. She would come to the rocky shore in Monterey every night, when he lived farther north, already slurring her words. He never knew whether she believed he was real, or a side effect of the drugs. But he stayed with her as she sat by the ocean and nodded in and out. Then she stopped coming to the ocean entirely. He feared she had died, until one night, he heard her singing in an old wooden boathouse some feet from the shore. He dragged himself into the boathouse and stayed with her that night. In the boathouse were a few old blankets on the ground and a suitcase full of clothes. He realized then that she was homeless. He wished he could walk on land and bring her food. He would bring her fish, but their raw, dead bodies only nauseated her and he didn't know how to build a fire to cook them. So he gave her licks of seawater and bites of seaweed.

"I began to understand," he said. "The humans and I were not all that different. I didn't know that people on land were filled with so much yearning. I thought you all had it figured out, were satisfied."

"Hardly," I said.

"It was a beautiful realization," he said.

"So what happened?"

"One day she just disappeared."

"Did she die?"

"I don't know what happened to her," he said. "All of her things remained in the boathouse. But she never came back."

I could not take hearing all of that. I didn't like that it was she who had left him, even for death, and that he would always long for her. And perhaps as punishment or to regain control of the narrative—that I might be like her and have a moment like that, the beloved vanisher—I confessed.

"I suppose it won't matter with me," I said. "Now that you've been through it in such a sad way."

"What do you mean?"

"I mean, I guess you will be okay when I leave here."

"What do you mean 'leave'?"

"I'll be going away soon."

"For how long?"

"Well, for good."

I told him everything: that I was from a place where there was no ocean and would be leaving in three weeks to return there, permanently. I asked him if he knew what the desert was. He only stared at me. Immediately I knew that I had hurt him.

"Do you think—" I started to say.

I was going to backtrack, to ask him what could be possible. Could I take him with me? Could he ever exist in a desert? But he put his hands over his face and began moaning.

"Theo," I said.

He wouldn't answer me and seemed to be in a trance. It was like he'd become a Siren. As Homer said, the Sirens had gorgeous, melodic voices, but they could also howl with pain and agony. It was not pain as I had romanticized it: him beautifully bereft with aching for me. It was not the Sirens as we humans imagined them, armed with divine power. This was vulnerability, a bit of madness even, and what it revealed was that he truly loved me, and that love could be grotesque.

Dominic woke up in the other room and began barking along with Theo's moaning.

"Please calm down," I said. "I'm sorry."

I told him that maybe I could work something out. Maybe I could stay after all. I hadn't known how much he cared. But he said it was too late.

"You lied to me," he said. "I was going to keep coming to see you on land. I had even wanted to ask you to come join me under the water, seriously. And here you have been set to abandon me all along."

I didn't know exactly what "under the water" meant. Was he more delusional than I was? Did he know I couldn't live under there?

"Theo, no, it isn't like that. I really am in love with you. I want to stay with you forever."

207

"That you would think of leaving me," he said. "That you would let me grow so close to you and never tell me it was finite. It breaks my heart. It's humiliating too."

"I was afraid that if I told you there was an end date you would see me differently. I liked the way you saw me. I didn't want anything to change. And then it was too late, you knew me the way you knew me. I thought of finding a way to stay in Venice, but I was scared that you would reject me," I said.

"Can you help load me back in the wagon?" he said. "I need to go back to the ocean."

"Wait, can't you just stay and we will talk it through?"

"Just help me. Take me back, please. I'm asking you, help me back to the water."

"I didn't know you felt that way," I said.

"Didn't know what? That I loved you? When you said 'eternal love' I thought you meant that you wouldn't leave me ever."

"So then I won't. I won't. If you don't want me to, I won't. I don't want to either! When I said eternal love—when we talked about it—I didn't know you meant in body. I didn't know you would want me to stay here in body. I thought that it could mean in spirit or that it might be a game you were playing. I always thought that at some point you would swim away and I would never see you again."

"Why would you think that?" he asked. "When did I ever give you that impression? Did I do anything but care about you?"

Explicitly this was true. But under my lens, my paranoiac, insecure vision, my endless anticipation of abandonment, even the slightest lack of attentiveness was interpreted as a fatal lapse in desire. I couldn't tell him that I'd been looking for any sign that he was over me, or would never love me as much as he would love someone else. I couldn't say that the fact that he had loved anyone before me meant I needed to keep an out. I couldn't tell him that I wasn't sure if I was truly capable of love.

"You don't believe in love," he said, as though reading my mind.

"I do," I said. "I believe in love more than anything. But I think I am very bad at it."

It dawned on me then that he was more like me than I thought, his fear of abandonment so intense. Maybe we were identical, and because we were identical I had gotten to be someone else, without even really knowing it. I thought of my moon in Gemini, the twins, with their dual nature. I contained both man and woman. But Theo and I, we were two of the same. I thought of Pisces, the two fish, bound together by one string—one star—Alpha Piscium. In attempting to escape the monster Typhon, Aphrodite and her son Eros turned into fish and swam away. But who was Aphrodite and who was the monster here? I had threatened to swim away so I wouldn't be the abandoned one. Now he was trying to punish me by leaving first.

You never think, in your fantasies, that the object of the fantasy can be hurt. I had known that he was sensitive. But I hadn't trusted that it was real, or at least, that it was as real as my own sensitivity. I didn't believe that he could actually feel betrayed. Was it because he was a man and I was a woman? I thought that only I could feel that kind of shame, need, and rejection. I thought that only a woman could feel that. It all seemed crazy now. I was crazy when I was the one begging for someone to stay and I was crazy when I was the one leaving.

"I feel ashamed," he said. "I want to go. Would you help me go?"

I just stood there.

"Never mind," he said. "I'll do it myself."

He pulled himself off the sofa and began to drag himself across the rug, naked, nothing covering his genitals or ass. I just stood there watching, shocked. I didn't try to help him, but I didn't stop him either. I wasn't crying. I didn't feel sad. I was just stunned that my fantasy of him had been so wrong—that he could live and feel so far beyond it. At first he had been just a hot young surfer boy who could only hurt me—never someone whom I could actually hurt.

I watched him crawl to the door and flop up and down until he got some momentum. Then he reached the handle, turned it, and dragged himself outside, naked, into the night. He looked like a dying fish. It was only then that I began to cry.

"Wait!" I said, and ran to him. "Stop, let me help you at least!"

"You've done enough," he said.

I followed him out, down the cement pass to the boardwalk, where he was scraping his tail as he dragged himself. He was moving slowly. But he was moving, getting there. I felt so nervous I didn't know what to do. Suddenly I felt like laughing, but not at him. Maybe I felt like laughing because the whole thing was so bizarre. Just when I thought that things couldn't get any weirder than waking up covered in doughnuts in Phoenix, here I was in Venice with a half-man half-fish I had somehow fallen in love with, who was dragging himself away from me. Or maybe I felt like laughing because I was scared.

I walked with him across the boardwalk slowly and onto the sand. In the dark, in some ways, he looked just like one of the other junkies, if one of them were wearing a strange fish costume. Or he was a veteran amputee who, having fallen out of his chair, was trying to drag himself back: what remained of his legs wrapped in a sparkly, scaly bag.

"Goodbye," he said.

I began to sob. I ran back into the house, where Dominic was now barking crazily.

"I'm sorry," I cried to the dog. "I'm so sorry for everything. Here, come here."

I put my arms around his neck and cried into his fur. Then I ran up the stairs and Dominic, still loyal in spite of everything, followed me up. From upstairs I could see that Theo had made it only halfway to the ocean. I called to him, but he didn't turn around. When he finally got to the tide, he didn't climb up onto the rocks, but simply dragged himself into the sea, never once pausing or looking back. Pulling himself across the sand he looked so helpless and pathetic, but as he crawled into the ocean and disappeared, he suddenly seemed so in control of himself. I thought, He is the laws of nature, though I didn't know what that meant.

I ran back down the stairs and over the sand to the water's edge—Dominic racing behind me. I sat down in the sand and waited. I waited there all night with no blanket, just me in my sundress. I huddled against the dog to keep warm. Once in a while I would call out Theo's name, but he never came back.

45.

By morning I was very sick: in the spirit, the mind, and the body. I couldn't stay in Venice any longer. Clearly something had gone very wrong, and I was getting worse. Group therapy had only led me to a merman with severe abandonment issues. Fuck this whole situation. I had come here to get away from Jamie, in the hope that the distance would help me recover. Now he was pursuing me and I didn't even want him anymore. Didn't that mean my mission was accomplished? Hadn't I won? It was time to return to Phoenix and claim my prize. I decided to call and tell him the good news.

"It's me," I said.

"I know." He laughed.

"How are you?"

"I'm okay. I haven't heard from you. I've been worried."

"I'm sorry. I needed some time to do some thinking."

"Oh yes?"

"Yes."

"And what are your thoughts?"

"Well, I was wondering first if you are still with—Megan. Or has that already burned out?"

"Well, there's been some complications with that situation, actually."

I knew he would fall out of love fast, but this had ended quicker than I thought.

"Oh really?" I said.

This was going to be good.

"Yes, I've been wanting to talk to you about this. But I didn't want to text it to you. And when I wasn't hearing back I figured I would talk to you in person when you returned."

This was it. He wanted me back. He was leaving Megan for me, he just needed to be sure I still wanted to be with him too before he ended things. Men are cowardly. But I could understand that and had sympathy for him. Five minutes before, I had been lovesick over Theo. The heart contains multitudes. We all need someone in our lives, because ultimately, humans are weak.

"Actually, I'm thinking of coming home early," I said.

"Oh yeah?"

Now he sounded nervous.

"What do you think about that?"

"Listen, Lucy, I don't know how to say this. I—I hope you aren't thinking of coming home early for me."

Oh no.

"No, not for you," I stammered.

"Okay, good. Because, uh, things have changed a little with Megan and me."

"How so?" I snapped.

"Well, it appears—it appears she is pregnant. And she's going to keep the baby. So we're going to be parents together. She's going to move in with me, at least for a while."

I was silent.

"Lucy?"

I couldn't say anything. All those years I had tried to get us to cohabitate, and all it took for this blond scientist bitch was some little womb booger and there he was, boom, ready to commit. I didn't want to show him I was angry. I didn't want to curse him out, give him that satisfaction of knowing he had won. Where I thought I had all the power in my pocket it now belonged to a fetus. But I couldn't say anything. No words would form. I was totally alone.

"Hello, Lucy, are you there?"

I was in a fetal position on the floor with stomach cramps. I didn't say a word, just let him yammer a few more times until he hung up. What was I thinking? Jamie would have only been a bandage. It was Theo I really needed. But now he was gone forever. I was withdrawing fast. I didn't know what to do or where to go. The hospital wouldn't be right. What could they give me that could fix this? It wasn't a real drug I was coming off of. It was way worse.

46.

Somehow, I found my way to group. Dr. Jude took one look at my unwashed hair, my skirt covered in sand, face drawn and skinny, and nodded knowingly as if to say, *This is where the addiction takes you.*

Yes, this was where you ended up: disheveled, lovesick, alone. Wherever you thought you would end up, wherever you thought the worst could be, was nothing like where you actually ended up. There was a reason they all kept coming back to group. Somewhere, in the backs of their minds, they must have remembered what the pain was like. They didn't want it anymore.

But Sara was still seeing Stan and she seemed like she was doing okay. She chirped about how she was integrating her Stan life into her self-care life.

"This time, I'm still doing me," she said. "I'm still self-dating. But it's also nice to always have a partner now at salsa dancing. He does warm-ups with me before improv class too. True, I have to pay for everything. And technically he has nowhere else to go. But he's here for me now. The way I see it, if he didn't want to be with me he could still be sleeping at the Korean spa. Those floor mats are not so uncomfortable. He does have a choice. He's not forced to live with me. He's choosing me."

Sara said she wanted to stay in group and also stay with Stan. Dr. Jude said she didn't recommend it, but she wasn't going to kick her out.

"You'll see," said Sara. "I'm really flourishing. I'm even thinking of getting into spoken word."

I wondered if Sara was totally kidding herself or if she

was proof that the seemingly impossible could be done after all: the mending of an old, unhealthy relationship into a new, healthy one that didn't destroy you. Should I have been more responsive to Jamie when he had first started texting? Why had I ignored him to chase a relationship that was only sustainable when confined to a rock? Clearly I had made some kind of wrong decision or I wouldn't be back here, head in hands, seated next to Dr. Jude's framed poster of Jungian archetypes. What was worse, still, was that the others all seemed to have gotten better without me. Even Diana had been totally clean, off the tennis boys for over a week, and was paying more attention to her children.

"Regardless of how I feel about my husband, whether I lust after him anymore or not, my children are what I really live for. I'm doing this for them. So that I can be present. It wasn't fair to be sitting at the kitchen table with them while they ate pizza, running off every five minutes to check my phone in the living room to see if a twenty-three-year-old had texted me. I wasn't able to be there for them. And they could sense it."

"How do you feel?" asked Dr. Jude.

"A little sad," she said. "But so much better. I'm not as on edge as I was. My worth isn't dictated by text messages."

Brianne, too, had found some solace in her son.

"When I told my son about the OkCupid guy, he said, 'Mom, that just sounds like a lot of drama. Do you really need that?' And I thought, You're right. Drama. It really is that simple. So I set some healthy boundaries. I told the guy that I would still love to see him when he got back to the States but that I wasn't going to give him any money. I said that I wished him the best of luck and I believe in him: that he would be able to make it work to find his way back here."

"Awesome," said Sara, biting into a Bosc pear.

"But the strangest thing was, the very next day, my son and his girlfriend broke up. He said that he was sad, but he knew it was for the best, because now he could see there was drama in that relationship too. Then he said, and I'll never forget this, 'Mom, I'm so glad that we can have a nice relationship. It means so much to me that I can tell you these things.'"

What a pussy, I thought.

But was he a pussy? He probably knew more than all of us. Maybe children weren't the worst thing after all. They couldn't be any worse than anything else. I had always judged these women who derived such satisfaction from their offspring. I thought they were weak and nauseating, like they had given up on their own lives. But I liked Diana. And Brianne, well, at least she had something to live for besides plastic surgery. Something to tether her to the Earth. Maybe she wasn't totally lying when she said she had a full life. Or, at least, that her life felt full. Who was I to judge anyone? I certainly didn't know any more than they did, crawling in here on my hands and knees.

I told them about Jamie and the pregnancy. I pretended that was the cause of my tears. It was something legible, a rejection they could understand. To recount the tale of Theo would be too far beyond their comprehension. What could I even say? I'm mourning a man I've been seeing secretly this whole time. He might be in his forties but he looks twenty-one. No, I didn't meet him online, I met him in the ocean. By the way, he has a tail.

It was hard to grieve like this, to mourn one man while pretending to be mourning another. Why were some sadnesses so much more permissible than others? Why did it seem like everyone was going to be okay except for me? Even Chickenhorse was in good spirits, letting the group know that she had finally decided to try going on a date. She met a guy at the dog park and he invited her to a pit-bull rescue benefit.

"I assume he's an asshole," she said. "But I don't think he's married. So I'm going."

When group ended I stayed back a minute to talk to Dr. Jude.

"Lucy," she said, blowing the dust off a book called *Low Self-*

Esteem and Addiction: The Siamese Twins. "It's good to see you back. I'm sorry you are suffering."

"Thanks," I said, wiping my nose. She offered me a tissue.

"Can I ask you a question?" I said.

"Sure."

"When you said that you were content without anyone—that a person could be content without anyone—did you mean it?"

"Oh, Lucy," she said.

"Because I just feel like that's a lie. I think everyone is looking for someone. And I think that if they aren't, they're just pretending."

"That isn't necessarily true," she said. "Me, I'm just happy to be alive. Do you really want to know what I think? Well, let me tell you something that you don't know about me. I'm a breast cancer survivor."

"I'm sorry," I said.

"It's okay," she said. "I had stage-three breast cancer when I was only forty-nine. I wasn't sure if I was going to make it. In fact, I didn't think I would. But after a number of very grueling years of chemo and radiation, as well as a double mastectomy, I was declared cancer-free. And I'm still in remission."

"That's great."

"It is," she said. "But after the cancer, going through that horrible experience, I took a good look at my life. I thought about what I wanted the next years of my life to look like, however many I had left. And one thing I realized was that I no longer wanted to be with my husband. It was a very hard thing to come to terms with. I have no children. My family lives on the East Coast. He was my family and had seen me through the whole ordeal. He still loved me very much. But I was no longer in love with him. And I realized then that I would rather be by myself, even if it meant never finding anyone again, even with my body looking the way it did postsurgery, than spend the rest of my life with someone I didn't love."

"How did you know you weren't in love with him anymore?" I asked.

"I just knew," she said. "Over time I realized."

"I get so confused," I said. "There were moments when I felt like I was no longer in love with Jamie at all. But after we broke up I wanted him back more than anything. So maybe it was the lust that had faded."

"Lust is lust," she said. "Any woman can have sex. It's not hard to find a man to sleep with you."

This was true. I'd never thought of it like that before. With Garrett and Adam, and even Theo, I'd felt like it was a sign that I was special when they'd wanted to have sex with me.

"But love is . . ." She paused. "Well, love might be something beyond words. It's funny, in all my years of doing this job, I still don't really have the words for it."

"Right," I said.

"I think the place for you to start, the question that you might want to ask yourself, isn't so much what is love," she said. "But is it really love I'm looking for?"

47.

The same smell of mashed potatoes and dirty scalps greeted me at the psych ward as I checked in to visit Claire. This time, though, I felt no stronger than the patients there. I guess this was how it came to that. This was how a person became crazy. I knew I was very close. I had known for quite some time, despite not wanting to know. Theo's sparkle had blotted it out. It eclipsed what, deep down, I already knew. I thought about what Dr. Jude had said. She sounded good. Her words were philosophical, wise, poetic even. But words didn't make me miss Theo any less.

Claire looked incredibly stoned. I had seen the med cups lined up near the front of the hall and the nurse dividing up all different kinds of pills. I assumed Claire was on quite the cocktail. The whole thing reminded me of a documentary I once saw on a methadone clinic. It seemed like they were just doing harm reduction, switching her from one dependency to another. Now, instead of dicks and whatever unprescribed pills she'd been taking, they were giving her an even stronger dose of prescribed shit. Meds for dicks. It seemed like a decent trade. And it seemed like it was working, at least as long as she could stay high.

She was strangely at peace with her surroundings, like a hypnotized yogi. Maybe she was too stoned to feel the vile aura of where she was. I guess the drugs transformed the stench into something more palatable, the way they did to one's own emotions.

I was glad to see that she still recognized me through her haze.

"You!" she called when she saw me.

"Hi, baby," I said. "How are you?"

She said she was doing well—so well, in fact, that she might not even have to go to treatment. But she wanted to go and had decided to go, regardless.

"Do you want to know what's strange?" she asked. "I find my-self enjoying the group therapy here, just listening to people. They have all sorts of fucked-up problems, far beyond mine—far beyond everyone from the women's group. It's like if Sara the foot-toucher were on acid all the time. It makes me grate-ful for my own problems. I would love to bring the two groups together into one big circle of healing. This way, when Brianne is complaining about Millionaire Match, she can be reminded that at least she doesn't have auditory hallucinations. Maybe I'm destined to lead a group-therapy exchange program."

"Wow, sounds like they really got you, didn't they?" I laughed.

"I don't know if they did or didn't. But do you want to know what's the weirdest? The strangest thing of all? I don't want men anymore. I feel finished."

"Wow."

"They say that you don't hit rock bottom until you hit rock bottom. Lucy, what if this is it?"

"What if it is?"

"All I can tell you is that I feel so bloody free right now!" she said, adjusting her hospital bracelet.

"I'm so glad for you, Claire," I said. Then I began to cry.

"Oh no, what's wrong?"

"Please. You have to help me. I am in so much pain. Theo is gone forever and I don't know what to do," I said.

"The swimmer?" she asked. "What happened?"

"He left," I said. "He just left and I don't think he's ever com-ing back."

"Oh love," she said.

"What do I do?" I asked.

"Ignore him," she said. "Ignore, ignore, ignore. Do not pursue. In your mind, you have to literally give him up."

"If I give him up do you think he will come back?"

"They always come back if you give them up—especially, as we know, if you find other cock. But what if you don't do that? What if you don't replace him with anyone? You don't have to give him up just so that he will come back to you. You could give him up just to give him up."

"Why?"

"Well, for one thing, it might behoove you to sit with yourself for a while."

Who was this talking?

"So that's it? Just give him up and sit?"

"None of these wankers are worth the pain," she said. "You have to dump them on the roadside and let them rot there."

"You don't understand," I said. "He didn't fuck me over. It was me who hurt him. It was me who lied to him, not the other way around. This isn't like the other ones. This time I'm in control. Sort of."

"You asked my advice and I'm giving it to you."

"I can't do that," I said. "I need love. Or if it's not love, then the power of that feeling. I love it. I love love. It's the only thing I have."

"Oh, Lucy," she said. "You have a lot. It's like your tits."

"What?"

"Your tits. You always say that you have no tits. But really, your breasts are ample. They're more than enough."

"I want a D cup. Metaphorically."

"And I want a thousand giant cocks. Or I think I do. But it's a lie. Because even a thousand cocks would never be enough. And it's crazy to think that they would. The fantasy is a lie."

"But I am crazy. And I don't want to live without the fantasy," I said.

"You can do it. We can do it together."

"I don't want to."

"Suit yourself," she said.

"Can I just tell you one more thing?"

"What is it?"

"Jamie got that woman pregnant. They're moving in together."

"No! The scientist?"

"It's true."

"How the hell did that happen?"

"They were fucking."

"No, I mean—oh Lucy, I'm so sorry."

"I know. How can I go back to Phoenix and face them?"

"You can and you shall. Let's just pray it totally destroys her pussy."

"She better get fat as hell."

"Well, now he'll really be pining after you."

"Yeah?"

"Oh yes. Nothing brings out a man's quest for escape like a lactating woman with somebody else doing the sucking."

48

As I left the hospital, I wondered if Claire was right. Was it possible that she had started seeing more clearly than me? The way she looked at me now was the way I had looked at Diana and at her before: lovingly, but full of pity. I decided it was she who was to be pitied. She had given up on the thing that made her most alive, even if it made her the most crazy. I knew the old way still sounded beautiful to her. But in an act of self-preservation, she was walking the path back to safety and sanity now. Even for Claire, the pain had just gotten too great.

Of course, this was today. Who was to say where she would be next week or next month or whenever she got out? For now she had convinced herself, or maybe done more than convinced herself. Maybe she had actually healed a little. But just because you had healed, it didn't mean the men could no longer get you. Love and lust were latent in her, lurking. For now she was free of the insanity. The cocktail of meds had certainly helped. I wondered if what she felt on the cocktail was as good as romantic obsession, better than that sparkle. You had to feel something truly heavenly to get over the chase. The chase was everything, all the hope and possibility of life. Very little else would ever be enough. Love itself would probably never be enough. You had to have the moment of almost touching, almost fucking, the moment right before he enters you for the first time, all the time.

I thought of a story I had read about Solon, an Athenian statesman, who one day heard his nephew singing one of Sappho's poems. He immediately asked the boy to teach it to him so he could have it memorized. When asked why, he simply said, "So that I may learn it and then die."

I was not going to stop hunting for him. I was not even at the place where the addict throws away her drugs only to buy more. I wasn't throwing anything away. Sappho had never given up on love, even when the longing was a dagger in her heart. When she fucked her lover Phaon, perhaps she thought she wouldn't get attached. I'll just fuck this young, hot creature and be done with it, she must have thought. Or maybe she thought she'd fuck him into loving her. But Phaon could not love her back: she was too old, or maybe too needy, and he was newly young and hot, having recently been rubbed with Aphrodite's magic ointment, which transformed an old man into a sexy boy. It would be difficult for any woman, but there was just no way that Sappho, being Sappho, would be able to play it cool or stay detached. And so she got hooked.

I had done all the drugs and now I was at the place where the addict goes to wait for her dealer. Even if she shakes and shakes, she waits. Even if he never returns, she waits. There is nothing else left.

So I returned to the rocks every night and sat by the sea with a blanket around me. As the days passed I became less inflamed with pain, and more just empty. I began to feel purified as though I were a gourd and someone had spooned me out. I felt spiritual, almost holy, like I could look down at myself from the sky. There I was, a woman on the rocks by the ocean, wrapped in a blanket, waiting for the return of her lover. Everything I knew about art would say that I was a painting. I was certainly a poem. Sappho was too—her life, perhaps, unknowable, but her feelings were mine. I was mythic. And though I was convinced that I would never see him again, it was too tragic to contemplate. My body cried. But I didn't let the nothingness eat me whole. Inside me was a small spark of hope that sent me out there every night.

I would bring the wagon, just in case he appeared. I wanted to show him I would labor for him. But I also wondered if maybe it was a jinx—that if I brought the wagon he wouldn't be there, like when you bring an umbrella and it doesn't rain. Still, the wagon was my totem and I had to bring it. It showed my hope to the gods I didn't even think I believed in. It was like an empty chalice waiting to be filled.

Every night, I promised myself that it would be the last night I drugged Dominic. But every night I had to do it, just in case. Should Theo return, I didn't want there to be any impediments when he came swimming up. I would take him home and we would be entwined right away. I would do anything to stay with him. I would never think of leaving him again.

Sometimes I would fall asleep on the rocks. As I drifted off I would imagine that he was watching me from somewhere, seeing if I was putting in my time, testing me. Perhaps it was the gods I didn't think I believed in who were watching me. But this is how it is with the gods and other mythic creatures. You imagine them watching you. You almost feel it. And so I waited for him. Nothing meant anything without him, except the hope of his return.

One night I dreamt that Sappho came over to the rocks and sat with me. She looked like Chickenhorse, only it was Chickenhorse as a hot, butch lesbian: her thick thighs in ripped jeans, hair styled in a pompadour and dyed jet black. Sappho-Chickenhorse told me I was stupid to wait for Theo. She touched my sternum with her palm and said, "Look at yourself, all of this over an asshole fish-boy."

"But you were once the insane queen of unrequited love," I said. "Shouldn't you, of all people, understand?"

"Just be careful you don't drown," she said.

In my dream I closed my eyes. She kissed each of my eyelids. I felt turned on, like I wanted to rub against those thighs of hers in her jeans. When I opened my eyes again in my dream, Sappho had become Claire.

"I'm sorry I can't drown with you," said Claire.

"That's okay," I said.

"I'm really sorry, Lucy."

"Nobody is going to drown!" I said. "Go get your nails and toenails done instead. You can pretend you're going on a date with David."

"Mani-pedi as the antidote to suicide," she said. "It all makes so much sense now. But I just got them done. What do you do instead of kill yourself when your nails are already done?"

"Maybe Le Pain Quotidien?" I said. "You should go get a Danish. But I need to stay by the water, just in case he surfaces."

"How long are you going to wait?"

"It won't be long now. I feel him watching."

49.

After four nights I began to lose hope. The sickness reemerged and it was deeper, all the way to my bones, the way addicts describe dope sickness. I shit myself constantly. I vomited into the ocean. Whatever he had done to me had made my body dependent. I literally needed him to survive. I had heard of people who died from drug withdrawals. Whatever was leaking from me could not be good. Was I going to die of the shits and the shakes? Was I going to die a painful, shitty death? Suddenly I became terrified of dying. It seemed like I was about to stop breathing. Even just the thought that I could stop breathing and disappear was terrifying. What was scarier still was that I had done this to myself.

I needed help. There were two hours until group. I needed some kind of emotional methadone, some advice at least about what they had done to tone down their withdrawals. I showered quickly, then walked from Venice to Santa Monica, afraid that if I took a car I might vomit or shit inside of it. Stopping at CVS to buy Pepto-Bismol, I felt terrified, like an alien, as though I were Theo on land. This trip to CVS was so unlike last time—the urinary tract infection where I had felt that strange closeness to myself. Now I was totally estranged and out of my body, as though I had no idea how to move. I saw my feet walking, felt my heart pumping, but I didn't know how I was breathing on my own—how my lungs knew to breathe and my heart knew to beat.

.   .   .

"Well, I did it again," said Diana. "I slept with one of the tennis pros again. This time an even younger one. Barely eighteen. It's like they're just passing me around now. I don't know how everyone in my social circle is not going to find out."

Everyone looked at her in awe as though we were watching a soap opera. Sara was popping cashews like popcorn.

"I just—I don't even know how it happened. It was like I was in a blackout. One minute I was getting into my car, the next minute I was talking to him. Then he got in the car with me and we started making out right there in the club parking lot. I took him to the Loews on the beach and got us a room, because only tourists go there and I knew we wouldn't see anyone. The whole thing lasted less than an hour. He didn't even ask for my number."

"Did it come on spontaneously? Or was there any moment leading up to it where you noticed the idea in your mind? Anything that could have been a trigger?" asked Dr. Jude.

"Besides the fact that he was eighteen with rock-hard abs? And wanted me? No. Oh, there was a moment—the night before. I was at a party with my husband, an industry thing. And I looked at him from across the room. He was dressed up in a tux and I was wearing a cocktail dress. He was talking to a director, a famous one. And if there was any moment where he should have seemed attractive to me—it would have been that moment. But I looked at him and just thought, 'I do not want that man. I do not want him at all. And I am going to be trapped with him for the rest of my life.' And I felt like I was sinking. Like I was sinking through the floor."

What was wrong with us? There were women on the planet who so easily accepted their paths. They were destined to like what they were given, and were given just enough, so that everything fell into place. Those women instinctively knew how to get a man and keep a man, each man interchangeable with the next: a torso, a dick, a pair of hands. Those women knew how to embrace whichever assembly-line man they were given. They knew how to breathe new life into him day after day and see what they had as special. They were like living psalms. There were no holes in their lives. Those women had never met a void a day in their life. They simply didn't see any.

"Can I just say something?" said Sara. "Diana, I'm sorry, but if I had a husband who took good care of me—and I looked like you—and had young children who loved me, I would be so happy. I would just—be happy."

"Dr. Jude, I'm feeling judged," said Diana. But Sara didn't stop.

"Stan left again. We got in a fight about a historical documentary. *The Roosevelts.* He said that I was the most annoying woman he had ever encountered and then he just left. I don't know where he is staying. Maybe the spa? Maybe another woman's house? I don't know who would want him. We were supposed to go to a workshop this weekend. An 'Opening the Heart' course—a refresher for me, and basics for him. I was so excited. I was finally going to have a workshop boyfriend. I paid for both of us and everything. And you know what? I don't even want to go now. I don't want to open my heart! Now I'm going to have to go by myself. I'm going to be the woman alone again."

I looked around the room and felt sad for all of us. We were built differently from other people—constructed in some fundamental way that was unlike those who could cope with love. Maybe we felt the same emotions as everyone else, but we felt them more intensely. Sappho felt more too, this I knew. Sappho was one of us. If she wasn't overwhelmed by emotions, why then would she have needed to sing?

Chickenhorse said she had canceled her date with the guy from the dog park. She said that she had gotten a weird feeling from him.

"Weird in what way?" asked Dr. Jude.

"I don't know. He was wearing one of those newsboy caps. And when I thought about the cap, I felt triggered. I just don't trust any man in one of those caps. It's like a flashing red no."

"What is it specifically about that hat? Have you had a negative experience with a man in one of those hats in the past?" asked Dr. Jude.

"No," said Chickenhorse. "The truth is . . . maybe it's me. I know you want me to start dating again. I know you think I'm ready. But I don't think I'm ready. I don't know if I'm ever going to be ready."

I wondered if this was what recovery looked like, the only option for women like us. Was it better to be somewhat sane without a man than to be crazy with one? Dr. Jude seemed to think it was possible that we could date consciously, eventually come to be in healthy relationships. She believed in us, and our ability to get better. But I didn't believe in us. Chickenhorse didn't believe in us either.

Brianne had stuck with her decision to give no money to the faux businessman. Now he'd stopped speaking to her. He had sent a final email a few days prior, stating that it was all her fault they couldn't be together, because she couldn't front him the money to return home. He called her selfish and said that he would be back when he was back. But he said he didn't want to be with a person who lacked trust and generosity in that way.

"My life is very full," she said, her lower lip—newly pumped with collagen—trembling a little. "It really is a very full life and I feel grateful for everything I have in it. But I was hopeful about this one. I thought that after I've done so much work on myself in here that maybe I was being rewarded for all of my efforts. I let myself get excited. Maybe that was my mistake."

Everyone murmured that it was better she knew now that he was an asshole. But they didn't say asshole. They said "unable to commit" and "love avoidant" and "terrified of intimacy." It was sweet the way they wanted her to be okay. They seemed like they were really rooting for her. Strangely, in that moment, they all looked like children to me. I saw them each as they might have been as children: not in body, but an innocence inside. I remembered that each of them had mothers who once loved them. Their mothers loved them and just wanted them to be happy. How strange that every person had a mother. It made me sad that people had mothers who stuck around a very long time. I imagined the mothers who didn't die would play with their daughters' hair every day, brush the stray pieces off the forehead, tickle their necks, stroke the crowns of their heads.

After my mother died and Annika went back to school, my father offered to play with my hair before bed. It was a kind gesture, but we both knew it was just too weird. He wasn't the touchy-feely sort. More of a head patter.

"Play with my hair," I would say to my teenage friends, but when they played with my hair it was never enough. I needed more than the friends were able to give. I envied my friends who could have their hair played with for a few minutes and then simply be done with it. They could take it or leave it. They knew that their mothers could come in later to finish the job, without them even having to ask. So they took it all lightly. They did this with their lovers too.

I looked at Brianne's cheeks, straining desperately to be young, and wondered what her face had looked like as a little girl. She found it unfair, terrifying, that time was actually passing. Time wasn't supposed to pass. Or it was supposed to pass for everyone else but her. I understood this. I was scared too. I wanted to stroke her cheek and tell her that she didn't have to put anything else in it. That she was still young in some essential way. A wave of pain rose inside me that I had never known could be so palpable. I felt that it was going to kill me, and tried to shove it down. The pushing back against it left me with a choking feeling. Who even knew what was killing me more: the pain itself or the fight against the pain? I was seeing, hearing, and feeling too much. I felt that if I did not leave the room in that moment that I would suffocate on something—the feeling or the resistance to the feeling—and I would die.

I ran from the room clutching my throat and out onto the sidewalk. I crouched down in a squat with my head between my knees. Just to be alone again, away from all of that human- ity that echoed my own, made me feel better. The sadness and nausea began to subside. Then I heard the door of the building open and footsteps behind me. It was Chickenhorse, coming to check on me. I wondered how she got elected.

"Hey, just making sure you are okay."

"I'm not," I said.

"Do you want to come back inside?"

"No, I need air."

"Do you think I should sit with you?"

"I should probably just be left alone."

"We aren't going to hurt you, Lucy."

I looked at her face. For a moment she didn't look chickeny or horsey. Her eyes were big and brown and with her mouth closed she had nice, plump, red lips. Was it possible that she was actu- ally pretty?

"Listen," she said. "I don't know what's going on with you. What it is exactly that you're doing. I mean, aside from the Jamie thing. But, whatever it is—you don't have to do it."

I laughed out loud, a crazy-sounding laugh. I was crouched on a sidewalk in the middle of the day. Whatever I was doing, of course I had to do it.

"You don't really know me," I said.

"Maybe not," she said. "But I relate."

I didn't want her to relate. I didn't want to be like her. But I knew she was being honest.

"So what's the solution? Never date again?" I asked.

She looked at me.

"Honestly, I don't know. Things were so bad for me by the end—the end of my last run. It could have killed me, easily. If I ever end up in that emotional space again? In a way, I think I'd be lucky to be dead. It would be worse to roam the planet, a tormented soul, for the rest of my life."

Maybe this was why I was in group, to remind people like her

233

of the hell that awaited them just on the other side. I was here to be a cautionary tale.

"How did you get through your withdrawal without dying?" I asked.

"I just kept going. One minute at a time. And gradually I saw that the feelings didn't destroy me."

"But you were forced to give him up, right? You didn't choose to do it. I mean, he got a restraining order?"

"What does a restraining order mean to people like us? In the face of our kind of obsession? But I guess, technically, yes, I was forbidden from being with him. I didn't make the choice."

So there it was. She hadn't so much recovered as she was stopped by the law. I pictured her like a marionette, a marionette of obsessive love, with a judge pulling the strings. She was running in place, like a boxer, but could not move toward what she thought she loved.

"But what if you could be with him? If you could be with him again, wouldn't you do it in a heartbeat?"

"No, I wouldn't," she said quickly.

"Come on. What if he was standing right here on the side-walk?"

She thought about it for a second and the corners of her mouth twitched downward.

"Do I still miss him? Yes, I do. I'd be lying if I said I didn't. But I don't miss what being with him took away from me."

"Like what?"

"Everything," she said. "Dignity, sanity. My life."

"What was the restraining order for anyway?" I said.

"It's embarrassing."

"Come on. I'm in child's pose on the sidewalk."

She laughed. I'd never seen her laugh before.

"Fine," she said. "One day I saw his wife out walking. I'd never met her, only stalked her on the Internet. But there she was, power walking down Montana right in front of me. And I thought about how unfair it was that I knew so much about her, from the stalking, and she didn't even know I existed. I just felt livid about it. And I sort of chased her down . . . with my Prius."

"No!"

"It's true."

"You chased her down! Like tried to run her over?"

"I wouldn't have said that at the time. But yes, that's what I was doing."

"My God, that's amazing." I laughed.

"It's not," she said. "It's pretty disgusting."

"I suddenly like you so much more," I said.

"You shouldn't. None of it was her fault. It was her husband's fault. Really it was my fault."

"Huh," I said.

We were silent for a little while.

"Do you want to come back inside?" she asked.

"I'll be back in a minute. I just need a little more air."

But I didn't have the strength to go back in. And I knew that if I tried to walk home I wouldn't make it. Laughing had given me vertigo and now the sidewalk was spinning. I felt the cement with my palm and it was cooler than the afternoon air. I wondered if perhaps I should just lie down right there. Should I just lie down with my cheek against the sidewalk, just lie down and go to sleep? If I die in that sleep I think I would be okay. But I didn't want to die there in public in front of whoever could walk by. Suddenly I was afraid again. I took out my phone and pressed the buttons to get a car to take me home. This was just what people did now. We went from emotion to phone. This was how you didn't die in the twenty-first century.

The driver, whose name was Chase, pulled up in a silver Honda. He was cute, with a gap in his front two teeth—maybe age twenty-six at most. He looked like he was trying to grow a mustache, and his brown hair was past his ears under a baseball cap that read FML. He babbled that he was an actor, or was trying to become one. His favorite philosophy about acting was Uta Hagen's, something about being a student of humanity. Well, for a student of humanity he was shitty at reading people. In my head I just kept saying, *Shut up, shut up!* I wanted to say, *Don't you know I am dying?*

But even in my dying I couldn't be mean to him for fear that he would think I was a bitch. Why did I even care what he thought? Was my death that unimportant? How could I prioritize the feelings of this vacant, mustached kid over my own—me, who was probably dying?

I repeated, "That's nice" and "Oh, interesting," and lay down in the backseat. I didn't announce that I would be lying down, I just did it. He wasn't paying any attention to what I was doing, instead going on about an upcoming audition for a prescription allergy medication where he would play the son-in-law of a woman with adult allergies. He said he had mixed feelings about it, because he didn't want to limit his range to pharmaceuticals. The part he really wanted was at an audition for Samsung next week. He was trying out to play the phone.

"It's not easy to make it in this town. I'm going up against two hundred other potential phones, at least," he said, looking in the mirror at the traffic behind him.

I noticed he had green eyes. He really was cute. I waited for him to comment on me lying supine in his backseat, but he didn't ask if I was okay. I suppose this was normal behavior in California. I closed my eyes and concentrated on my breathing. I wasn't dead. I was breathing in the back of this cute idiot's car.

When we pulled up at Annika's house, he stopped and said, "Okay, we're here. Wish me luck with Samsung!"

I opened my eyes and squinted at him. I wanted to tell him that I hoped he never got a part.

"Wanna fuck?" I said instead.

I was shocked when the words came out. He must have been too, because he turned around to look at me for the first time.

"Are you serious?"

"Totally."

"Here? In the car?"

"Sure, why not."

"Someone might see us."

"I don't care if you don't care," I said.

"Man. I've been driving for three years and this has never happened. Yeah, why not? YOLO, right? Hold on," he said, and put the car in reverse.

This was not really the response I was looking for. I wanted more of an "I'm floored by this request, because you're so beautiful" and less of a "Well, since you asked, carpe diem!" But he pulled into a side alley and shut off the car.

"Come up here," he said. "Come around to the front."

I got out of the car, walked around to the driver's side, and crawled onto this mustached man-boy's lap. I was facing him, straddling him. He put his seat all the way back and I took off his FML baseball cap. His hairline was receding. We began kissing and he put his hands up my shirt. He sort of grabbed at my breasts and twisted them, like they were handles on a door. I felt like he was feeling for there to be more, trying to stretch them into being bigger, but they would only stretch so far. I wanted to say, *Be gentler*, but instead I said, "Yesss."

He slid his dick out of his jeans but left them on. He didn't put on a condom, or ask if he should wear one. His dick was small, but firm, like a dill pickle. I lifted up my skirt and slid my underwear over to the side, sat on the dick. I moved up and down saying, "Yeah, fuck me," even though I was the one doing the fucking. A few of my pubic hairs got caught in his zipper. I kept hitting my head on the roof of the car with every few humps. Each time I hit my head I said sorry.

"That's okay. Rub your clit," he said.

"Don't tell me what to do."

"Sorry," he said.

"And don't come inside me."

But he came inside me, and in less than a minute, making a face that looked like a dying warrior, a hissing sound escaping his open mouth.

"Damn," he sighed after he had finished expelling his load of little Uta Hagens into my vagina. "That was great. Did you come?"

"Um, definitely not." I laughed.

Was he kidding? I would have to be a better actress for that. I guess he thought I was hypersexual and came instantly, tossing orgasm after orgasm into the wind. Who else would fuck a stranger in his car? Most people wanted to avoid being fondled by their driver.

I imagined his sperm in there, trying to talk to my egg, and my egg ignoring them. What were his sperm saying? *It's a tough town, but I'm hoping to get an agent this year,* said his sperm. *Just shut the fuck up,* said my egg.

"Well," he said, patting me on the ass. "I hope you give me a good rating."

"Oh, for sure," I said. "Five stars."

50.

I got into the bathtub and ran the water, soaking and scrubbing away Chase's semen, which had formed a crust on my thigh. I could see it leaking out of me too in the bathwater, like passing clouds. Really, what was wrong with me? Why couldn't I be a person who was content to just lie around and watch the clouds, without trying to consume anything? Was there something wrong with just being alive? Why was I so defective? Then again, it wasn't my fault we were put on the planet and left to make our own meaning. I was making mine and doing the best I could. Drying off, I put on one of my sister's silk kimonos, then went downstairs and got a glass of white wine. Was I cool? Was I glamorous? Was I living a life that others would crave, or was I out of my mind, fucking some strange driver? Part of me felt glamorous and part of me felt insane, the two feelings rotating over and over.

I lay down on the floor and noticed that I felt better. I was relaxed, somewhat high even. The bad sex had served as some kind of methadone. Dominic came over and licked my face, whimpering. I would take him out later, so what if he shit in the pantry. I could just go to sleep, I thought. Now I felt certain that it would be sleep, and not death. I knew that it would just be sleep.

But as I was drifting off, my phone rang. It was a Phoenix number and I answered it quickly, thinking that it might be Rochelle calling from her office to say that Megan had miscarried, or another piece of news involving Jamie. But it was the advisory committee, both the English and classics chairs, on the line. They were calling to let me know that they had read the outline and sample from my new thesis. Their voices sounded enthusiastic. Well, this was good! They were responding much more quickly than I expected. And having both of them on the call definitely signaled something big. Maybe they were so impressed that they were going to offer me more money? It was strange but I was so worn out that I couldn't visualize either of their faces, only the rosacea nose of the classics chair and the hatching chick from the Easter sweater of the English chair. When they spoke, I imagined it was the nose itself speaking, with the chick chiming in as it emerged from its egg.

"There's an unorthodox fluidity about the new work that's very refreshing," said the nose.

"Yes, the decreased omniscience, the infusion of romanticism. This new iteration is very powerful," said the chick.

"The voice of critical omniscience wasn't your strong suit," said the nose. "Or perhaps, you didn't believe what you were saying before and that's where the thesis faltered. After all, if you couldn't convince yourself, then how could you convince the reader?"

"I don't know," I said.

"The new thematic scaffolding creates a much more sound dialectic," said the chick.

"Great," I said.

"Having said that, we regret to inform you that the departments will no longer be able to fund this project," said the nose.

I was stunned.

"What? Why?"

"To be frank, with this new infusion of personal thoughts and feelings, it can no longer be considered a scholarly text," said the nose. "This sort of personalized narrative just isn't what we do around here."

"The truth is, as readers, we are genuinely glad you've pivoted," said the chick. "Your prior thesis clearly wasn't working."

"But unfortunately, the departments only receive funding for projects that further scholarship—not hybrids of scholarship and creative writing," said the nose.

What was I going to do for money? How was I going to live?

"Can I reapply for it somehow?" I asked.

"Unfortunately, we won't be able to instate it," said the nose.

"Can't or won't? Don't you decide what gets funded?"

"To some extent, yes," said the chick.

"But we can't deviate too much from what the university has traditionally focused on," said the nose. "We have to retain a tonal continuity."

"So what you're telling me is that this version is much better than the last version. But you were willing to fund the last version and not this one?" I said.

"That's right," said the nose.

"Well, what if I just go back to the old version? Hammer away on that?"

"Unfortunately, that isn't going to work," said the chick.

"Why?"

"We were always skeptical of the original premise of the thesis and now you've convinced us that the reasoning was faulty."

"Plus, we want to encourage your creative breakthrough."

"Great," I said.

"We suggest that you seek out a mainstream trade publisher, or reapply to a program with a more creative bent than Southwest State," said the chick.

"But you won't pay for it?"

"No," they said at the same time.

51

I returned to the rocks. I knew I belonged there. If there was going to be desolation, no number of terrestrial men could fix me. I needed to go to the ocean, the primal tap, where the catalyst of my illness swam freely. If I was going to be alone and full of despair, let me at least be desolate here. Let me go cold turkey in the place I now loved most. Maybe it wouldn't be so cold turkey after all? Maybe the fumes of memories could bring me down more gently. Only once in that week of waiting by the rocks did someone bother me. A lifeguard drove by in a jeep and asked me if everything was okay. I wanted to say, *Well, actually, if you really want to know . . .* but instead I said that I was fine. Then I told him I was a scientist conducting a study of the waves.

"You know you're not supposed to be out here this late at night," he said.

"I know. But it's for the good of the tides."

"Are you sure you're okay?"

"I'm okay."

Then everything fell silent and he drove away.

I took this to mean that I was supposed to be there. I was surely being tested, to see how strong and devoted I was. It was like I was part of some ancient worship ceremony, only instead of leaving candles, food, or wine at the altar, I was leaving myself. And instead of an altar there was the ocean. I would look out into the waves and for a moment I would really believe that I saw him. I had never seen him out in the waves, he never swam close enough to the surface, but now I constantly hallucinated him. Usually he was a bird skimming across the water. Once he was a dolphin. And every time, when what I thought was him would turn out to be only seafoam, or the wind blowing on the water, I wondered how much of everything I had seen or thought I'd seen in my lifetime had been only illusion like that. I wondered if anything was really living or if anything had ever lived.

52.

One night, asleep on the rock, I awoke to two hands on my shoulders. They were his hands. I was not dreaming, because they never moved or loosened their grip. I was not dreaming, because I had just dreamed that I was alone, back in the desert, and the dream still vaguely lingered in my mind. I dreamt that I was in a diner outside of Phoenix trying to choose a cake from a glass spinner case of desserts. I was having difficulty seeing the cakes. They were blurry, crumbling, old, and stale. In their staleness they were turning into dust right in front of me. They were turning into nothingness. But the waitresses insisted they were there. The waitresses were all members of the group: Diana, Sara, Dr. Jude. Everyone was urging me to pick a cake. They had formed a circle around me and they were cheering me on. But I couldn't choose a cake, because I couldn't see them. And when I tried to explain that I couldn't see them, the group would echo in unison, "But they're right there."

When I awoke, I thought that I was still in the diner for a moment. Then I felt his hands and I knew that I was on the rocks, by the ocean in Venice Beach. Immediately I knew whose hands were on me. It was as though I had become the rocks and this was the first time we met, when I saw his hands on them for the first time. Only now, some other part of me was witnessing the whole thing and his hands were on me. Then his face was in front of my face, a wet lock of hair in his eye.

"Hi," he whispered.

He had always been there.

He kissed my forehead and kissed my mouth.

"Hi," I said.

There was a surge of euphoria, a deep peace inside me, but also a return to normalcy, fixed, as though I were supposed to feel this way all the time. This was how junkies described getting well. There had been a missing piece and now the piece was back. It felt good to have the piece back, but also just normal. The sickness that had overwhelmed my head, my heart, my guts was gone. It didn't matter what nature had intended for me. It didn't matter that I had ever lived without him. He was not an extra part, but the thing. This was the new nature.

He pulled himself up onto the rock and we sat there, hugging. We stayed in total embrace and didn't speak. I forgot where we were, and that seemed most normal of all: to be nowhere. I could hear the ocean, but forgot that it was the ocean. I forgot that I hadn't always lived at the ocean or that it was even a separate entity. This was the only life I had known.

"I'm so sorry," I said, but he hushed me.

"I know," he said. "I've seen you every night on this rock."

"You have? But where were you? I came here and came here and never saw you."

"I was far away. I was in a deeper part of the ocean, much deeper than you have ever been. But I could see you there. I could see you there and I just hoped you would keep coming. I wanted to go to you every night. All I wanted was to swim to you and be with you. But I was afraid. I needed more nights. I needed all these nights before I knew. But tonight, you looked so finished. You looked so finished with the Earth, so surrendered. I could tell in your sleeping that you were finished. I could tell that if I came back you wouldn't return to the desert. I knew that you no longer had it in you. That is good. It has to be your choice. It has to come from you. I saw it in your face that you would never speak of the desert again. I knew you were finally mine."

"I never want to live apart from you," I said. "I will live on this rock, I don't care. I'll sell mango on the beach, or bad jewelry.

Those shitty crystal necklaces they sell on the boardwalk. I don't care."

"Would you give up your dog?" he asked.

"Yes!" I said. "He isn't even my dog!"

"What about fire?"

"Fire?"

"Yes, fire. Would you give up fire? Would you give up walking around?"

"YES!" I said. "I hate fire. I hate walking. I don't like any of it. I would give up anything you ask me to give up. I don't need any of it. Whatever you want me to give up, I will give up."

"I want you to come under the water with me," he said.

When we had been fighting, when he said that he was going to invite me to live with him in the ocean, I didn't understand what he meant. I wondered if he thought I had gills. But now I knew exactly what he meant. I knew what he meant in the sense that suddenly I envisioned myself with him in the infinite depths, infinite blackness. But this time I was not kissing his eyelids or his forehead as he slept. This time I was the one with my eyes closed. I was dead.

Or maybe he didn't mean death, not completely. I couldn't bring myself to ask, *What does this entail exactly? What does it mean, me following you under? Do I become a mermaid myself? Do I drown?* What if when I followed him into the ocean it was only death on one level, but on another level it was eternal life? Maybe I would grow a tail. Maybe I would become immortal, or close to it. I was scared not to know the journey before I took it, but I was more afraid to ask. I feared my questions would break the spell again and he would disappear. If I conveyed a lack of trust I might never see him again. And then what? I would be flinging myself into the water with rocks in my pockets soon enough anyway. Or quietly eating all the Ambien. I couldn't show any doubt. I couldn't show any hesitation.

It is said that Sappho became so devastated by Phaon's rejection of her that she could no longer stand to live. So she threw herself into the sea, believing that she would either be cured of her love for him or she would drown. She drowned. That was only one story. But in every Siren and mermaid myth I had read, it always meant death for the humans who followed them under. Men diving off the backs of ships at night. Men walking into the water with rocks tied to their ankles. Many men. This was the choice they made if they wanted to be with their mermaids forever. Perhaps it wasn't a choice at all? Once you had made love with one of these creatures you couldn't go on living on land without them.

Did this mean he wanted me dead? It wasn't exactly the romantic scenario I had envisioned. If I was dead and he wasn't dead, did that mean he had all the power? If I died for him, it was kind of like him not texting me back on a cosmic level. Or maybe the one who died had the power, as the other person was left to live without them. When Romeo cried for Juliet, because he thought she was dead, it was Juliet who had the power. But then she cried for him when he was really dead, and he had the power. It's the dead one who is most cherished in the end.

"I want nothing more than to be with you," I said.

"I'll hold your hand the whole way."

"Could you give me a little bit of time before we go? Maybe we can just keep meeting on the rock a little longer?"

"So you aren't going to come."

"No, I want to. But I need to straighten out some things for my sister first. I just need a little time."

"How long?" he asked suspiciously.

"Just a few days. Until Thursday maybe?"

He was silent. I kissed him on the forehead.

"You can't tell anyone you're going," he said, pulling away from me. "They will think you're crazy and lock you up."

"I know. I won't tell them anything," I said.

"Good," he said.

"In the meantime, how about you come stay at the house with me for a little while? As I'm preparing. The dog is asleep. I've been making him sleep every day now just in case you were here so I could bring you home with me."

"No," he said. "I'm finished with the land."

"Oh," I said.

"This is as far as I can go. I hope you understand why."

I didn't want to understand, but I did. He had sacrificed for me. The thought of him dragging himself back across the beach that night, the danger he put himself in, was scary. Now he wanted me to sacrifice for him. But hadn't I done that? What had this whole week been?

"I'll meet you here each night until Thursday," he said. "And you can tell me whether you are still coming."

He looked different to me now, more bloated in the face and jaded. His eyes looked darker. I didn't know how I felt about the fact that he needed me as much as I needed him. It scared me to be needed.

"I'm coming," I said.

"Good."

We brought our faces together and kissed gently on the mouth. He put one of his hands at the base of my neck, under my chin, and tightened it—not enough to cut off my air supply, but just so I could feel him pressing a bit into my larynx. My throat felt full of pleasure and emotion. I opened my mouth wider on his and made an "ohhh" sound. We kissed wetly.

"I wish we could live the rest of our lives on these rocks," I said. "Why isn't it possible to just live at the edge of both, the ocean and the land?"

Of course I knew why. The edge was an uncomfortable and dangerous place for both of us. The rocks were nowhere to live. I had wanted him to come to my world for that same reason.

"One day these rocks won't be here," he said. "The ocean will waste them away."

"Then we could find new rocks," I said.

"Eventually you have to choose," he said. "That's how the story has always been and that's the way it will be forever."

"But why?" I asked.

"Well," he said, thinking, "I guess because the choice is always there."

53.

When I got back to the house, Dominic didn't bark. This was odd, because he always smelled Theo on me. I went into the pantry to check on him. He was lying there on his side, perfectly still.

"Dominic," I said. "Domi."

Then I saw his face. His tongue was hanging out of his mouth. His eyes were open, hazy, as though they were made of plastic. He looked like a grotesque stuffed-animal version of himself. The floor was covered in vomit and drool.

"Oh no," I said out loud. "Please, no."

He was motionless. I didn't even have to touch him. I didn't have to feel his flank or check for breath to know he was dead.

The whole summer came flashing in front of me: each of the men and behind them sweet Dominic, waiting for me in the background the whole time. What had I done? I had poisoned him. I'd been dosing him heavier and heavier, because he seemed to be getting more resistant.

"Please come back. Please," I begged, kneeling beside him.

His eye seemed to be looking at me, or through me into space. His ear was flapped up over his head and I adjusted it so it faced downward again. It felt cold when I touched it, and detached from anything living, like a piece of loose suede. I began to cry. I thought of how he didn't like being stroked on his ear, but he always let me. The rest of his body was cold too, heavy like stone.

I shook him a little. Where was he? How was his body here but he was just gone? Everything about him had been warmth, softness, the most gentle parts of life. But now he was the opposite: rigid and empty.

"I never wanted you to suffer," I said. "I only wanted you to be comfortable. I didn't want you to be scared of Theo."

But a quiet voice inside me said, *No, that isn't the truth.*

The truth was I'd wanted him out of the way so I could wander the labyrinth of my fantasy life. I had been given pure love in the form of this dog and I had destroyed him.

I sat there and waited. I waited as I had waited for Theo, because I didn't know what else to do. And sitting on that floor, the truth was further revealed to me that I was not capable of love for anyone. I'd always imagined that there was a subjective reality. But there was nothing subjective about this. I was objectively selfish and cruel. Suddenly it occurred to me that there really were gods who could smite us. The gods were just nature itself. If you didn't follow the gods, you blew it. I had gone against nature. I had done it all wrong.

I'd been wrong about death too. There was no gentle escape. When I had taken those Ambien in Phoenix I thought there was a peaceful way to just kind of disappear. But death wasn't gentle. It was a robber. It stole you out of yourself, and you became a husk. Dominic's warmth was all gone. But his spirit had to be somewhere. Where was his spirit now? Was he still in the room, hovering over me and his body? I hoped he couldn't see himself like this. Was he watching me, angrily? Or was he already with Annika in Europe? Could she feel him?

What was I going to say to Annika? I couldn't tell her. She was going to be devastated and blame herself. Worse yet, what if they performed an autopsy and she found out I'd killed her child? Though there was the diabetes. Maybe that was what had happened, something with his blood sugar. But I'd neglected him horribly. And Annika never had a chance to say goodbye.

I remembered my first group therapy session, when Claire had said to Dr. Jude, "Who cares what I'm doing? I'm only hurting myself." And Dr. Jude had told her that wasn't true. She said there would be casualties, that there were always casualties. This was what she meant.

I was too scared to get in touch with Annika right away. I decided I would go to the hospital to see Claire before contacting my sister. I cleaned up the vomit and drool, then wrapped Dominic in the blanket I had used to smuggle Theo on the wagon.

"It's going to be okay," I said to the poor baby, even though it wasn't.

I sat with the dead dog on my lap and stroked him through the blanket for a long time. It was the most care I had given him in weeks.

This time Claire looked alive again—not overly drugged.

"My darling," she said. "What a pleasant surprise."

"Yes, for both of us," I said. "You look like you again. You look like you're back."

"Oh I'm back, baby."

"I really thought for a minute there that you had become sane."

"Never." She laughed. "I will never give up on suicide again. They thought the meds were making me too *Valley of the Dolls,* I guess, so they changed them. Well, that didn't work and I had another attempt. I tried to hang myself off the bathroom door handle with a four-hundred-dollar cardigan from CP Shades. They had to break in the door and found me naked on the floor of the bathroom, not dead yet, but passed out. It was brilliant."

I laughed with her, but also I shivered. This was what happened to girls like us. We were wired to die.

"Are you still giving up men?" I asked.

"Christ no! Do you want to know the best part of all this? David found out about this last attempt. He's been writing me letters compulsively. Two of them a day, pages and pages. He doesn't even mail them; he comes here and drops them off for me. It's like the more suicidal I am, the more he wants me. When I get out we are going to try and live together. Arnold is going to get full custody of the kids in the divorce and I can't be arsed to give a fuck. So I'm too crazy to be a mother? Well then, that's fine. I didn't make myself this way. It is what it is."

"You sound . . . good," I said.

"I'm great," she said, tugging at her hospital gown. "And what about you?"

"I'm a mess. I think I may have poisoned my sister's dog."

"Oh my God." She giggled. "You did what?"

"It's not funny. He's dead."

"That beast you brought to my house? You poisoned him? With what, bad Alpo?"

"No. Tranquilizers."

"Oh shit."

"Yeah."

"A junkie dog. Jesus, who would have thought? You know, I could tell he had a drug problem. He tried to steal my TV." She snorted.

Now it wasn't comforting at all to have the old Claire back. Why was she laughing? She was like one of those young boys who shoots animals with a BB gun and then has no remorse. Except I was the one who had killed Dominic. I wondered if we were both inherently evil people. Bad women. Were we? Evil people rarely know they're evil. Someone had told me that once. What if we were put on the planet to fill some purpose but that purpose was bad? Maybe this was why we had to die.

"He was such a sweet dog," I said. "It's horrible. My sister is going to be destroyed. I don't think she will ever forgive me."

"Listen," she said, "it's not your fault he couldn't handle his shit. Never trust an addict, Lucy, not even a dog."

"Stop it. I feel irredeemably awful."

"Well, you're not."

"Do you ever feel that way? Like you're the worst one and there is no hope for you?"

"Darling, I *know* I'm the worst one," she said. "And of course there's no hope."

I began to cry.

"Oh, love, don't be so hard on yourself. I'm guessing it wasn't intentional."

"No, of course it wasn't intentional. And he had diabetes. So maybe it was that."

"It probably was."

"I really fucked up this time."

"Listen," she said, and put her hand on my shoulder. "Your sister can find another dog. But there's only one Lucy."

I wanted to believe her. I kept trying to wriggle out of the reality of the situation, find some way to prove to myself that I wasn't a dog killer. But no matter how I looked at it I was a murderer, third degree at the very least. I wanted to see myself the way Claire saw me. She was so nonjudgmental. But she only withheld her judgment of me so she didn't have to judge herself. She couldn't have me be a villain, or she would be one too.

"What about your swimmer?" asked Claire. "Did he ever come back?"

"Yes, he did."

"And?"

"We're going to run away together."

"To the desert?"

"No," I said. "To the depths of the ocean."

"Dark," she said. "Like a suicide pact. So romantic, I love it."

"Sort of," I said. "Sort of."

54.

Annika and Steve immediately got on a plane and headed home. I was terrified for their return. I sat on the white sofa, thinking of all that had gone on there, and dug my fingernails into my gums. When they bled a little, I imagined wiping the blood under the sofa cushions where my period bloodstains were. Now I understood the desire Claire had to hurt herself. I couldn't drink anything or take a pill, because I needed to be clearheaded for their arrival. But the last thing I wanted was to be lucid. I needed an out, something to release me from the feelings of shame. So I took it out on my gums.

When they pulled up in the driveway, Annika refused to get out of the taxi and only Steve came in. He had never liked me to begin with, but now he clearly hated me. I thought of his trench coat, covered in Garrett's semen, in a dumpster somewhere. He issued a brusque hello and went into the pantry, where Dominic was still covered with the blanket.

"Goddammit," he said. He sounded angry.

Then he went back outside. I crept over to the window and saw him talking softly to Annika, coaxing her out of the cab. But she refused to come. I heard her crying and saying, "No, no, no."

She looked up and our eyes met through the glass. She opened the cab door and came rushing into the house. I thought that she might yell at me, but she took me in her arms and hugged me. I sort of stood there as she cried on my shoulder, not knowing what to do.

"I loved him so much, Lucy," she said.

"I know."

"He was the most special baby in the whole world. I just, I never loved anything like I loved him."

"Let's sit down," I said.

We sat down at the kitchen table. She was tan from the Roman sun and smelled like orange blossoms. Her ass had gotten bigger under her yoga pants and she wore a blousy shirt to cover it. I sat with my hands under me, clenched in fists, and squeezed them hard every time she spoke.

"What am I going to do now? I mean, what the fuck am I supposed to do now?"

"Do you want me to go out and get you something to eat?" I asked.

"Eat?" she looked up at me. "Oh no, I can't eat."

"Okay."

"I wanted so many more years with him. There was so much life we had left together. I mean, I would have eventually outlived him. But not for so many more years. He wasn't even old. And to me he was still a puppy. He will always be my puppy."

"Annika, I'm so sorry," I said.

But she didn't blame me. She didn't say, "How could you have let this happen?" Instead she stared blankly, her full lips slightly parted, as though she too now knew the nothingness. Maybe it was the first time she could see it. Even when we lost our father she hadn't had this look. This was the face of a mother who had lost her child. It made me think about my mother. I wondered, if my mother hadn't died—if it had been me who died instead and my mother had lived—was this what she would have looked like?

Steve came over and put his hands on her shoulders. He said that they were going to have Dominic cremated, because California law would not allow them to bury a body so close to the beach. The vet tech would come pick him up in the morning. With that Annika began to sob. She went inside the pantry. I followed her to the door and saw her lie down on the floor with her dead dog, her hair fanned out beside him. He was hers, the creature she loved most, and I had taken him from her. I could smell him from the doorway. Neither Annika nor Steve said anything about the smell, but the scent of death was wafting up from his body and through the glass house.

After Steve had gone to bed and Annika fell asleep on the floor of the pantry, I crept out to the rocks in the dark to see Theo. He hadn't come out of the water and was resting his arms on one of the rocks, bobbing in the waves.

"You're late," he said, looking up at me. "I thought maybe you weren't coming."

"I know, I'm sorry. But I'll always come. And tomorrow, the water."

"I'm glad," he said without smiling.

I took his hand to reassure him. His fingers were chilly. I thought about how cold and lifeless Dominic's body was, how death was not the warm bath I had imagined. The water was going to be freezing. I was scared of it, scared of feeling the freeze rush into me, or maybe scared of the warmth rushing out of me. I had never thought of that warmth as something I would miss. And Theo was being so distant from me now too, sulking. I felt lonely.

"I wonder what the experience will be like, how my life will— manifest under there. Also, how I will stay under the waves and not just bob to the surface."

I was hunting for a potential answer.

"You have to trust me," he said. "It's going to be beautiful. I will help you go. You will have chosen, but I will assist you. Then we will have a very long time together."

"And we'll still make love under there?"

"Of course we will," he said.

"Okay," I said. "I'm just a little scared."

"Here, let me come up and join you."

257

With that he pulled himself out of the water and took a seat next to me.

"I love you," he said, cupping my face with his cold, wet hand. He kissed me softly on the cheek in a way that made me feel like a sweet child, no longer horrible. I felt that I was again back in the womb he and I shared, an innocent. Was this all it took to be cleansed: one beautiful person to treat you kindly and gently, and you were exonerated? How could Dominic's death and Theo's love both be true at the same time? How could I have killed Dominic and still be worthy of such tender affection? I was either awful or I wasn't. Which one was it? I didn't think I could be both.

His kisses moved from my cheek to my nose to my lips. I gently kissed and licked his beautiful mouth, one lip and then the other. He lay back on the rocks and pulled me on top of him. My thighs sandwiched his pelvis. As we kissed more, I felt him get hard under his cloth. I was excited to still have that remaining life force in me, the kind that could make his cock come alive. I began rubbing my body against him, moving up and down on his thigh and then on his pelvis. Then I moved my pussy back and forth on the length of his cock, over the cloth, as though I were anointing him. I rubbed faster and faster as we stayed in an embrace, our mouths locked on each other. A warmth spread from my pussy up through my stomach and into my heart. It radiated out through the top of my head. Everything was suddenly warm, the cold completely eliminated.

Was this what the eve of one's wedding was like? I felt that we were being held on the rock by Aphrodite herself. Tomorrow she would drop me into the water, but maybe the water was only her lap. What if I would only be dropping to a warmer, deeper embrace?

I moved against him again and again. As I moved, I imagined us beside a giant underwater sand castle. The walls of the castle were made of coral and sea crystals of all colors, textures, and sizes: peach, silver, pastel mint, cyan pieces embedded in translucent white chunks, big slabs made of thousands of tiny sparkling dark-green crystals, rusted gold rocks, transparent indigo pyramids, rosy sea glass, neon-orange honeycombs of coral. The castle had tall turrets and spires, and Theo and I were beside it, preparing to enter.

But then I began to come and, as I did, the castle melted slowly to the ground. He and I clung together as the castle vanished, eclipsed by a wave of pleasure, disappearing from my inner vision. I didn't stop moving until I rode over the peak of that orgasm. If anyone had looked at the rocks they would have seen a woman, thirty-eight years old, hopefully a little younger-looking, writhing against what looked like a large fish. Or maybe they would have seen her just riding the air. I wasn't sure which was crazier.

When I got back to the house Steve was awake at the kitchen table, eating cereal, wearing a pair of blue striped pajamas, hairs sticking out from his balding head. I was drenched with sea spray and grime. He looked at me sternly.

"Late-night swim?" he asked.

"Just a beach walk," I said.

"I don't know what went on while we were gone," he said calmly. "But why is it that every time you come here, disaster strikes?"

"Don't worry, I'm leaving tomorrow night," I said.

"That's not what I'm saying. I'm not telling you to leave. I only mean—your sister just wants to be good to you. She only wants you to be happy."

"I know."

"But you can't not make a mess."

"I guess I can't."

"If it were up to me, we would have hired a dog sitter. But Annika wanted to give you the time here. You know she'd do anything for you."

"Would she?" I asked.

"Yes!" he said, as though it were crazy that I didn't know. But the truth was, I didn't.

"Whose blood is that? What happened?" he asked, pointing to the sofa. He had turned over the pillows.

"It's—"

But just as I was about to answer, he cut me off.

"No, you know what? I don't know what happened and I don't want to know."

"Okay," I said. "But it's my blood. There was no one else here but me."

55.

The following evening I packed my suitcase. I thought about my little sweaters and dresses floating in the water as I packed up each one. It made me feel sad. I kept thinking the words *belonging* and *my belongings*. Dominic was no longer in the pantry. I wasn't sure who had come and taken him away. It smelled heavily of ammonia, but I swore I could still smell death.

Annika had gone back inside the pantry. She was just sitting there on the floor with Dominic's bowl and a squeaky toy in the shape of a duck.

She looked up at me.

"This was his favorite toy," she said, giving it a squeeze. "Did you know that? Did I tell you that?"

"Yes. We played with it together a lot," I lied.

"Good." She smiled. "I wanted him to have the most beautiful life."

"Annika, I am so sorry. I want you to know I'm grateful to you."

"I knew I should have come home. I should have listened to my intuition. But you told me you could handle it. You said that nothing bad was going to happen to him, that he would be fine."

"I know. If there is some way I can make this up to you—"

"No, it isn't your fault," she said. "It's my fault."

"You couldn't have known. Even the vet didn't know how sick he was exactly."

"I will never forgive myself," she said. "Never."

"Annika," I said.

There was nothing else left to say. I held out my hand to help her up. She took it, but instead of standing up, she brought me down to the floor to sit with her. With our backs pressed against the wall I held her hand with both of my hands. I softly stroked her skin, so that it was warmed. I felt nervous doing this, as though I wasn't sure if it was appropriate. Why wouldn't it be appropriate? We were sisters, after all. It was such a small act, but it felt so intimate. It was the gentleness and surety of the way I touched her hand that made me feel strange, as though I didn't know I knew how to do this. I wondered who or what inside me was doing it. It was motherly, almost.

"Do you want me to play with your hair?" I asked her.

"Yes," she said.

I put my knees up so she could lean against them. Then I rubbed the back of her neck and the scalp area behind her ears.

"Mmmm, that feels nice," she said.

"Lie back," I said, folding my legs into a cross-legged position. She put her head in my lap and closed her eyes. I traced each of her eyelids with my pointer fingers. I softly rubbed her eyebrows and between them, moving in circles up to her forehead and slowly tickling her scalp. I became less aware of time passing. I seemed to drift in and out of myself for a little while, as though the act of giving this sweet nurture somehow relieved me of having to be a person—or made being a person bearable. But every time I'd almost let go of myself completely, disappear into the experience, I remembered that I had somewhere else I was supposed to be. I didn't want to remember. I wanted to forget all about my plan. But I felt that I had to go through with it, as though some other part of me that was not my head or my heart—more like an internal magnet—was grabbing me and pulling me toward another magnet.

"I'm going to have to go," I said to her, giving her one final pat on the head.

"Where are you going?" she asked, looking up at me.

"The airport," I said. "My cab will be here in a moment or two."

"The airport?"

"Yes, I booked my ticket."

"Oh no, don't go," she said.

"I felt like I should leave you guys alone."

"No, I don't want that!" she said. "Please stay. Steve is at work all day and it's going to be so lonely without Dominic. I'm scared to be alone."

"I can't," I said, standing up. "I have to get back to the university."

"But I need you," she said.

Suddenly I wanted to stay. For maybe the first time in my life, I didn't want to abandon an uncomfortable feeling. I wanted to give her motherly love in the way she had tried to give me motherly love. Hers had always been from a distance, but it was there. And I wanted to give her motherly love in the way that she couldn't give me motherly love: by staying, even when it was uncomfortable. Wasn't it time that I showed up for her?

I also wanted to give her love in the sisterly way I had given Claire and Diana love. The group had taught me how to do that, imperfectly, but I knew what it was now. You just sat there with someone and listened. That was all you had to do. I wondered if Diana had finished fucking her way through all the tennis pros—if she had moved on to her son's friend. Or if she was doing better again. I thought about Claire and wondered if I stayed in Venice how long we would stay friends. How long she would stay alive. Had I chosen her as a friend because she had an end date too?

I wanted to leave my suitcase at the foot of her stairs, sit down beside my sister, and tell her that I would stay for as long as she needed me. I wanted to put my arms around her and thank her for needing me, for being unafraid to share the same space. I wanted to thank her for asking, risking that rejection.

But that magnet kept pulling me out. It was as though what was to come was already written and I was just fulfilling my part of the story. And so I held on to my suitcase firmly, and all I could say was, "I'll come back. I promise, soon, I'll be back."

I walked down a few houses with my suitcase so she and Steve couldn't see me. Then I turned around toward the beach. Was this my last walk? The wind was blowing and it was cold. Annika hadn't told me how cold Venice could be before I got there, even in summer. It was something I had to figure out for myself.

With the wind blowing, the beach houses looked warm and inviting. From the outside they made it look so easy to be alive on Earth, to hunker down all cozy and warm. I wondered if it felt that way for the people inside them, like a relief to be out of the elements. Or did they quickly forget about the chill outside and take the warmth for granted?

I sat on the rocks waiting for Theo. As I looked at my suitcase again, it filled me with sadness. How was I going to get underwater and stay there? What did he mean when he said he would help me? It was crazy to go into it so blind, but I felt I had no choice. Also, didn't everyone go in blind? No one knew what was going to happen next. I hoped that it would be peaceful. I was just looking for peace.

When Theo swam up to the rocks I saw there was a full moon hanging low over the ocean like a big fish egg. I didn't notice it until he appeared, though I don't know how I could have missed it. As he crawled up, tail slapping against the rocks, I felt that I was seeing him again for the first time. He looked like a surfer, or not a surfer, just a creature, maybe a fellow human, but more beautiful than anyone else and in that way not human like I was human. How much beauty was I projecting upon him, and how much was the moon? And if I was not projecting the beauty, and it was not the moon, how much of him was real beyond the beauty? I wondered if we were ever not projecting. We think we've grown or learned something, but maybe it's always just a new projection. Were my incessant thoughts and feelings just a mechanism to escape the nothingness, or was the nothingness comprised of my thoughts and feelings themselves? Was there another way out besides out? It didn't matter now.

He smiled at me and I felt like he was looking at me at the altar. I felt like I had more control of him than I'd ever had. Even though I was the one who was surrendering her life to join him, the sacrifice seemed to give me power. It was the dead-girl thing. The dead girl was always the one with power.

"I didn't know if I would need a suitcase," I said.

"You don't," he said. He had a rope with him.

"Will you take it with us anyway? So no one knows what happened?"

"I'll take it under, yes."

A shot of adrenaline surged through me. I felt scared.

"So how does this work?" I asked. "I've always heard that humans can't drown themselves—that you need to attach a rock or something. Apparently the human body, however stupidly, always fights to live. What do we do? Do you tie me up with that rope and pull me under, to the bottom?"

"You will tie yourself up," he said. "It is true that the human body does fight to the surface, sometimes even against your will."

I noticed that he said "fight to the surface." He did not say fight to live. Never once did he explicitly mention my death in this. He still wouldn't. But he hadn't contradicted me either when I said drown. I dipped my hand into the icy water. My fingers went numb almost immediately.

"I cannot help tie you," he said. "I can only guide you down to the bottom. I will never fight you. I will never pull you under harder than you want to go. In the past, with the others, this is how I always did it. I need to feel you are there of your own will."

"The others?" I asked.

I knew that there had been others on land. Alexis in the boathouse and who knew what else? But I hadn't known any others had gone under. This made me hurt instantly. Then I felt stupid. Why hadn't I thought of that? I didn't want to think of it. He had such a want for me, a desperation that I go under. He had wanted so badly that it be my own want that brought me under, that was how vulnerable and powerless he was over his own feelings. His need was so big that he couldn't own it. He needed it to be my need. But this didn't mean I was the only one. I never considered that whoever came before me might also be under there. Now I shuddered.

Who was he? An incubus needing so many women to want him? Needing so many women to die for him? How many women? In my own desire to feel chosen by this beautiful creature, I had never thought to ask if others had gone before. It had seemed impossible that his need to be wanted by others was more ravenous than mine. Sexually, I had encountered that kind of need amongst the playboys and assholes. But theirs was purely a physical desire. They sought nothing from me but sex, especially not love. They didn't want my life. It was me who forced it on them. Now here was a man who needed my love and my life. But my love and my life, and the lives of how many other women? I felt a stinging in my eyes. I was crying.

"The others?"

He looked away.

"How many are there, Theo?"

"Some," he said.

"How many?" I demanded.

He looked down at his hands.

"How many bodies are under there?"

He paused for a moment. I could see he was trying to decide whether to lie or not.

"Just tell me the truth," I said.

"Seventeen," he said finally.

So he had a harem. Of what I was not sure. Maybe it was just their bones that were left, or whatever didn't decay in the saltwater. I was not a scientist. But whether they were alive or dead, sand or flesh, I needed to maintain my singularity. What was I going to do now? Suddenly I thought of what Chickenhorse had said. *Whatever it is you're doing, you don't have to do it.*

But I did have to do it. What else would I do? I could not go back to Phoenix, languish in my apartment. There was nothing there for me. And every day I would have to face consciousness, cursing myself for not dissolving in the most beautiful of ways when I could have. Suddenly, though, this dissolve no longer seemed beautiful. It seemed all wrong. If I were to die for him, if I were to be dead—and I knew within myself that I was to be dead—I could not just be a dead girl among many. The dead girl among many is not worshipped. I wanted to be the lone dead girl or nothing at all.

"I fucking hate you," I said coolly.

I was shocked that these words came out of me. Immediately I thought to correct them, but I didn't.

"Lucy."

I looked at him carefully. Did he really love me, or had it been just a game?

In a way it was both. It was a game he was playing with himself, a very serious game, in which I had occupied a crucial role. Theo had hoped that I could fill his emptiness, at least for a little while. Then, once he had me under the water—once my want for him was proven—he would have no need for me anymore. I would begin to dissolve in that emptiness and he would need someone else to fill it. This was a game I knew well. Like Claire, I too wanted a thousand cocks. Didn't we all just want a thousand hard cocks attached to the bodies of boys who have died for us, still warm, to plug our infinite holes? It was a whole way of life, really, the pursuit of that satiety. And it felt like life or death for him too.

I wondered if I was looking at myself. Was I that beautiful and cold? What had always felt to me like an overabundance of want, too much desire, had not been the problem. It was my fear of having to feel it that hurt me. Theo was afraid too. That innate desire was something warm, lovely even, but his fear had turned it into something cold.

Maybe it wasn't such a bad thing to need, even if you risked rejection. Annika needed me now. When she put it out there on the line it moved me. In her it didn't seem weak or disgusting, but like a beautiful quality. Her need brought something out in me that I didn't know that I could be. It was transformational.

I could go back to the beach house. I could go back to the house and I could stay, she told me so. In fact, she not only wanted me to do that—she needed me to do it. Maybe I could even finish the book on my own terms. Fuck the university. I could find a real publisher, at least the book wouldn't be garbage.

"Never come to this beach again," I said to him.

"Lucy—"

"Do you hear me? I never want to see you again."

"I am so sorry," he said.

"Sorry I'm not dead."

He was silent. We both knew that I was oversimplifying things. But he didn't correct me either.

"I do love you, Lucy," he said.

I loved him too. But at the same time, who knew what love was exactly? I still didn't have it figured out. I remembered what Dr. Jude had said. *The question is not what is love, but is it really love I'm looking for?*

"I just thought—I don't know what I thought," I said.

"You thought that we were better than some mythic story."

"Yes," I said. "I thought that your choosing me made me special—special enough to defeat the story."

"You are special," he said.

"No, I'm not," I said. "But I don't want to be part of that story."

He looked paler than ever, as though the full moon or my rejection had blanched all the blood from his face. He was beautiful and yes, I loved him, in one of infinite ways a person could love. I knew that I would wish a thousand times that things could have ended differently. But I also knew, somewhere in me, that there was no soft ending. That kind of ending—the soft and loving ending—would have me back on the rocks, then under the ocean, for dead. One of the dead.

"Goodbye," I said.

"Lucy."

But he knew I was not coming. We both knew it was the end.

"Goodbye," he said.

I watched him push off the rocks and dive into the ocean. It looked like he was entering a giant vagina, as though another woman had come to take him from me already. I wondered if he would always have other women, if he had loved me the most. Even if the other women were just bones in the sea, even if they were nothing, they had dissolved for him. They were his nothing.

But what, then, was he? Was he really even anything? Mythical creatures were born and died all the time. They were born when we needed them and they died when we no longer saw them through the same eyes. In that way he wasn't so special. How many had been born before him? How many died when a human vision, powerful but ultimately fragile, was effaced by time and dirt? He would be reborn when the next woman needed him. He would come to occupy another space again.

I picked up my suitcase and walked back across the beach. A line of palm trees at the edge of the boardwalk rustled in unison in the wind.

"Fuck me," I said to the palm trees.

I still didn't love myself. I wasn't sure how or when that was going to happen. But maybe it would if I continued to stay alive.

"Forgive me," I said.

When I got back into the house, Steve was in the kitchen eating cereal again. He eyed me skeptically over his reading glasses. In front of him was the newspaper, with a headline that read FIRES IN THE VALLEY.

"I made a mistake," I said.

He blinked and kept chewing.

"I'm not going to leave yet after all."

"Is that so?" he asked.

"Yes," I said.

He was silent. He rose and put his bowl in the sink.

"Try not to bleed on anything," he said, and shuffled up the stairs.

It dawned on me that I hadn't gotten my period in a while, not since Theo and I had bloodied the sofa. That was at least five weeks ago. Maybe I was hitting menopause? Did women hit menopause at thirty-eight?

I didn't bother opening my suitcase, brushing my teeth, or washing my face. I stripped down to my underpants, braless, and climbed onto the sofa, snuggling up under the blanket. It was strange to be there without Dominic or Theo. Why could they never coexist in the same space, Theo with his fantasy love and Dominic with his pure love? Theo was so afraid of Dominic, how his pure love might hurt him or even eliminate him. I was afraid too, which was why I had chosen to hide him away. I had hoped that fantasy would triumph. Now I was left with neither. But I had my sister.

In a way it was kind of nice to be alone. The euphoria was gone and the silence was gone—those were Theo's. In his place, some of the nothingness had clearly returned. But I felt different about it, like it was laughing with me or maybe I with it. It was my own nothingness to have and to hold. In my mind I called it a fucker and turned off the light.

Acknowledgments

Thank you to Meredith Kaffel Simonoff, my agent and mermaid, for being a believer from the beginning. Thank you to my editor, Alexis Washam, for your vision, and to Molly Stern, Liz Wetzel, Rachel Rokicki, Lindsay Sagnette, Roxanne Hiatt, Lisa Erickson, Jillian Buckley, Alex Larned, Rachel Willey, and all of the other amazing people at Hogarth. Thank you to the passionate ladies at Bloomsbury UK: Alexis Kirschbaum, Philippa Cotton, Alexandra Pringle and Rachel Wilkie—you make me feel lucky. Thank you to my Hollywood mafia: Michelle Weiner and Olivia Blaustein at CAA. Thank you to Olive Uniacke and Erik Feig at Lionsgate, and to Anne Carey for keeping it (sur) real. Thank you to Libby Burton, whose initial edits were vital to this book. Thank you to my foreign publishers, especially Aylin Salzmann at Ullstein! Thank you to Amy Jones, Susanna Brisk, and Karah Preiss. Thank you to my parents for my education. Thank you to Pickle for showing me the love of a good (bad!) dog. Love and gratitude to Nicholas Poluhoff, without whom—for so many reasons—this book would never have existed.